RAISING WINTER

A CANDLEWOOD FALLS NOVEL

STACEY WILK

RAISING WINTER

Copyright © 2021 by Stacey Wilk

Cover design copyright © 2021 by Jen Talty

ISBN: ebook: 978-1-7364714-4-9

ISBN: print: 978-1-7364714-5-6

Printed in the USA

To Darlane
Because you can read my mind.

Happy Reading

Stacey Wilk

HAVE WE GOT A STORY FOR YOU!

Dear Readers:

Welcome to Candlewood Falls!

Each Candlewood Falls story stands alone. However, the end of one story doesn't mean the end of your favorite characters. They can show up in any Candlewood Falls book at any time!

Candlewood Falls is a unique world of connected stories by different authors whose characters, business, and events appear in each others' stories.

Think of Candlewood Falls as a literary soap opera!

Be sure to check out the Ready For Another Trip to Candlewood Falls page at the end to discover which other books include your favorite characters.

Happy reading!

Stacey Wilk, K.M Fawcett, & Jen Talty

PROLOGUE

B rad Wilde didn't understand all the uproar over two people tying themselves together for their entire lives like a grafted tree. He was thankful it wasn't him getting married. But here he was at The River Winery toasting his friend Malbec River and his new fiancée Eliza Jane at their engagement party. He couldn't imagine spending his entire life with just one woman.

Even his twin sister had fallen prey to the wedding bug. Brooklyn and Caleb were engaged and planning a wedding. His sister wanted him to put on a monkey suit for hers. He preferred life in his jeans and work boots. Getting dirty from the soil and trees of his orchard suited him. And he would not apologize ever again for who he was.

He had mingled a respectable amount of time at the engagement party. But he was ready to take off and get back the orchard. He had some paperwork to do for the apples going to grocery stores and the farm stands still open in November. In the morning, he'd fix the roof on the storage shed when the light was better.

Putting his beer down on a tray with other empty bottles and dirty wineglasses, he made his way to the small circle of people he needed to say goodbye to. Their conversation about doctors and medicine drifted toward him like a ferocious wind. He patted Malbec on the back and interrupted their squawking.

"I have to be going. Thanks for having me."

Malbec shifted and gripped his extended hand. "Thanks for coming, man. The party wouldn't have been the same without you."

"Wouldn't have missed it. Text me. We'll grab a drink next week. Eliza Jane, are you sure you want to marry this guy?" He punched Malbec in the arm and leaned in to kiss Malbec's lady on the cheek.

"I've never been surer." Eliza beamed up at Malbec with a range of emotions flashing over her eyes like a movie montage —love, wonder, and some that definitely spoke of lust.

His friend seemed happy. Brad guessed it couldn't hurt to have a woman looking that way at him.

"Brad, we were just talking about the new doctor," Brooklyn said. His sister had returned to Candlewood Falls about nine months ago after a terrible attack up north. She had come home to lick her wounds at their grandmother's alpaca farm. Not only had she healed up nicely, but she bought the farm from their grandmother and managed to fall back in love with Caleb Ransom. He had tried to stop her from getting involved with the ex-con. He had been an idiot about that one.

"Everyone is talking about it. Like nothing new ever happens in this town. Well, I guess it doesn't." Caleb shrugged and shoved his hands in the pockets of his dark jeans.

Candlewood Falls was like most small towns. Everyone knew everyone and their business. Keeping secrets was a difficult thing to do, though he had managed to keep one big one from everybody, including his whole family. Sometimes he couldn't believe he had pulled it off. He had thought for sure Brooklyn would have figured it out just by looking at him, but she hadn't.

"They need something to talk about now that they can't talk about you." Malbec threw an arm around Caleb's shoulders and gave a tug. Caleb shoved Malbec away.

"I heard that was why you were back, Riesling," he said. Riesling was Malbec's younger sister and a physician's assistant. She was too young to hang with them when they were in high school, but he remembered her always running after them with a stethoscope trying to listen their heartbeats.

"That's right. Old Doc Harden is finally retiring. I came back to help with the transition. And to celebrate with Malbec and Eliza Jane, of course."

Eliza Jane did that looking delighted thing again. The wine tasting room was suddenly stifling. Sweat broke out over his skin. He needed to get some fresh air.

"I'm encouraging everyone to make an appointment for their physical. That includes you, tough guy." Riesling poked him in the chest with a long finger.

"Not me. I'm as healthy as a horse. I never need a doctor."

CHAPTER ONE

H e needed a doctor.

Brad cradled his right arm against his middle and cursed up a storm. He was pretty sure he had broken his wrist. Stupid. He had been in a hurry and hadn't checked the integrity of the ladder before he climbed. The ladder was old and hanging around as many years as him, but it had been close by.

He had wanted the roof patched on the storage shed. The work on the orchard slowed down in the cooler months. All the apples from this year's harvest had been picked, sold, and stored. His crew was smaller from now through May. The men worked in the pressing barn, making cider and applesauce. Today was a good day to get up into the loft and patch the roof.

The day was good until the rung on the wooden ladder had broken clean through. His feet fell out from under him. He had reached for the edge of the loft, but his fingers slid over the wood as if it were made of ice. He landed with the full force of his weight on his wrist. His right wrist. His dominant hand. Shit.

He couldn't move his fingers and the swelling had already begun. He could cook a steak on the heat rolling off his skin. He used his good hand and pushed himself to his feet. He needed to get to Doc Harden. But his feet tangled under him when the room spun, and he fell to his knees.

Looked like he wasn't going anywhere by himself. Some of the ladies were working in the bakery. He didn't want those women clucking over him. He wanted someone who wouldn't ask a thousand questions. He could call Caleb. He would race over, but then Caleb would tell Brooklyn. So, he was out.

He dug his phone from his front jeans pocket. Sweat broke out on his upper lip. His wrist hurt like a mother…. He tapped at the screen with his good hand and put the phone on speaker.

"Hey, man. What's up?" Raf Alvarez was the one person he could count on for complete discretion. Raf was the brother he didn't have. Brad had plenty of male cousins because the Wilde family was big. He also had several uncles, but he was closest to Raf. Raf knew all his secrets, except for one. And he knew all of Raf's. At least he assumed he did.

"I need a ride." He choked on those few words because his throat was dryer than dead leaves. The pain in his wrist was worse than he realized.

"Are you okay? You sound terrible. Where are you?"

If he ever had to fight in a war, he would want Raf by his side. Raf had been by his side since they were eighteen and Raf had walked onto the orchard's property looking for a job to support his younger brothers.

"I'm in the storage shed. I don't normally ask like this, but please hurry the fuck up."

"I'm running. I'll be there in five minutes. Do you want to tell me what this is about?" Raf's breathing became labored. He was, in fact, running. But Raf would remain calm. No drama with Raf. They had that in common.

Brad pushed to his feet again. The room stayed straight. He sucked air in through his teeth. His wrist pulsed more. "I broke my wrist falling off the ladder."

"You need the doc."

It pained him to say it as much as his hand hurt. "I need the doc."

"So much for never needing the doctor." Riesling River entered the exam room holding what had to be his file and tossing one puckered smirk his way.

"I guess I deserve that." He cradled his arm against his chest. She had done an X-ray.

"The wrist has a fracture. You broke the distal radius when you landed. It's the larger of the two bones in the forearm. It commonly breaks at the lower end near the wrist." She pointed to that spot on her own wrist. "For someone like you, I usually see this kind of thing in a skiing accident or dirt biking. Falling off a ladder?" She snickered.

"It's not funny."

"It's only funny because I've known you my whole life, and you and Malbec are the same personality."

"Yeah, what's that? Cool big brother?" He and Riesling never had a thing. For one, she was too young for him, and for the other, growing up with her brother Malbec by his side most of the time made them all like family. Cousins at best.

"Big brother, definitely. Cool? Not so sure about that one. Let's try for arrogant enough not to know when to quit." She opened the cabinet in the corner. "I'm going to give you a brace. You'll wear it for the next five to six weeks. Then you'll probably need physical therapy."

"I need to be ready to prune the apple trees by February."

"The brace will be off probably after the first of the year. But if you don't do the PT, you'll miss your season. Raf will have to run the show."

Raf could do it, no problem. And he trusted Raf to take care of the orchard since he was Brad's second-in-command out there. But the orchard was his responsibility. And he always took care of his responsibilities. Every single one of them.

"Okay, Doc, I'll do what you say."

"Not the doc. But close. Do what I say, and you'll be fine. You can go back to pretending you don't need the doctor. I'll be back in a minute. This brace is too small for you. It's more appropriate for a ten-year-old girl." She left and closed the door behind her.

Any other day that remark would have flown straight over his head. But sitting here with his wrist throbbing, and his mortality a mark on his radar because he fell off the ladder, that little comment hit the bullseye. Would he ever get to see his child?

CHAPTER TWO

Lyra Ryan watched the newscast for the hundredth time. She couldn't look away. The segment was worse than a train wreck. Well, in fact, the news segment was a huge train wreck for the whole world to see, and she had been hit by the train. She kind of wished she had actually been hit by a literal train instead of this figurative one, but she had her two boys to think about. She had to take care of them. Somehow.

She muted the volume of the television in her bedroom. She didn't need to hear what they were saying. She had heard enough. But she couldn't stop watching her husband being escorted out of a fancy hotel by two FBI agents sporting the regulation windbreakers and with his hands cuffed behind his back, wearing only his white dress shirt — unbuttoned and exposing that chest he was so proud of because of all his hours in the gym — his black boxers, and black dress socks pulled up to his skinny knees. At least it was November. She hoped he froze his overused balls off.

How had her life fallen apart so expertly? "Well, Lyra, if

you had been paying better attention to your husband's behavior, maybe you would have noticed the cracks in the foundation," she muttered under her breath.

Husband. Now that was a word that tasted like liver in her mouth. She and Michael may have been joined in matrimony for fifteen years and cohabitating under the same roof, but a marriage they did not have in the true sense of the word.

The whole miserable mess Michael had caused made her stomach roll. He had lied about what he was doing at work every day. He had lied about his infidelity too, but to bring knowing harm to so many people…she couldn't bear the thought.

She didn't give a damn about the hooker that he had been with when the federal government arrested him. Hence the open shirt and exposed underwear. She only cared about the fact he had built their lives on a stack of cards—and allowed others to do the same. And when the carefully placed cards fell, they had taken her personal therapy practice with it too. Because no one could trust a therapist married to a fraud.

She had been a fool to believe as long as he gave her the space to do as she pleased, which really amounted to her going to work every day because she had always been compelled to counsel people, and tending to the boys' needs, she was content. She could live behind the illusion of a happy marriage. She didn't need passion or love. She needed everyone to believe she had succeeded. A professional Christmas card once a year, the preplanned social media posts, and their fancy house and cars was all it took to maintain the smoke and mirrors.

"Mom, I'm all packed." Theo bounced into the room the

way only twelve-year-old boys and Labrador retrievers can pull off and flopped onto the corner of the bed. "What are you watching?"

"Nothing." She turned off the television. Theo and Lucas had been hurt enough. Theo didn't need to see his father's half-naked perp walk.

She had stayed married too long because of the boys. And if she were being honest, which was something she wasn't sure she had the stomach for at the moment, she had stayed because Lyra Chambers Ryan could not have the black smudge of divorce on her appearance. And now she had far worse. *That'll teach you.*

"Are you sure you packed everything? The movers are coming in the morning to take us to Candlewood Falls."

Thankfully, she had had enough sense to keep her own banking account for her business. The Feds couldn't touch what was hers and hers alone. And thankfully, she had squirreled away a little money because every once in a while she entertained the idea of leaving Michael and starting over. She would have needed something to hire a divorce attorney, if she had ever been brave enough to follow through. Which she hadn't. And boy, did she need a good lawyer to get her out of her marriage as quickly as possible. She didn't want Michael's mistakes around her neck anymore.

"Why can't we live with Grandma and Grandpa?" Theo had asked that same question a dozen times.

"Grandma and Grandpa need their space and so do we. I rented a small house in town. You'll be able to see them all the time." The very last thing she had wanted was to move back to her childhood home and be under her parents' roof again. Returning to Candlewood Falls was bad enough. But she would need help with the boys and her parents were her only option. Beggars couldn't be choosers.

"Is it as big as this house?" Theo picked at a scab on his arm.

"No, sweetie. You still have to share a room with Lucas." Neither boy was too happy about this new arrangement, but her money would stretch only so far. And she had no idea what to do for more. She certainly couldn't be a therapist anymore. Who would trust her? She didn't trust herself. She had completely missed Michael's sociopathic tendencies. She couldn't have been much of a therapist if she hadn't seen what was right under her own nose for so long.

Theo pouted and she brushed his hair away from his eyes. "It's going to be okay." If she continued to say it, then it would be true.

"When can we see Dad?"

In twenty-five to thirty. "I don't know. How about we get pizza tonight for dinner?" It would be the last time for a while she could allow such a luxury. Her boys deserved one last night to feel like themselves because starting tomorrow when they crossed the town line into Candlewood Falls, they all would be anything but.

"Pepperoni?"

"You bet."

Theo bounced off the bed, yelling for his older brother to order the food on the app. She picked up the remote and tuned back in to the train wreck, still unable to look away.

Lyra turned into the long driveway of the new rental house. The driveway was losing its battle with nature which seemed determined to take back the space. Grass and weeds poked through the packed dirt, making it difficult to know where the driveway even was. She lined up the tires with what looked like the space to drive on and clenched her jaw to keep her tongue from getting bit with each bump and groove.

Lucas sat in the front seat beside her. His wireless earbuds were shoved into his ears so conversation had been nearly impossible for the last hour and twenty minutes. She wanted to reach over and squeeze his shoulder just to let him know she was there for him, but every time she thought about it, she changed her mind. He was mad at the world right now. And with every right. His father, and to Lucas, his mother too, had ripped away the life he knew, the life he was settling into as a fourteen-year-old boy.

Theo was asleep in the back seat and had been from the second she jumped on the New Jersey Turnpike and headed south. She envied the way sleep arrived effortlessly for children and honestly, every man she had ever known.

The rental sat on five acres of overgrown and pretty much unusable land. The good thing about Candlewood Falls was everything was spread out in this small town. The bad thing about Candlewood Falls was the very same thing. She was grateful that the house next to her was on ten acres. The realtor had told her the neighbor was on an old horse farm. She hadn't asked who the neighbor was. She had found a realtor from another town to show her the place—a realtor who didn't know her from before. From the good old days. She would avoid the new neighbor for as long as possible. She had no interest in making friends. She had come home to lick her wounds in private and to give her boys some sense of security. Candlewood Falls

STACEY WILK

was good for that. Small towns often were a place of safety.

She pulled up to the house—that wasn't much to look at —and parked. The house was a compact thing in the shape of a square with a few brick steps that led to a front door. Dirty siding. A couple of windows in the front. The kitchen and two bedrooms were in the back. A living room and a undersized dining room in the front. But the rental was secluded, and she could avoid waving to people who would be out walking their dogs or doing their morning runs.

"We're here." She forced a lightness into her voice she didn't actually feel. The movers would be there in a couple of hours and a lot of work would need to be done. She doubted the boys would be much help.

"This place is a dump." Lucas opened the car door and unfolded from the seat.

"It's our forever home." Or at least forever for now. An option-to-buy clause existed, but she didn't want to think that far ahead. This was what she could afford on her savings.

She would need to find a job soon. She just didn't know what she wanted to be anymore. "Theo, honey, wakeup. We're at the new house." She shook his leg until his eyelids batted opened.

"We're here already? That was fast." He stretched, yawned, and rubbed his eyes with his fists. "Where's the house?"

"It's right there." She pointed through the windshield and laughed.

"All three of us have to live in there? Are you sharing a room with me and Lucas too?" He leaned between the front seats and stared at the house with confusion etched on his

14

young features. She brushed back the tendrils of dark hair that fell over his eyes.

"I know it's smaller than we're used to, but you'll see it's going to be nice." She had plans to make it a real home for them. Plans that included bleach.

She hopped out of the car and went to the front door. Lucas dragged his feet behind her.

"Can I check out the back?" Theo said.

"Sure. But don't go far." She worked the key in the lock, hoping the key wouldn't snap off in the process, then had to hip check the door to get it open.

"Great. The door doesn't even work right." Lucas pushed past her into the empty living room. "And it smells in here." He covered his mouth and nose with his hand.

"We just need to open a few windows, and the door works fine. We will get used to the house's little quirks. It will be fun. Like a mystery."

The rooms were empty which she was grateful for. Carpet covered the floors in the living room, dining room, and bedrooms. The mauve color was stained and had faded over the many years of use. She didn't want to think about what had left those stains. But she had checked underneath when she came to see the place. Hardwood floors were under there. She could rip out the carpets. Hopefully, the floors were in decent shape.

Lucas ambled toward the bedrooms. The boys could have whichever they wanted. They were both the same with the same narrow closet and a view of the neglected backyard.

She opened the windows and the back door in the kitchen even though it was cold out. At least the sun was shining. New Jersey in November could be overcast and the kind of damp that seeped into her bones.

"No daughter of mine is going to live in a place like this."

She spun at the screech of her mother's voice. Lyra's heart dropped into her canvas sneakers. "What are you doing here?"

She had told her mother she would call her when it was okay to come over. She absolutely did not want her mother here before she had had a chance to fuss over the place a little.

"Do you think I wouldn't come by on the day you moved back home?" Clarisse Chambers swept into the room, her blond hair sprayed into place. Not even a hurricane would dare to move a single piece. Her makeup was applied with expert precision. And she wore a deep-red wool wrap that flowed when she moved as if it were a queen's cape. Or a witch's.

"I told you I'd call. I want to get us settled in first." She had hoped to make that call in a few days, a week, a month if possible.

"Why don't you let the boys stay with me and your father? Why should they have to live in a hovel?" Her mother wrinkled her nose.

"The place just needs a little TLC."

"It's not respectable for a Chambers to live like this. What will people think?"

"There is nothing wrong with living here. It's what I can afford. And considering what else has been going on in my life, my living arrangements pale in comparison in the gossip department." And there would be plenty of gossip if there wasn't already. Many people in Candlewood Falls would have a field day with what happened to her. She suspected she was already the talk around a few dinner tables. *Did you hear about Lyra Chambers? Talk about the fall from grace!* The person who would cackle the loudest would be Weezer River.

"This house still isn't right. But you're stubborn and you're going to do what you want no matter how much it affects me and your father."

She bit her tongue to keep the retort in her mouth. This was not the time or the place for a fruitless discussion on her decisions or her mother's selfish beliefs that she should consider her feelings before she made a move. Never mind that she was a middle-aged, grown woman with a husband who had affairs and stole millions of dollars from unsuspecting people, or that she was raising two boys or that she had once operated a very successful counseling practice. No, Clarisse Chambers still believed that her child should think of her needs first.

"Perhaps you should come back after the movers have left and I have had a chance to set up the furniture. You might be more comfortable that way." She couldn't bring a lot of the furniture because the bank saw everything as an asset that could be sold, but she had managed a few pieces from the basement that she'd had for decades.

"Lyra, think about the boys. Don't they deserve to live somewhere where they can spread out? Or have friends over? This isn't a place for entertaining."

She was right about that much, but she hadn't planned on having any parties. Her only friend in town was Michelle. In fact, Michelle was her only real friend—ever.

"If the boys want to have friends over, they can. I took the big screen TV from the house. It's perfect for their video games." She had also brought the TV from her bedroom because she wasn't sure if she'd ever sleep again. The television kept her company. She wasn't sure if she should have taken the big television, but if the bank wanted it, they could come and get it.

"Grand Mom." Theo bounced into the room with dirt on his face and hands. He lunged for his grandmother to wrap her in a big hug, but her mother jumped out of the way.

"Oh, Theo, sweetheart. Grand Mom has a lunch date with her lady friends. You can't get my wrap dirty. Go wash your hands and face and we can try again."

Theo's smile fell.

"Come give me a hug." She held out her arms, and Theo walked into them. He was always willing to hug her, and she loved that about him. She inhaled the fresh air clinging to him, then turned her gaze to her mother. "Is Dad around? Maybe he could take the boys for something to eat. I'll deal with the movers and the cleaning."

Her father always came to her rescue. She adored him and often couldn't understand how he put up with his wife. Sometimes she was angry at him for tolerating so much. If he had drawn a line in the sand more often, maybe all their lives would be different.

"I'll call him." Her mother retrieved her phone from her designer purse and went outside.

"Go tell Lucas that Grandpa is coming. He'll take you two for whatever kind of food you want. Okay?"

"Ice cream?" The glee returned to his features.

"Sure." Ice cream for dinner one night wouldn't hurt anything.

"Lucas." Theo yelled, running from the room.

Lyra wiped a hand over her face. Maybe returning to Candlewood Falls had been a mistake. What she needed now was love and support, not judgment. What made her think her mother was capable of what she needed?

But her parents loved her boys. That much she was certain of, even her mother did in her inflexible way. And Candlewood Falls was familiar. She hadn't wanted to start over in a completely brand-new town where she didn't even know the location of the post office. After her life turned upside down, she needed something to ground her. Her hometown could offer that much.

A text came across her phone. She pulled it out of her back pocket. Michelle.

Are you here

Just got in

Do you want help

Thanks. All good. Call you tomorrow. She could count on Michelle. They had been friends since high school. They were so different in many ways, Michelle's family not as well off as hers. Michelle had lots of friends from all walks of life where she preferred to keep her circle tighter. Michelle wore the craziest fashion trends. She had never been brave enough to wear anything but what was in for fear of not fitting in.

Her mother stood in the doorway. "Your father will be here in five minutes. He's thrilled to spend time with the boys. Are you certain you want to live here?"

"Yes." Not at all. Her parents' house was charming. It sat up on the hill of their property with a wraparound porch and double glass front doors etched in gold. The second floor had more than enough bedrooms and bathrooms for all of them. Their house didn't smell as if an animal had died in the basement.

"Suit yourself. But don't say I didn't warn you this is a

mistake. I'll be going. I'm late for my lunch." Her mother swooped off.

"God forbid you were late for a lunch date," she said under her breath.

"Late for what?" Theo stood inches behind her.

"What? Oh, nothing. I didn't hear you come in. Grandpa will be here any minute. Are you all set to go?"

Theo held up his hands streaked with dirt.

"Try again, buddy. I have stuff in the car. I'll be right back." She had packed some essentials like soap and paper towels, cleaning supplies, and paper plates. She even had their sheets and blankets along with a few changes of clothes.

She navigated the uneven ground back to the car. The tree line between her place and the neighbor's was sparse. Most of the leaves had already fallen, making the branches barren and giving her a view next door. The lot might be ten acres, but it looked as if the house was closer to her side. She stood a good chance of bumping into someone between now and April when the trees filled out again. She only hoped she wasn't living next door to someone who wanted to be friends or worse someone whom she had been unkind to in her youth.

A tall man with a brace on his right wrist and tattoos above that walked up the driveway from the road toward her. His shoulders were broad, and he held what looked like the mail in his good hand. She stopped short and stared. He turned his face toward the sun, maybe closing his eyes. She couldn't be entirely sure.

If she didn't know any better, she would assume this rugged man with long hair, wearing a t-shirt that stretched over his biceps and chest along with his dirty blue jeans and work boots could be the caretaker of the property. But she knew better, all right. This wasn't the caretaker.

Oh no. She had rented the house next door to the boy most likely to succeed in her grade. The boy who had every girl following him around, hoping he'd look their way. She had never been interested in him because of his eccentric father, absentee mother, and the family-owned orchard. She had had her eyes set on a bigger prize then. A prize she had thought she achieved until Michael had stolen her life from her with his lies and deceit.

Returning home was embarrassing enough, but to have to live next door to Brad Wilde on top of it all was a bit much. He would probably have himself a good laugh at her expense because she had been foolish enough to tell him once that he was nothing more than a dirt digger. Just thinking about how awful she had sounded could still make her face burn. She would deserve it if he acted as if he'd never seen her before. And hopefully he would.

She grabbed a box out of the trunk of her car. She wanted Theo cleaned up before her father arrived. Dad wouldn't flinch over the dirt the way her mother had, but she still wanted to make a good impression on him. She had been taught appearances were important. Which was why her life crumbling in such a royal fashion was almost too much to bear.

Her father's silver sedan turned off the street and bounced down the drive. Without thinking, she raised a hand to wave. He beeped the horn in return. Even through the glare on the windshield she could make out the smile on his lined face. At least her father was happy to see her.

"Lyra? Lyra Chambers, is that you?"

The voice made her whip around. She fumbled with the

box, catching it right before it hit the ground. Brad peered through the tree line from his driveway. His brows creased with uncertainty. Or maybe it was disbelief.

Her mouth opened and closed, but no words came out. Did she tell him no one called her by Chambers anymore, but she was thinking of returning to it? Did she lie and say he had the wrong person? But she would be found out soon enough. As soon as her father parked and got out of the car, in fact.

She managed to give him a slight nod of her chin. Gripping the box with sweaty hands, she held her head high and marched inside her dump of a rental, leaving Brad Wilde unanswered and among the trees.

CHAPTER THREE

B rad scratched at his brace. What the heck was Lyra Chambers doing next door? That old house had sat empty for at least a year. He couldn't imagine why someone with their nose in the air would be there. Maybe she was helping a friend move in.

He hadn't seen her in at least fifteen years. She hadn't changed. Still as beautiful as ever, though he never knew her to go without makeup and wear something as casual as the sweatpants she had on today. Even in high school, she had dressed as if she were attending a fashion show. She had looked down at his clothes more than once back then.

He had never cared much for fancy clothes. He was like his dad in that way. Keep it simple, and something he could wear on the orchard and not care if it got dirty. Because it would. He missed work. The orchard was his whole life, and he couldn't do anything more than paperwork, answer calls, and bark orders. He wanted to be with his men. This time of year there were apples to press, cider to make. Even though it was only November, he could get ready for the planting season.

He went inside and dumped the mail on the kitchen counter. He grabbed his phone and went to his favorites list, tapping on Raf's name.

Raf picked up on the first ring. "Hey, man. What's going on?"

"How are things?"

"Do you mean how are things with me? I had a date last night. Pretty lady, but I don't see it going anywhere. I spilled coffee on your dad this morning. He was pissed off about that one."

"Raf, man, tell me about work. I don't care that you spilled coffee. Did the roof get fixed yet? Did you regrade the apples in cold storage? What about the coring and peeling machine? You don't want any problems with the sauce. We have those extra hundred and fifty cases that have to go out."

"My Spanish grandmother would say you are *desagrad-able*, ornery. I wish you'd get laid. Maybe you would calm down."

"Raf, the orchard." Ever since he broke up with Beth, the last woman he had been serious with, he avoided the complications of a relationship. Ironically, he'd had enough of meaningless sex too.

"All right. All right. Everything is under control. I have told you that every day since you fell off the ladder. Take it easy for a few weeks. Do your PT and get better so you can come back for pruning season."

"I want to be there." He wanted to run a hand through his hair, but stopped right before he would get the brace caught. He should get a haircut now that he was down his good hand.

"Listen, I know this is hard for you. But you don't have to worry about work. Enjoy the holidays with your family. Take that vacation you always talk about but never do. When it's time to prune and plant, you'll be back yelling at everyone."

"I don't yell."

"Yeah, okay. I got to go. Do you want to catch a beer tonight?"

"Sure. I'll meet you at Murphy's around six." It wasn't as if he had anything else to do. Work was his life. Without it, he didn't know what to do or where to go. He had been roaming his house and his office at the orchard, driving himself crazy.

"See you then." Raf ended the call.

He moved around the kitchen, pulling together lunch. He hadn't bothered with breakfast because his hand was hurting and trying to do everything lefty usually ended with him cursing. He was starving now and could manage a turkey sandwich on a sub roll. He hoped.

His phone lit up again. Another call came through with a number he didn't have saved in his contacts, but looked familiar. He hesitated before answering, but then why not? He wasn't exactly busy. He grabbed the turkey from the fridge.

"Brad Wilde." He put the phone on the counter and hit the speaker button so he could move around. A tomato would be nice on the sandwich, but he didn't have the patience to cut one with his left hand.

"Hello, Brad. It's Nora Reis." Her curt voice stopped him cold.

A roar echoed in his ears and a bead of sweat rolled down his back. A call from Nora Reis was an unpleasant surprise. "What's up, Nora?"

She cleared her throat. "I'm sorry to have to be the one to tell you this…but Maggie died in a car accident last week." Maggie lived in Stowe, Vermont, where winter came early, Maggie's favorite time of year.

He dropped into a chair at the kitchen table because his knees buckled out from under him. "What happened?" He and Maggie had a very tangled history. A history that only three people knew about—him, Maggie's sister Nora, and Maggie.

"She was coming home late from work. She hit some black ice at the start of a bridge…she…she didn't make it." A sob cut off her words.

"I'm sorry for your loss." He couldn't get his mind to accept Nora's words. Maggie gone? That wasn't possible. Maggie was the same age as he was. They had had a few good times together, but that was over ten years ago. More recently, she refused to speak to him. Nora and Maggie were very close. Losing her would be hard for Nora and Maggie's daughter—his daughter.

"Is Winter okay?" Maggie had loved the winter season so much that she had named their child after the season without mentioning it to him. She hadn't consulted him about anything. Plenty of times he wondered why she had told him at all that she was pregnant.

"She's holding up."

"Is there something you need me to do?" He would always help Maggie in any way he could. That had been his promise to her, even though she hadn't wanted that from him.

"I need you to take Winter for a few weeks." She blew her nose.

"Excuse me?"

"You heard me, Brad. I have to return to work, and I can't bring her with me. I'm going to be in Ecuador, traveling through the rain forest. I can't drag around a ten-year-old girl who should be in school. I'll be back after the new year."

"I can't take her." He didn't know how to care for a child. He struggled to take care of himself these days with only one hand. Winter didn't know him. Maggie could not have wanted this.

"You have to take her. There is no one else. And believe it or not, Maggie made you the second choice for guardian if anything should have happened to me."

"She did? Why?" His head spun. He couldn't keep up with all the runaway thoughts.

"Do you really have to ask that question?"

"She didn't want me in Winter's life, Nora. On any level. I had to beg her to take money from me. Why would I think that she would want me to be Winter's guardian? Maggie made me agree to stay away." Maggie had never even hinted at the idea he could end up as guardian. She probably didn't want to encourage him to get involved in Winter's life.

Nora let out a heavy sigh. "I never agreed with her on that. I thought she was making a big mistake by pushing you away, but it was her choice, good or bad. Winter needs you now. Just for a few weeks. Just until I can finish up my assignment and come back. After that, I'll get a more suitable job. I'll raise her. You can go back to your very convenient life."

"What is that supposed to mean?" He jumped up and

banged his bad hand on the table. He stifled the string of curses.

"Look, I may not have agreed with Maggie's decision to keep you and Winter apart, but you sure as hell didn't do much in the way of trying to convince her. Sure, you put up a small argument, but in the end you went ahead and took the coward's way out."

"Hang on a second. I asked her to marry me."

"She didn't love you. And you didn't love her."

"So? Was this way any better?" He had been denied his child. And he had never told a soul about her. Not his twin sister, not his father, not his grandparents, and not his best friend. He had suffered in silence for ten years, not knowing what his little girl was up to, what she liked, who her friends were. The only relief he had was knowing Maggie cashed his checks every month. That was all he could get her to agree to because she had told him in no uncertain terms that he would be a lousy father. She didn't want him in Winter's life. She was going to tell Winter she didn't know her father at all.

"Keeping your identity hidden from Winter was not Maggie's best moment. She really believed she and Winter would be better off without you. And can you say they weren't? Were you really ready to be a parent?"

"I'm not having this discussion with you." He had it several times with Maggie while she was pregnant. When he had been served the restraining order, he gave up. He had no say in what Maggie did with the baby. But that didn't mean he liked being kept in the dark.

"Winter has a right to know who her father is, and since I need your help, now is the best time. She is my only concern."

"Did you tell her?"

"I did."

He dropped back into the chair. The air left his lungs. His daughter knew about him. He would have liked to see her face when she found out. "What did she say?"

"She's mad and with every right. She just lost her mother, her only parent. And now she found out she does have a father after all. She doesn't appreciate being lied to."

He didn't blame her. He never liked being lied to either, not that anyone ever does.

"Brad, will you take her?"

And do what with her? He wanted to ask. He didn't know how to be a dad. She must have questions about where he'd been all these years. Would she believe him if he said this was the way her mother had wanted it? "Does she go to school?"

"Of course, she does. She's in the fifth grade. I've arranged for her to have her assignments done online. Because of the circumstances, the school agreed. She only has about a month left before winter break."

He could handle a month of this, couldn't he? He had wanted a chance to be in her life once, but because Maggie wouldn't allow it, he had shoved the truth of being a dad so far into the back of his mind, he sometimes forgot he was. Well, he only was in the biological sense. He wasn't a real parent.

"Okay. When are you bringing her?" He should probably get some things a young girl would like. He had plenty of space in the house. Winter could pick one of the extra rooms for hers. He should also go to the grocery store and stock up before she got here. Maybe Nora knew her favorite foods. He wished his grandmother Cordy were still in town. She could bake for them and maybe give him some advice.

"Tonight."

"Tonight?" He needed more time to prepare. He had to tell his family about her.

"I have to catch a red-eye. I'm going to put her on the train in Newark."

"Hang on a second. Are you in New Jersey?" He paced the kitchen, trying to get his mind around what was happening. An hour ago, life was on autopilot, and now it was as if a hailstorm had blown in, tearing his life to pieces.

"We drove down from Vermont. I didn't want her switching trains by herself. I'll put her on the train to you, and I can catch my international flight out of Newark Airport."

"You're putting a ten-year-old girl on a train alone? Is that safe?" Would it be okay for Winter to be on the train for forty-five minutes alone? What if some sleazeball got on and sat near her? He would have to kill somebody.

"She has a cell phone. I programmed your number in it. She pulls into the Candlewood Falls station at four. If you're not there, she's instructed to call the police for help."

"Why did you wait until the last minute to call me?" He would have liked more than a few hours to make sense of all of this. He didn't even know if Maggie really had put him on the list for guardian, but Nora had no reason to lie. If she hadn't called, he would never have known one way or the other what happened to poor Maggie. For all that they had been through, he would never have wanted this for her.

"I kept trying to change my mind. And now it's too late to do anything else. Will you be there? Can she count on you?"

He didn't seem to have a whole lot of choices. And neither did Winter. He wouldn't turn her away. He'd have to figure out what to do with her. And it was only for a few weeks. "I'll be there."

"Thanks, Brad." Nora ended the call.

He stared at the phone. He had other calls to make before Winter's train arrived because he couldn't have a little girl appear out of thin air without an explanation. He never believed he would spend one minute with Winter — but he had imagined.

He tapped at the screen and waited while the phone rang.

"Hey, son." His father's familiar deep voice came across the line which was unusual, because his dad rarely answered his cell phone. He didn't even like having one, but Brooklyn and he had made Dad get one so they could reach him when they needed to. He needed his dad now.

"Hey, Dad. I need to talk to you. Do you have a minute?"

"I don't think you should both be here." Brad paced the train platform in front of his father and sister and checked his phone for the tenth time. It was almost four o'clock. "I don't want to overwhelm her with an entire family right away. She doesn't even know me." He had never met his own daughter. He wasn't even sure if he would know what she looked like. Maggie had sent him one picture right after Winter was born. He had put it in a safety deposit box, and it was still there with a will that left a life insurance policy to her if anything happened to him. When he had asked Maggie for other pictures or mementos, she had refused.

"Are you kidding? I find out that I have a niece and you want me to stay away? Not happening. This is one of the greatest days ever." Brooklyn rubbed her hands together with a wide smile on her face.

He should admit he was grateful for having his family by his side. He had never been so out of his game before. Until today, he understood his life and its direction. Work. The orchard. The occasional relationship that never got too serious. Because of work. Now a child had dropped into it like a hot air balloon. His child.

"I agree with Brooklyn. I want to meet my grandbaby." His father chewed on a piece of hay while he leaned against the station's stucco wall. He took in his father with his wool plaid shirt and relaxed jeans. His skin had creased and pocked because of the years in the sun and the hard work of living off the land basically. He and Brooklyn shared the same blue eyes as their father. He shared his father's work ethic and love of soil and trees. He hoped he could be a quarter of the father his was. Even if he only had the job a short while.

"Look, let's not get ahead of ourselves. She doesn't know us. We're not her family in the real sense of the word. She just needs someone to babysit her for a few weeks. Maggie and Nora have no other family. There isn't anyone else to leave Winter with, and Nora couldn't take her. But when Nora returns, Winter will go back to Vermont and live with her aunt. The way it is supposed to be."

Brooklyn put a hand on his shoulder. "I know we don't always agree on things, but what that woman did to you is wrong. Plain and simple. You would have and will make a great dad. She stole that from you and from us."

"Brooks, women raise babies alone all the time," he said.

"Sure they do. And that's great, but when the dad wants to be in the picture he should be. It's not like you're some deadbeat. And just because she didn't love you that way doesn't mean Winter won't love her dad. What the hell was Maggie thinking?" Her face contorted in anger.

"That I was too arrogant. And I wouldn't know how to be a dad because I was selfish like Mom." He didn't have the heart to say the other thing Maggie had said. Maggie didn't like his dad and his eccentric ways either. She thought something was wrong with his father because he lived in a one-room cabin up the mountain with a generator for power and an outhouse for a bathroom. Maggie had said he didn't have good role models for parents as if he had inherited a genetic curse.

Her words had ignited his temper that day. She had made him completely helpless by refusing him rights to his daughter. That was the day the restraining order came.

But her words had rung with a bit too much truth in them. He wouldn't make a good father. Maggie was right about his mother. But not his dad. His dad had done the best he could, and he loved his dad very much. Maybe love wasn't enough when someone was a parent and Maggie knew that somehow.

Ten years ago he had been twenty-eight with plans and dreams. Children weren't one of them. He would have married Maggie, but he didn't really want to. So when she had shoved him out of her apartment with hateful hands on his chest, yelling that she wanted to raise her baby alone, he had given her what she wanted. And when he could admit it to himself, he regretted that choice. Maybe he had been a coward after all.

The train's rumble shook the ground before he could see it coming. The speck in the distance spread to the silver machine's massive frame as it drew near. The afternoon sun reflected off the train's roof. He squinted against the glare while the whistle announced the train's arrival. The brakes hissed and squealed, stopping the train in front of them.

"This is so exciting." Brooklyn gripped his arm.

Excitement wasn't exactly the word that came to mind. He scratched at his brace. The spiders in his stomach ran up his throat on their skinny legs. He swallowed back the nerves about to choke him.

"It's all going to work out," his dad said.

The train doors slid open, and two conductors jumped down. The commuters in their suits and business casual wear with briefcases and backpacks stumbled off the train. He held his breath as the flow of passengers slowed to a trickle.

"Where is she?" he said. He checked the time again. Had Nora said something other than four o'clock? He hadn't asked for Winter's cell number either. That was stupid. Five minutes in and he was already screwing up.

"I can ask the conductor if he's seen her." Brooklyn stepped around him, but he grabbed her arm.

A pink sneaker popped out first followed by the long legs of a skinny girl in pink pants and a white sweatshirt with light-brown hair like his pulled back the way Brooklyn sometimes wore hers. Like a horse's tail. She dragged a pink suitcase down the train steps with a determined look etched on her face. She righted her backpack and checked left, then right. Her blue eyes grew wide when she spotted the three of them. They were the only people standing on the platform. But she didn't move.

"My god, she looks just like you," Brooklyn said. "Well, don't just stand there. Go to her."

He forced his feet to move. Winter didn't budge. He closed the space between them, fixing the smile on his face. But it wasn't a fake smile. No, a warm feeling had started somewhere in the middle of his chest as soon as he saw her and spread up through his neck, over his lips, and into his eyes. She blurred before him.

"Hi, Winter. I'm your dad." The words tasted foreign, but sunlit. At least his voice hadn't failed him.

She stared up at him with a definite set of her jaw and said nothing.

"Can I take your suitcase?" He held out his good hand.

She gripped the handle and pulled it against her leg. *Guess not.*

"I'm really sorry about your mom."

Still nothing. Maybe she couldn't speak. That might have been a good thing to know ahead of time.

"How about we go back to my house and we get you settled in? Um…I brought my sister Brooklyn and my dad Silas to meet you. I hope that's okay." He took a quick glance over his shoulder. Brooklyn waved like a loon. His dad stood there strong and solid with a goofy grin on his face. He shook his head at their ridiculous display, but he was grateful for their presence.

"What happened to your hand?" Winter said.

He looked down at the brace then back at her, a little unsure of where she was going with this. She didn't say hello, but she had asked about his hand. Strange, but if she wanted to know... "I fell off a ladder."

"Oh. Sorry about your hand."

"Thanks." Maybe this whole visit wouldn't be so bad.

"But I still don't like you. And I never will."

CHAPTER FOUR

"But you're a therapist." Lyra's mother sat at the table in the dingy kitchen of her rental with her legs crossed and her lips pinched. Mom had made sure to put a dish towel down on the chair before she placed her expensive navy-blue-clad backside on the chair even though the set had come from Lyra's house in North Caldwell.

Clarisse had stopped by to ask if Lyra's father could pick up the boys after school and her parents would take the boys to dinner over in Lambertville. They wanted to bring the boys to the toy shop in town. Theo would love it, but Lucas might not appreciate a small town toy store that didn't sell the latest gadgets. But she had agreed because the afternoon hours slipped away like grease in a hot pan, and she still had a lot of cleaning to do. School would be out soon. Today was their second day, and if the second day was anything like the first, even though she wanted very much to hear how their days went, she could hold off a little longer for the *this place sucks* recap. She already thought she was the worst mother on the planet for moving the boys away from everything they knew.

"I was a therapist, but I'm not any longer thanks to Michael." She climbed down the stepladder and wiped her hands on her pants. Her plan was to clean out the cabinets today while the boys were in school so she could put their dishes and pots away. She was tired of living out of boxes even if it had only been a couple of days.

"That's ridiculous. He didn't steal your license." Her mother waved her hand through the air, as if she could swipe away her objections so easily.

"He stole my reputation. Every single client I had told me they didn't want to work with me any longer. Some even asked to see my tax returns. As if I would overcharge them for my services." That one stung, and only two clients had asked that, but still. She wasn't a therapist for the money. She liked helping people. When that light bulb moment crossed her clients' faces, and they knew they would be okay in the end, she felt like she was a part of changing lives.

"Well, you're back home now. I'm sure there are plenty of people in Candlewood Falls that could use your services."

"I'm not going back to being a therapist. End of discussion." No matter how much she enjoyed helping people, she didn't understand human behavior the way she thought she did. All the classes and workshops and silly letters after her name and she was still duped by her husband. She knew about one of the affairs, but not the first one. And she had no idea he was stealing money and making up profits and just plain lying to everyone. How had she screwed up so royally?

"Then what do you want to be? Because you can't sit

around here all day. This house is enough to make the happiest person depressed."

She had no idea what she would do for a living. Maybe one of the stores on Main Street was hiring. The holidays were around the corner. Someone might need seasonal help. She could learn to operate a cash register.

"Do you want to work with your father? He still keeps a few clients just to give him something to do and something to talk about on the golf course."

"Absolutely not." Her father was a retired investment banker. He had mainly worked local, but he had several big clients in the city back in his heyday. That was how she had met Michael about eighteen years ago.

"Fine." Her mother stood and smoothed her perfect pants. "Why don't you come with me tomorrow night to my knitting club? We're down a member since Cordy Sutter moved to Arizona last month. Sometimes her granddaughter Brooklyn shows up, but she's a terrible knitter. It might be nice for you to get reacquainted with some of the old crowd."

Her mother was referring to Brooklyn Wilde, her unexpected neighbor's twin sister. She and Brooklyn were never friends. Lyra had been too busy running for class president, planning the proms, and organizing her cheerleading squads. Brooklyn had run with a different crowd. One that included her brother. Brad had never looked twice at her in the old days. But she had never given him the time of day either. If only she could go back. She would do things differently. At least be nicer.

Brad had aged well. She hadn't missed that while she stood in her driveway like someone whose tongue had been cut out, unable to utter a single syllable. He had filled out over the years. Probably went to the gym every day based on the size of his arms and chest. She would take a guess that he hurt his hand throwing around those humongous tires in that crazy fitness class so many people liked. He fit the image of a gym head, maybe a boxer even, with those tattoos and long hair. She did like a man with a little hair on him.

"I'm not up for any clubs right now. I just want to finish cleaning these cabinets." They were covered in layers of dust and dirt and a few other things she didn't want to name for fear she'd go running out the front door. She planned to lay paper down on each shelf too. Easier to clean that way.

"Suit yourself. Your father will bring the boys back after dinner."

"Thanks again for picking them up after school and spending time with them today. It's a big help."

"That's what parents are for."

"Did you know Brad Wilde lived next door?" She shouldn't bring the subject up with her mother, but Mom might have a little information about Brad. She only wanted to know because they would be living next door to each other.

Clarisse arched a perfectly shaped brow. "I did indeed. I didn't think you'd care about that. He's not exactly your type."

"I'm not looking to date him." And what was her type? Michael? Not anymore. No, thanks. "I didn't realize how close the house was considering the amount of property it sits on. I thought I saw him the other day walking up the driveway. Never mind. I was just curious." She had more than seen him. She had nearly dropped that heavy box on her foot when he called out her name.

"He's lived there for several years now. Owns it outright. Paid cash. That was impressive. I won't lie. But he still works with dirt. I don't understand why he doesn't hire someone to do the grunt work. Honestly." Her mother huffed and puffed.

"Maybe he enjoys what he does."

"No one enjoys that much physical labor, except maybe his strange father. And what was I thinking? Brooklyn just bought the alpaca farm from Cordy. The whole family is in the mud up to their eyeballs. Maybe you shouldn't come to the knitting club. Brooklyn might not be a good friend. Though, you two do have something in common. She gave up her perfectly good job as a nurse to play with animals. And you have given up your perfectly good job to clean a house." Her mother pecked her cheek with a kiss and swept out of the house. Lyra looked out the window to see if she flew away on a broom.

"That went well," she said to the empty house. Her mother's visit might not have offered the kind of emotional support she could use at the moment. But it did give her one thing she hadn't thought about before.

She now had an idea for a new career.

Brad didn't know what to do. Not too many times in his life had he been at a loss when making a decision. He trusted his gut, and his gut rarely let him down. Until now. He hesitated outside Winter's room. She had picked the room at the end of the hallway farthest from his. Hers did have its own bathroom and he could argue that's why she picked it, but he wondered if there wasn't something more to that decision. She had barely said two more words to him since they returned from the train station.

Did he open the door without knocking? But what if she was changing? Did he knock first and open the door at the same time? Or did he wait to be allowed in? He scratched at his brace. He was the damn VP of Operations for Wilde Orchards. Something this simple should not be so complicated.

"Winter?" He knocked and waited.

No response. Did she take naps in the afternoon? He pulled out his phone and jotted down the question in his notes app. He was quickly constructing a list. He planned on searching the internet for some of these answers. There had to be a book about raising kids. Someone must know what they're doing.

He knocked again. "Winter, I'm coming in." He eased the door open, almost afraid of what would jump out at him. She sat on the window seat, staring out at the backyard. Her knees were tucked close to her chest. She hadn't changed out of the clothes she wore off the train yesterday.

"Are you hungry? You never ate your lunch. I thought maybe we could have a snack."

She didn't turn away from the window. He took a slow step closer, afraid to spook her and make her run from the house.

"Do you like apples? I have a bunch of apples from my orchard. I could cut up some, or I can dip them in caramel if you like that."

She shot him a sideways glance. Maybe she liked caramel.

"You have an orchard?" She kept her gaze on the window. Seven of the ten acres stretched out behind the house. Most of that space was tree-filled. A county park went on beyond that.

He had liked the seclusion when he first bought the place. He still did. "I do. I have an apple orchard, and it has a pumpkin patch."

"How do you have a whole orchard?"

"Well, it's my family's." Her family's too, but he didn't know if he should say that. After Nora returned for Winter, he would never see her again. Nora would make sure of that because Maggie had wanted it that way. He didn't think creating too much of a bond would be a good idea for either of them. "My dad and his brothers own it. I could take you there." He took another step closer.

"No, thank you."

"Is that a no to eating the apples too?"

"I'm not hungry."

At some point, she had to want food. She couldn't keep telling him no, could she? How long did he let her go without eating? He pulled out his phone and typed in that question too. He took a risk and sat on the end of the window seat. "What are you looking at?"

She pointed.

From this angle, he could see the edge of Lyra's backyard. Two boys threw a Frisbee back and forth. So, Lyra had children. He might have heard that somewhere. Maybe at a class reunion.

"Do you want to play Frisbee?" He could run out and get one. He wouldn't be very good with his left hand, but she was ten. She couldn't expect much.

She shot daggers at him and hopped off the window seat. "No. I don't like Frisbee." The words spat out of her mouth as if he had said the most ridiculous thing. She plopped onto the bed, grabbing the pink lamb and tucking it under her chin. "I like to fly kites. And bike ride."

Kites. He wasn't sure he ever flew a kite. His mother was never into doing any outside stuff with them. And Dad was too busy when Brad was a kid to pull out a kite. He would need two hands for that anyway. Maybe he could ask Brooklyn to help out.

As for bike riding, he had a mountain bike, but riding wasn't an option with his hand in a brace.

"Do you want me to get you a kite?"

"No, thank you."

So much for that idea. "Okay. If you change your mind about the apples, come downstairs."

He pushed off the window seat and pressed his good hand to the tight feeling in his chest he kept getting every time Winter told him no. Now would not be a good time to have a heart attack. He stole a glance at Winter who was still cuddling the lamb and staring at the ceiling. This whole arrangement was a bad idea. He had no idea how to even babysit a kid, never mind be a father.

"Brad?"

He stopped at the door and turned, hoping she would follow him to the kitchen. "Yeah?"

"Why do you have long hair?"

That was what she wanted to know? "I don't know. I like it this way, I guess. Why do you have long hair?" Two could play at that game.

He had grown his hair out several years ago for something to do. Right around the time he got his last tattoo on his arm. He figured he'd cut it as soon as it hit his shoulders, but he hadn't. He pulled the sides back when he went to work, but mostly he just let it hang.

"Because I like it that way," she said with a huff and shrug of her shoulders. "Your hair is the same color as mine."

"It is." He wanted to know how she felt about that, but he didn't ask in case she stopped talking or got upset because he had spoken.

"Can I ask you something else?" She turned her gaze away, but seemed to grip the lamb tighter.

"Sure."

The doorbell rang. He wasn't expecting anyone and didn't appreciate the interruption now that Winter had decided to use full sentences with him even if she only wanted to talk about hair.

She swung her gaze his way. Her eyes were wide with wonder. She must have been surprised by the bell too. Or relieved.

"Can you hang on a second? I'll go see who that is, and then you can ask me whatever you want."

"Never mind. It's not important. I have some homework to do." The expression on her face snapped off. She slid from the bed and pulled a book out of her backpack.

The bell's jarring ring echoed up the stairs. Whoever it was, wasn't going to go away, and the mood in the room had been broken. He trotted down the steps and opened the door.

"Dad, what are you doing here?" His father stood on the porch in his faded jeans and broken-in flannel shirt, his hands in his back pockets. His face creased into a smile.

"Two reasons. One, I was hoping to say hello to Winter, if that's okay. And two, you and me, we need to talk." He dipped his head toward the yard, his smile a little less bright.

"Is something up?" He closed the door, but not all the

way in case Winter yelled or got hurt or something he didn't know how to plan for. He hoped there wasn't a problem at the orchard. Raf had assured him he had everything under control.

His dad stopped at the end of the walkway near the driveway. The laughter of boys drifted in his direction. Lyra's kids were still outside playing Frisbee. He craned his neck to see if she might be around, but he didn't see her.

"I didn't want to push when you first called me about Winter. Shock is the best way to describe what I was feeling." He shook his head. "You have a child. I have a grandbaby and you didn't tell me. Why is that?"

He swallowed the lame explanation. "Maggie insisted I stay out of Winter's life. I didn't see the point in telling you because you would never have known her."

"Why did she want you out of your own daughter's life? And more importantly, why would you allow it? I thought family meant something to you."

He reached for his hair, but stopped. He didn't need the brace tangled up. "Look, Dad, Maggie had her reasons. She didn't love me. I didn't love her. She wanted me out of her life completely."

"And you didn't argue about it?"

"Of course, I showed up with a ring." He had gone to a pawn shop thirty miles out of town because he wasn't ready to share the news and bought a respectable ring. It wasn't huge, but it was nice. She had laughed when he showed it to her. After that, he donated it to a church a few towns over. Told the pastor to hock it, use it, whatever.

"And she said no." Dad scratched at his chin.

"About a dozen times."

"So, why not raise Winter together, then? Did some-thing else happen between you and this woman?"

"No, Dad. Maybe Maggie was the one who was unsta-ble. You know me. Am I the kind of guy who would harm a woman and a child on purpose?" The hurt and disappoint-ment he kept bottled up for the past ten years fought its way out. He never totally understood why Maggie would cut him out completely. But right now, he needed his father in his corner, not judging the worst time of his life.

"You're a Wilde. We don't duck responsibility."

"Dad, can you give me the Wilde lecture some other time? I have a ten-year-old girl in my house, and I don't know how to talk to her. I don't know what to do with her. She won't even eat. I'm in over my head. Okay?" He fisted his hands without thinking and pain shot up his right arm, stealing his breath. He bit back a curse and shook his hands out.

"I'm happy that I have a grandchild. I hope to have more from you and Brooklyn. But I think you should have stood your ground with that woman. Your daughter had a right to know her father. I don't understand your decision. Work, the orchard, will never be as important as family."

"I didn't want a family." The words came out in a harsh bark before he could stop them. He could blame his anger on the pain in his wrist. Or his father's pushing a subject he didn't need to hear at the moment. He didn't mean the words the way they sounded. He hadn't planned on a family then. He thought he was still too young, that he had time. He didn't love Maggie, and that wasn't the way to live a life, but because he was a Wilde, because his father had drilled into him that he should always do the right thing, he did.

When she said no, go away or else, he left. Winter was never supposed to show up here.

A squeak came from behind him like a chipmunk racing across the field. Winter stood in the open doorway. Her bottom lip trembled. Her eyes had grown to the size of apples. She ducked her head, but he didn't miss the hurt on her face. Damn.

"Winter, I didn't mean…"

She ran.

CHAPTER FIVE

Lyra wanted to peel off her dirty clothes and sink into a hot tub. Every muscle from her eyelids down to her ankles complained. She imagined her old bathroom in North Caldwell with the jacuzzi soaking tub, and her body ached more. She would have to settle for the simple cast iron tub in the one bathroom this house had. At least the door had a lock.

She had spent the day cleaning the thick black mold that had covered the edge of the tub where it met the tile and all the mold along the tile grout. She had used three bottles of bathroom cleaner with bleach before she saw white again. She almost passed out from the fumes. The tub itself had an inch of soap scum all around it. More bleach. She had also scrubbed the bathroom floor on her hands and knees. They would no longer have to come in here in flip-flops. Tomorrow she would tackle the window and slap up a coat of paint just to freshen up the walls because she couldn't do a thing about the ugly pink tiles.

Theo continuously asked when he could speak to his

dad. Lucas never said a word about Michael. That had her more concerned than Theo's complaining. She didn't know what Lucas was avoiding. She suspected he was embarrassed and angry. But there would be more. Her therapist brain was on high alert.

The idea of dirtying up her tub after cleaning it, didn't completely appeal to her, but she wasn't going to get a massage anytime soon. She didn't have the money for that kind of luxury. The hot water and a glass of wine would have to do. Right after she made dinner and the boys went to their room. Hopefully, there wouldn't be a fight tonight over who was on whose side. Lucas had put a piece of string through the middle to keep Theo away.

She checked her phone. It was a little early to start dinner. She wanted to review her business plan for her new cleaning venture. The business plan wasn't much except an extra-long to-do list. But she was ready to work again. Working gave her a feeling of accomplishment. Since she wasn't going to be a therapist any longer, cleaning was her only other marketable skill. There had to be people in Candlewood Falls who would hire a cleaning person. Even if it was her. Surely, not everyone would hold a grudge against the young girl with the silver spoon in her mouth, and her need to flaunt it.

She should be ashamed of herself for such behavior. But a Chambers had to keep up appearances. That was what her mother said on a daily basis. She shook the memories away.

"Mom, Mom." Theo's voice echoed through the house. "Mom, you need to come outside. Quick."

She hurried from the bathroom and around the corner to the kitchen where Theo stood. His cheeks were flushed, and his chest heaved as if he had been running.

"Are you okay?" He didn't look hurt.

"It's not me. Come now." He ran back through the slider without waiting for her to ask another question—and she had plenty.

She forced her legs to move. The afternoon sun hung right above the treetops, blinding her as she stepped outside. She blinked away the white floaters in her eyes. Lucas stood with a scowl on his face, and his arms crossed over his chest.

A small girl lay faceup on the ground with her arms and legs stretched out like a starfish. Her dark hair spilled around her. Her eyes were squeezed shut.

"What happened?" She ran to the girl. "Honey, can you hear me? Are you okay?"

"She ran into the yard through the trees," Theo said. "She was coming fast. Lucas was trying to catch the Frisbee I had just thrown. Then bam. They collided." Theo smacked his hands together.

"You should have said something, dork." Lucas glared at Theo.

"Lucas, that's enough." She turned back to the girl and placed a hand on her little shoulder. "Are you hurt?"

"I hit a wall," the girl said.

She bit back a laugh. Lucas was tall for his age and all skin and bones. He was fast too, like Michael. He probably didn't see the girl coming.

"Can you sit up?" She held out a hand.

The girl opened her eyes. They were wide and blue like a still lake and filled with an intensity too strong for a child. The girl pushed up on her elbows.

Theo dropped down beside her. "Hi, I'm Theo. I'm twelve. We just moved here from North Caldwell. Do you live nearby? I didn't see you in school. What grade are you in?"

"Theo, sweetie. Let's give her a little room to breathe. But I do need to know if you're hurt and where you came from. Your parents might be looking for you." And worried sick if they didn't know their child had run through the trees. She could have come from the county park behind them. The park had walking trails.

"I don't have parents." The girl sat up and rubbed the back of her head.

If this child had a concussion because she collided with Lucas, her parents could want to sue her. She searched the girl's face. Her pupils didn't seem to be dilated, but it was bright out. And she had no idea how long it took for concussion symptoms to show up.

"Of course you have parents." She must have an adult watching her.

"It wasn't my fault," Lucas said. "I didn't see you."

The girl looked at Lucas with narrowed eyes and her top lip twisted into a snarl. Lyra tried not to laugh. The girl could match Lucas's looks glare for glare. "Is that an apology? Because my—" She clamped her mouth shut. Tears filled her eyes.

Oh, crap. She was hurt. "What's your name, honey?" She needed to call her parents or her guardian or whoever was responsible for this girl. Too much time had already gone by.

"Winter!" a male voice called from the tree line. "Where are you?"

"Is your name Winter?" she said.

The girl nodded.

"Is that your dad looking for you?"

"No. I don't have a dad." She blinked away the tears.

The hairs on Lyra's arms stood up. "Were you running from this man?"

"Yes. He's mean."

"Lucas, run and get my phone. It's in my bedroom." Lucas didn't move. "Now," she said with as much conviction as she could muster without totally scaring Winter. They needed to get Winter inside before this man found her. Lucas ran and Theo followed.

"Let me help you up." She took Winter's hand and pulled her to her feet. "We'll go inside and call for help."

A rustling came from the trees as if a strong wind had picked up. Her feet froze in their spot. The man was coming through the trees. She was a trained therapist. She could handle an escalating situation, as long as the man didn't have a gun.

A large male body rippling in muscles pushed through the brush. A branch smacked him in the face, knocking him backward a few steps. His head whipped back, and he cursed. His long hair tangled in the branch. She laughed. She couldn't help it. This wasn't a mass murderer. It was Brad Wilde. She was pretty sure he wasn't a kidnapper either, but he was looking for the little girl next to her.

She stole a glance at Winter. She had crossed her arms over her small chest and set her jaw. Her blue eyes had chilled over, and she tapped her foot. This little girl was anything but afraid.

"There you are." Brad wiped at the blood on his face from the fight with the branch. He stopped short when he saw her next to Winter. "Oh, hi. I'm Brad. I live next door."

"You're Brad Wilde." They grew up in a small town where everyone knew everyone. It stung a little that he could think she wouldn't know who he was even if she couldn't remember the last time she saw him. Maybe high school graduation and that was twenty years ago.

She must look like a mess in her work clothes covered in bleach spots, the sweatshirt with the tear at the hem, and the hole at the knee of her sweatpants. She hadn't showered, and it was almost dinnertime. Even she could smell the sweat and cleaning chemicals coming off her in waves. She smoothed her hair down in some lame attempt to pull her appearance together.

He narrowed his eyes. "You know who I am?"

"Sure. Your family owns the orchard in town." She wondered if he knew anything about the scandal. He would have to. Unless someone lived under a rock, they would know what happened with her husband even if he didn't know the culprit had been her husband. And she wasn't about to tell him. It would be nice not to be judged for five minutes by her husband's bad choices. Though Brad might be judging her soiled clothing.

"I thought that was you the other day. I saw you moving in. Sorry about the interruption. Winter, we need to get back to the house." He waved Winter over, but she didn't move.

She glanced between the two and wondered what the showdown was all about. Whatever it was, it certainly wasn't her business.

Lucas came up beside her with her phone. "Here." He shoved it at her and went back inside. She put the phone in her pocket, not needing it now. She had overreacted. Too many crime shows and too many years as a therapist. It really was time to move on.

"Winter, we need to go back now. Grandpa came over to see you."

A gasp of relief almost fell off her lips. Winter had a grandfather. That must mean a parent was nearby. She still couldn't fathom why Winter didn't like Brad, but he was a little rough-looking with those tattoos, along with that hair. Though she found them insanely attractive. A rugged man had always made her lady parts sing.

But why would Winter's grandfather be next door? Unless… She squatted down beside Winter to be eye level with her. "Winter, I need a little truth at the moment. Do you think you can be completely honest with me?"

"Yes. I never lie."

"Good girl." She stole a glance at Brad. He had fisted his hands on his hip, the one with the brace was at an awkward angle. He was expertly scowling.

"Who were you running from?"

"Me. She was running from me," Brad said before Winter could answer. "Winter, can we please go back to the house so I can explain?"

Winter shook her head.

"Why was she running from you?" She stood to her full height which only made her come up to about Brad's chest. Even though he hadn't moved from the brush line, she could tell she would have to stand on her tiptoes to meet his smoldering gaze.

"I said something that she misunderstood. I didn't mean what I said, Winter."

"But you said it."

"I did. I shouldn't have said it like that. Can we go now? I'm sure Ms. Chambers would like to get back to whatever it is she was doing before you showed up at her house."

The idea of the bath and the glass of wine seemed far away at this point. She hadn't expected to get dragged into the middle of a family squabble, but she didn't mind helping out.

"You should know, so you can tell her grandfather or her parent, that she bumped into my son while running and went down pretty hard. She hit the back of her head and got the wind knocked out of her."

"Does she need a doctor?"

"I don't think so. But I'm sure her parents will keep an eye on her for any signs of a concussion."

"Concussion?" His eyes bulged from their sockets. "What do I do if she has a concussion?"

"I don't know for sure that she does. Wait a second. Are you watching her?" Where was this grandfather? And who was this grandfather Brad mentioned?

"Until her aunt comes back." His face turned the color of ash. He rubbed at his bad hand.

"What if she doesn't?" Winter said.

Brad cleared the space between them and dropped down on his haunches to look Winter in the eye. "She's going to come back for you. You'll see. Then you can live with her just the way you and she want. Okay?" He lowered his voice into something more soothing than before. "I'm sorry about earlier."

"What if Aunt Nora doesn't come back?" Winter's bottom lip quivered.

She seemed more concerned about this Aunt Nora returning than what Brad may have said. Everyone has said things they've regretted. She certainly had, even to the boys. But it couldn't have been too bad. At least she hoped it wasn't.

"She will." Brad placed his good hand on Winter's head. "Does this hurt?"

"A little. Do you promise she'll come get me?"

"I promise." A sadness passed over his blue eyes. Blues that resembled Winter's...

"My shoe is untied." Winter stuck out her foot. "I think I tripped on it when I bumped into that boy."

"Can I tie it for you?" he said.

She should slip away and allow this conversation to happen without an audience, but she stayed put as Brad softened into a teddy bear. She wanted to ask them questions, to learn more about their dynamic, but she wasn't a therapist anymore. She had no right to pry.

"I can tie my own shoe."

She stifled a laugh. A future independent woman. Lyra liked Winter more and more.

"I bet you can. I bet you're good at it too. You're probably better than me."

Winter scrunched up her nose and kept her gaze on Brad. Brad just squatted there with an adoring grin on his face. "Okay. You can do it." She lifted her leg to bring her foot closer to him.

He looked downright endearing while he propped Winter's foot up on his knee and tied her sneaker. Winter pushed Brad's hair behind his shoulder and smoothed it down. His head snapped up and that small smile burst wide open, igniting the lines around his eyes.

"Thanks, my hair was in my face," he said.

"We can go home now." Winter held out her hand for him to take, then turned to her. "Thank you for helping me."

"Yeah. Thanks." Brad stood, taking Winter's hand.

"No problem. Winter, if you want to come back over to

play with Theo, he would like that. Or maybe you two could ride the bus to school together."

"I'm being homeschooled."

"She's only here through the new year. Her aunt arranged for online classes while she stays with me." The light in his eyes went out.

Winter tugged Brad's hand. "Can I come back to play?"

"If it's okay with Ms. Chambers."

"You can call me Miss Lyra or just Lyra. Whatever you're more comfortable with. And yes, you can come over anytime. Theo loves company." She debated on saying something for a minute, but her curiosity got the best of her. "I should probably mind my own business, but may I ask a personal question?"

"I'd rather you didn't."

"How are you two related?" The words blurted out before she could stop them. She should know better than to pry; she never forced her clients to answer anything they weren't comfortable with, but she had been enamored with their dynamic. She needed more information like a flower needing the sun.

"She's my daughter." He squared his broad shoulders and set his jaw, his gaze never wavering.

"I don't understand. You said she's only here for a short time."

"Like you said, it's none of your business."

CHAPTER SIX

His secret would spread through Candlewood Falls like a bacteria. Brad kept his grip on Winter's hand because when she had slid her small fingers into his, his heart nearly stopped in his chest and a warmth rushed over his skin. Nothing he had ever done had made his skin tingle that way. Not even when he became vice president at the orchard.

Lyra stared at him with her mouth half open. She had full lips and amber-colored eyes. Kind of like whiskey. Which he could use a shot of since Winter ran off and scared the crap out of him. Those amber eyes were hooded and dark circles bruised the skin below her pretty eyes. Her clothes were splotched with white spots. Bleach maybe. She was a far cry from the put together princess he remembered who walked around like she owned the place. Her keen observation had cut him, though.

"Brad, I'm so sorry. I shouldn't have said anything." Lyra tugged at the hem of her shirt, ripping it further.

"I'm sorry too. I was rude. It's a long story."

"I didn't know you had a child. My mother never mentioned it. Not that she gossiped about you or anything. It was just when I would call her, she liked to give me the highlights as if I was missing out on something by not being here. She likes to hear about babies being born."

"Brad, your face is bleeding." Winter pointed up at him.

He wiped at his face with his brace, scratching the spot already cut open by the damn branch. Blood stained his brace and coated his fingers. "We should go. Sorry to bother you." He turned, but stopped. He didn't want to tangle with the brush again. He'd had enough for one day. "I would rather not walk back through the trees. You okay with us walking through your yard?"

"Would you two like to have dinner with us?"

Not the answer he was expecting. He wanted to go back to his house because his father was still there. He had no idea what he would do about dinner. Before Winter showed up, he just decided on the fly, usually picking something up on his way home from work. Now, he needed to learn how to plan for this kind of thing.

"Thanks, but we should get back."

Winter tugged at his hand. She motioned for him to come closer. He squatted to be eye level with her. She leaned in and placed her lips against his ear. "Do you have a girlfriend?"

He leaned back to get a better look at her. Her face was covered in innocence. Her question seemed to be legit. "No." He wouldn't elaborate in front of Lyra.

He had broken it off with a woman he dated over the summer a few times. Nothing serious there.

He had only been in love once and never dwelled on that

time for long. They had been complete opposites and at first he had loved that she was so different than he was.

"I would like to have dinner with Miss Lyra." Winter tipped her chin in defiance.

He kind of owed her after his remark about not wanting a family. But he didn't want to sit down with Lyra and make small talk. He wasn't up for a new friendship. Based on what he knew of her anyway, she was just another woman who didn't like to get her hands dirty and would disapprove of his hair and tattoos.

"It's not any trouble. I always make extra. I think the boys would like to have someone their own age to talk to instead of me." Lyra's face shone with eagerness. "Let me make up for my nosy behavior."

He stifled a groan. Women would always be the death of him, his useless mother, his sister who had fallen in love with an ex-con—albeit Caleb and he were friends now, Maggie shoving him out of her life, Winter, and now Lyra. Thankfully, he had Raf and Dad in his life. "Okay, I guess. What time?"

"In a couple of hours?"

"Sure. I need to clean up my face, and my dad is back at the house waiting for us." Dad wanted to spend some time with Winter. He couldn't deny his father that chance. He hoped Winter would go along with the idea.

"How is your dad?"

"The same." Lyra and her family never understood Dad's desires to unplug from society. He did distinctly remember Lyra razzing Brooklyn about living in a house without a bathroom on more than one occasion and in front of a group of people. He should have said no to this lady and her dinner invitation. He didn't like anyone who hurt Brooklyn.

A quick glance at the rental Lyra and her children lived in told him the princess had fallen off her throne. He wouldn't ask what happened, but the kid in him was kind of glad.

"Okay, then. I'll see you soon," Lyra said.

"Yay." Winter jumped up and down, clapping.

He was going to regret this.

Lyra wished she had a nice patio set to sit at, but all she had was the patio, if it could even be called that. Faded red pavers made a square space outlined by old, worn-out railroad ties. The wood was drier than an old woman's skin and with as many creases. Thanks to the large oak tree's roots poking through the ground, the bricks were popping up in random fashion, making the patio more of an obstacle course than a place to sit with a glass of wine. So, she stood.

"Can I get you anything else? Another glass of wine?" She only had a couple of cheap bottles of wine in the house and they were white. Michael had always teased her about her wine choices while he sniffed and swirled a mouthful before each bottle. She had tried to take it in good stride when they still liked each other, but she had never acquired an interest in fancy wines. She wished, though that she had something a little fancier to serve Brad. He ran the whole orchard now. She had been impressed with his climb up the family ladder.

"No, thanks. One is enough for me." Brad held up his empty glass. He wore a Wilde Orchard sweatshirt, jeans, and work boots. The night had grown cold from this afternoon when he had worn just a t-shirt. The sweatshirt molded to his sculpted arms. And his jeans hugged his thick thighs.

She had no business noticing him, but it had been ages since she had sex and all her female parts were at attention. Not that she wanted to have sex with him, but he was easy on the eyes. She had remembered him being tall and narrower in high school, like most boys who hadn't finished growing. He had filled out nicely.

"You don't have to sit on those awful steps. I can bring a chair from the kitchen out here." The light from the kitchen spilled down the steps. Woodsmoke floated on the crisp night air, and the stars poked through the black velvet sky. A hush of quiet covered them like fleece. She had forgotten how beautiful Candlewood Falls was.

Brad sat on the rickety steps that swayed back and forth when she walked down them. He didn't seem to mind their instability, but this wasn't how she was used to entertaining. She needed to stop comparing her old life to this one, but she missed her high-end conversation set with white cushions. Even in November.

"That's not necessary. But you're going to want to reinforce these stairs from underneath. You should call the landlord."

She had already called the landlord three times with a list of things to fix, but he had told her he didn't have the time to run out here. Her argument about paying rent had fallen on his deaf ears.

"I'll take care of it myself."

"That's what landlords are for."

"Decent landlords which this guy is not. Do you know Andy Johnson?"

"Nope. Never see him. Not that I'm home much. Well, before this." He held up his injured hand. "So, Andy Johnson won't come out here and fix his property, but he's willing to take your money. What are you going to do about it?"

"Right now? Nothing. Then I'll go onto YouTube and find a video about fixing stairs."

Brad barked out a laugh. "It's not that simple."

"I'm sure it's not that hard."

"You don't strike me as the kind of person who likes to climb under steps and roll around on the ground." Brad arched a brow as if he had heard something ironic, then checked his phone, dismissing her before she could respond.

His gesture made her insides burn. "What kind of person do I strike you as?"

He met her gaze and stood. "I don't know. Just not someone who would climb under the stairs with a hammer and nails. Don't get your panties in a knot. I didn't mean it as an insult. Some people are better at looking pretty than hard labor."

"You think I don't like to get dirty, or I'm a snob or something. Right? Lyra Chambers thinks she's better than everyone. Go on. Say it. I know you've been thinking it all night." She would ignore the part where he called her pretty.

"Hey." He held his hands up in surrender. "I wasn't the one who brought out the good china and crystal for a dinner with two total strangers."

She had done that, hoping to make the dinner a little nicer. The kitchen was still in disrepair with the linoleum worn through to the floorboards in spots. A past tenant had written phone numbers on the wall. She had tried everything she could to remove the ink, but traces of it still remained. The front of the dishwasher was dented too. But she had scoured the refrigerator and stove. At least those two things were clean now.

"You can't have pasta and meatballs on paper plates."

"I have. It's getting late. We should go." He stood. The steps shook in response. She was going to have to fix those soon. And despite what Brad Wilde thought, she had used a hammer before.

"Don't you want to let the kids finish their board game?"

"I think I should get Winter back." He opened the slider and called for Winter to come.

"Does Winter see her mother much?" She had steered clear of conversation about Winter's mother in case she and Brad had a tumultuous relationship. Winter was getting along so well with Theo and even Lucas cracked a smile or two she hadn't wanted to create more tension by bringing up a possible bad relationship.

Brad leaned against the door. "Her mom passed away recently."

"Oh my. I'm so sorry. I didn't realize. How is Winter doing?"

"Damn if I know. She barely speaks to me." He opened the door again and yelled for Winter.

"Give her time."

"She's only with me through the first of the year. Her aunt is going to have to help her with the grief." The emotion went out of his eyes as if he closed a door on them.

"How do you feel about that?" Her therapist antennae went up. A child not living with a parent spoke volumes.

Was he abusive? She couldn't imagine that. Even during dinner, he had been sweet to Winter, trying to help her pour her soda, always asking her questions, wanting to know what she thought. Winter had given him a run for his money a few times with her defiant chin and snappy retorts.

"Me? I don't think it matters. Maggie, Winter's mother, wanted it that way." He slid the door open again. "Hey, Winter, we need to leave now. If you don't come, I'm going to go in there and carry you back like a baby. Is that what you want?"

She bit back a cringe. "May I make a suggestion?"

"Depends."

"On?"

"On whether or not you're going to tell me how to parent."

"I am…was a therapist. I have some experience with dealing with children. You and your daughter have your own relationship. I'm sure she knows you love her and only want what's best for her." Old habits died hard. She only wanted to help. He seemed frustrated, but maybe she was reading him wrong. She had been dead wrong about Michael.

Winter stood in the doorway with her pink jacket on and a scowl that matched Brad's. Lyra tried not to laugh at how alike these two were.

"I'm ready." Winter pushed past him. The red mark on her forehead had faded some.

"It's about time. Say thank you to Miss Lyra."

"I know to say thank you. My mother taught me that." Winter turned to her. "Thank you for having me. I had a great time." She oozed sugar and spice with wide eyes and a gooey smile.

66

"You are very welcome, and you're welcome to come back any time as long as it's okay with your dad."

Winter glared at Brad as if to dare him to say no. She wanted to know what was going on with these two. It must have something to do with Winter's mom passing away. They both must be grieving terribly.

"Thanks, Lyra. I'll see you around." Brad took Winter's hand and led her toward the front yard.

The darkness swallowed them up, leaving her alone. Again.

CHAPTER SEVEN

L yra opened the door to the Green Bean coffee house. The strong aroma of coffee was thick and full. People chatted about work, hospital visits, and children like a choir singing in the round. The voices echoed off the high ceiling and conflicted with the gurgle of coffee machines.

A man with a shaved head, blue blazer, and sunglasses laughed and smacked his leg at a table with a woman in a t-shirt and shorts who didn't seem to think whatever he said was anywhere near as funny. Lyra glanced at her own wool cardigan and leather boots and shook her head.

Her hands shook too. She couldn't believe she was doing this. She was going to start her cleaning business. She had made up business cards and flyers to leave around town.

"Lyra…." Someone whispered her name.

She spun around, but no one was looking her way. She must have heard wrong in all this noise. Her plan was to ask if she could leave up her flyer on the bulletin board. Other local businesses had done that.

A table of three women covered their mouths and

giggled like schoolgirls. The women were all about her age. All three of them were in activewear right down to the matching sneakers. Probably a group of moms. She sometimes envied the moms who didn't have to run off to work after they put their children on the bus. But if she had listened to Michael and quit her practice, she would have had nothing in the bank.

One of the women glanced her way. Her eyes widened, and she snapped her head back to look at the others at her table. She leaned in and said something. The second woman, with red hair pulled back in a ponytail, looked over. And wrinkled her nose.

"Well if it isn't Lyra Chambers." The redhead stood.

She didn't recognize this woman, but clearly their paths had crossed. She was grateful she had bothered with a little makeup this morning and picked her clothes with care. She hadn't brought everything she owned because she didn't have the closet space in the rental. "Hello."

"I heard you were back in town."

"Looks that way." She smiled and tried to rack her brain. How did she know this woman? One of her father's employees? Maybe someone who had been to her house when her mother entertained her garden club?

"You don't recognize me, do you?"

The other two looked on with earnest. "Sure I do. Of course. It's lovely to see you again."

"I know you don't know who I am because you never gave me the time of day in high school. In fact, you had made sure to trip me in gym class in front of everyone. You laughed the hardest."

She had behaved like a spoiled brat back then. It hadn't been until the last few years when her marriage fell apart that she realized. She had no friends of her own. Everyone had belonged to Michael. No one had been in her corner when the world fell in on them.

"I'm sorry if I did that." She still couldn't remember the woman's name. Her heart ached.

"I saw what happened to your husband. That's pretty embarrassing for someone like you, I bet. How does it feel to fall off that throne and land on your ass?"

"Phoebe…" One of the other women gasped in appropriate horror.

"I guess I had that coming. Again, my apologies. If you'll excuse me." The memory hit her like a freight train. Phoebe Van Doren had been in her grade. She was short and heavy with wavy hair that stopped above her ears. She had acne and wore oversized sweaters with long army-green skirts. She had been an easy target. Lyra's stomach churned acid.

She had to get out of the Green Bean. The noise and the crowd and the warmth from the coffee makers made her head spin. The business flyer could wait or maybe she wouldn't even put it up. She spun on her heel and crashed into a solid mass of male muscle. The wind went out of her, and she stumbled back into the corner of the table.

More laughter from the group of yoga pants wearing moms.

Brad grabbed her elbow and steadied her before she landed on her butt and really gave these women something to scream about.

"I'm sorry. Excuse me." She tore from his grip and hurried outside to the sidewalk. Main Street was quiet this time of day. Most people were at work or at home. This time of year the year-rounders weren't doing a lot of shopping. Christmas wasn't far off. The tourists showed up on the weekends for flea markets, farmers markets, and festivals, but during the week there was hardly a soul. And she thanked god for that one.

She sucked in the cold, damp air. November was fickle with its weather. One day would be sunny and crisp. The next day the sky would cloud over, and the world became gray. It never rained or snowed. But the dampness would seep through clothing like cold river water and into the densest of bones.

"Hey, are you all right?" Brad had followed her out.

"Please go away. I just need a minute." She moved to the side and pressed her back against the building where the corner turned.

"I saw what happened in there." His voice was deep and thick with a little gravel in it. She could jump into the voice and swim there, but not now. Now she wanted to be alone.

"Well, you can have yourself a good laugh. Maybe even grab a seat at their table and reminisce about how horrible I was back then." She would always be judged. Her mother had judged and was still judging her every decision. Her clients and acquaintances had judged her by Michael's mistakes, and the women she went to high school with couldn't take a moment to realize she had been a child too.

"Lyra, look at me."

She forced her gaze to stay on her boots, but it had as much power to avoid him as a leaf in the wind. She met his fierce stare. Those blue eyes looked right through her. He was sexy in his flannel shirt with the sleeve rolled up to accommodate his brace. The faded jeans with tears in the legs made her mouth water because there was something provocative about a man who knew how to use his hands for labor. Sweet lord, she needed to stop this ridiculous but delicious fantasy about Brad Wilde.

"Why won't you go away?"

"Because I don't usually do what I'm told." His smile was bright against his skin. She hadn't noticed that before. Maybe because today he didn't look as pale as he did when he ran into her yard looking for Winter.

"What do you want?" She could do without any more humiliation for the day.

"I just want to make sure you're okay. Those women were tough on you." Brad glanced over his shoulder as if one of them might appear around the corner of the building.

"I deserved it. I did all those things Phoebe said."

"I don't doubt it. You made fun of my sister pretty good too back in the day."

"Please, I can't take any more of my bad childhood behaviors under the microscope. But please, tell Brooklyn I'm sorry." She had zero memory of teasing Brooklyn. But isn't that the way it always went? The one doing the teasing barely had a recollection, but the one whose feelings were hurt could conjure up that memory on cue complete with a physical reaction.

"You can tell Brooklyn yourself. She comes here a lot. Were you in there to get coffee? I could grab a cup for you."

"Why are you being nice to me?" He had hightailed it pretty fast out of her house the other night after their argument. She never expected to see him again except the occasional wave from the driveway. Theo had been asking for Winter, but she had to tell her son Winter was busy because she didn't dare go next door and knock on Brad's door. She had overstepped with her "suggestions" for talking to Winter.

"I owe you an apology for the other night. I was acting like a jerk at your house. You were right to offer me some parenting advice. I don't know what I'm doing. I'm failing epically. Winter has never lived with me before."

"But she's ten. Were you and her mother never married?" She pushed off the wall and faced him. Parents had all kinds of relationships. They didn't have to be married to live together. But most of the time a child spent some time with each parent unless there was a problem.

"I don't want to talk about all that now. Maybe some other time. I just wanted to apologize and should have come over sooner. Can I get you that coffee?"

"No, thanks. I wasn't in there for coffee." So, there was a problem, and it was none of her business. She only hoped with Winter's mother gone, there was an adult in that child's life who could give her comfort and support, if Brad was incapable. Not that he was. She wouldn't assume anything.

"I don't get it. You want a muffin or something?"

Needing to put her therapist's hat to rest, she squared her shoulders and said, "I wanted to put up a flyer. I'm starting a new business. Something simpler than being a therapist." The words tasted sweeter than she thought they would. She hadn't told a soul yet about her plan, not even Michelle, in case someone tried to talk her out of it. Like her parents.

"Oh. What kind of business?"

He would laugh if she told him. But she was determined to do this. She would have to get used to more snickering in her direction. "A cleaning business."

"Like cleaning houses and office buildings?"

"I hadn't thought about companies, but sure. Cleaning is cleaning." She didn't want anyone to be around when she cleaned. She couldn't force homeowners to go out while she was there, but a business would want her to clean when they were closed. That idea had appeal tenfold.

"Give me the flyer. I'll put it up for you." He held out his hand.

"Thanks, but not while Phoebe and her friends are in there. They might tear it down. I'll come back."

"You're not going to let them scare you off, are you? I thought you were tough. You know how to get dirty." He arched a brow, but a mischievous smile tugged on his lips.

"I'm not scared. I just don't trust Phoebe. She seems determined to make me squirm for how I treated her." She should go before one of those women came outside and saw them talking. Then the gossip mill would really churn and it would all be fabricated. Not that anyone would care about that part. She didn't need any added grist in her life.

"If you're not afraid of them, then give me the flyer." He held his hand out again.

"You apologized. We're even. You don't have to hang my flyer. When I'm ready, I'll do it myself."

"Well, hello. Look who we have here." Weezer River floated around the corner wearing her fur coat flowing behind her, denim overalls, and muddy boots. Her short hair was shellacked into place like a piece of fine art and her makeup done up to magazine perfection. The same old nosy Weezer River who would be telling all of Candlewood Falls that Brad Wilde and Lyra Chambers Ryan were huddled close on the street.

"Hey, Weezer," Brad said as if he were unaffected by Weezer's appearance on the sidewalk.

But why would he be? He was the golden boy of this

town. Nothing could dent his armor. Rumors about the two of them would do nothing to him.

"Hello, Weezer." She met that Weezer inquisitive gaze she bestowed on everyone.

"Hello, Lyra. I heard you were back in town. How's that husband of yours? Or are you planning on staying married to him?"

Heat burned up her neck and cheeks. "I wouldn't know how Michael is. He's none of my concern any longer."

"Husband?" Brad said.

"Soon to be ex-husband." The paperwork was already in place. Her lawyer felt she could get a quick divorce considering the circumstances. Michael's lawyer wanted her to stick it out until after the trial so she could play the part of supporting wife. Michael's lawyer could kiss her backside.

"I just assumed you were on your own." Brad scratched at his brace.

"I am on my own." And had been for quite some time. Michael was a roommate and a co-parent, and a bad one at that.

Weezer turned to Brad. "Did you have a nice time at the engagement party?"

"Sure. I'm glad to see my friend is happy." He turned to her. "Malbec got engaged. You remember Malbec, don't you?"

"He was in our grade." Malbec River was hard to forget with his good looks and suave demeanor. But she had never been allowed to associate with the River children. Her mother didn't like Weezer or her husband Carter.

"Did Riesling help you with your hand after your stunt?" Weezer pointed at Brad's brace.

Brad held up his arm. "She's the best. I'll be good as new soon."

"And Bradford, is it true that you have a child no one knew about until a week ago? How did you keep that secret from me?"

Brad's jaw twitched, and his spine snapped straight. "Just Brad. If you ladies will excuse me, I have to get to work."

By the hard as nails look on his face, Winter was not a topic he wanted to discuss with Weezer. But there must be some truth to that statement.

She fought the urge to ask how no one in town knew Brad had a child. Who and why does someone keep a secret like that? But it explained some of the reason why Winter has never lived with Brad.

"Work with that hand?" Weezer said with a smirk.

"There's more to the orchard than picking apples. Lyra, if you need any help with what we discussed, let me know." He marched off without a look back. She wanted to go to him and offer some comfort, but she stayed put.

"You two were thick as thieves," Weezer said when Brad was out of earshot.

"He's my new neighbor. I have to be going too. It was nice to see you again." She hurried past Weezer.

"Oh, Lyra, one more thing."

She hesitated, but not seeing a way out of it, turned to face her and hoped her expression didn't give away her true feelings. She didn't want to hear a thing Weezer had to say. She was probably going to chastise her for something she'd done to one of her seven children. And Weezer would be one to talk. All seven kids had run as far and as fast from their mother as they could. At least that's what Lyra's mother had said. "Yes?"

"I saw what those witches did in there. I was sitting in the corner having my morning cup of coffee. That redhead is just jealous. Her whole life fell apart two years ago when her husband left her for a man."

"She has nothing to be jealous of. I haven't seen her in years. She's holding a grudge." It didn't appear even an apology would let that grudge go.

"That too. But only because she couldn't rise above her station the way she had hoped. And you did. Sure, you fell off the royal seat and landed hard on your ass, but we've all done that. Now, pick yourself up and wipe yourself off so they don't have anything more to say about you." Weezer pointed at her, then followed in the direction Brad went.

She had to lift her jaw up off the pavement. The last person she ever expected words of encouragement from was Weezer River. Maybe things in Candlewood Falls had changed after all.

CHAPTER EIGHT

B rad stepped onto the orchard and inhaled the sweet scent that covered the area like a blanket. Customers walked into the market. The apple trees were dormant, but he still loved the way the empty branches twisted, waiting for next spring to produce their crop. Some of his men were in the pressing room making cider. Everything ran like a well-oiled machine and that was because of him. This place was in his blood, and he couldn't imagine any other way of life. Which was why a woman like Lyra would never be for him. That didn't stop him from feeling bad for her when Phoebe gave her crap for something that happened a long time ago.

Her declaration about starting a cleaning business had surprised him. He couldn't figure out why she would give up being a therapist to clean someone else's house. But it wasn't any of his business. He had enough of his own problems.

"Why can't I stay home?" Winter came around the front

of his truck and stood beside him. The mark on her head from the Frisbee accident was gone.

"Because I want you to see your family's business." And because he didn't want to leave her home alone. He didn't know the rules about how old a child had to be to stay home by herself, and he couldn't find anything on the internet that pertained to the laws in Jersey. He wouldn't have brought her to the orchard if he wasn't afraid she might hurt herself trying to use the stove or something. He didn't think she'd like it here this time of year. Maybe in September when she could pick apples right off the trees. Or if he had put her on one of the school tours, but none of that went on in November. With Thanksgiving around the corner, mostly the bakery got the business. People wanted their apple pies and apple cider donuts.

"Is Grandpa here?" She turned in circles as if she were looking for Silas to appear like an apparition.

Winter had taken to Silas right away and started calling him Grandpa without Silas having to ask. Silas had walked her into the woods behind Brad's house and pointed out different types of birds and wildlife. She had squealed with delight with each discovery. His dad had boasted about how smart Winter was—which she was, and that made his little girl's face turn pink.

He had to tamp down some of the green monster climbing out of his gut while all that nature talk went on. Most days, Winter still scowled at him. He deserved it, but he was hoping she might give him a little slack. He had no idea how his father had raised two kids by himself. He would be sure to say thank you to his father when he had him alone.

"I don't see his truck. I'm sure he'll be here soon."

"What about Aunt Brooklyn?"

He swore Winter had begun embracing his father and sister just to punish him. "She's not here. She doesn't come here often because her farm keeps her busy. But I can take you to see her alpacas."

"She has an alpaca farm? Let's go there next." She bounced on her toes, her messy ponytail bouncing behind her. Winter had insisted on doing her hair herself. Not that he knew how to help her, and besides, his brace was in the way.

He tried not to chuckle. Winter's excitement for everything except him made his chest swell as much as this orchard did. He wasn't expecting to feel his ribs expand as if something had pumped him full of gas. He figured missing the first ten years of her life would put him at a disadvantage, making him unable to appreciate her, but from the second he saw her come off the train, he thought he might float away.

"I have some paperwork to do in my office. Do you want an apple cider donut or something?"

"You sell apple cider donuts? Those are my favorite with the powder on them." Her eyebrows climbed up her forehead. Maybe bribing her with sweets would get him on her good side.

"Not only do we sell them, we make them in the bakery."

"Can I make some?"

"Sure. But not today."

"Why not?"

"Because no one is baking this time of day, and I don't know if I can do it one-handed." His wrist had been aching a lot lately because he was doing more than he should be, but most things were difficult with his left hand. And he was getting frustrated with his limitations. He didn't want to embarrass himself in front of Winter, and he'd like to use the donut making as a way to get her to stop scowling at him.

Winter narrowed her eyes and pressed her lips into a thin line. Her skinny arms crossed over her chest. "Brad, can I ask you a question?"

"Sure."

"Why didn't you ever visit me?"

She picked now to ask that question? He looked around to make sure no one could hear her. He hadn't told his other relatives about her yet. He figured the news would get to them one way or another. It wasn't as if Winter was a secret any longer, but he didn't want to answer anyone's questions, especially his cousin Sam's. Sam would have a hundred questions about why he hadn't told anyone about Winter, and why hadn't he insisted that he be a part of his child's life. Not that Sam wasn't right to ask, but he couldn't explain it to his cousin in any way that would make sense.

He motioned her to follow him to the bench under one of the trees and patted the bench beside him. She wiggled onto the seat. Her feet dangled off the edge. He cleared the nerves from his throat.

"Did you want me to come see you?" He had never considered that. Maggie would not speak to him about Winter. Maggie had sent back the birthday cards he had sent the first two years of her life with a letter from an attorney saying he should not contact them anymore other than the support check.

"I asked my mom a bunch of times about you. She said you weren't a good man, and we were better off without you."

"That was what your mom wanted."

"But did you want to see me? Weren't you curious about me?"

"Of course. I wanted to know all about you, but I had to listen to your mom. She was in charge, not me." And that was the hardest thing he ever had to do. In his world, he called the shots, but when it came to Maggie, she would not let him have an inch. He had to believe she knew better about him than he did. He would have made a lousy father. He was doing a rotten job now.

"If she didn't want you seeing me, then why did Aunt Nora leave me with you now?"

"Aunt Nora was in a bind."

"If Mom hadn't died, then I still wouldn't have met you."

"Probably not." He had stopped reaching out to Maggie years ago. He didn't want to disrupt Winter's life by showing up and trying to explain his absence. He knew what it was like to have a parent who didn't really want to be one, and that's what he would appear to be to Winter. He often wished his mother had walked away and stayed away when he was a kid not much older than Winter. When his mother occasionally popped into his life pretending to care about him, his insides burned with a fury. He had never needed her, didn't want her.

"Do you like me?" Her question startled him back to the bench and their conversation.

"You think I don't like you?" He had been trying to send her the opposite message and clearly not doing it.

"You make weird faces when you look at me."

"I do not."

"Do too."

"Do not." He screwed up his face, and she laughed. The

twinkling sound lifted into the air and landed smack in the center of his heart. He put his face closer to hers, crossed his eyes, and stuck out his tongue, trying to touch his nose with it.

She laughed harder and placed her hands on his face as if she was trying to capture his bizarre look. The bubble of joy in his chest expanded into his throat, blocking the air. Another burst of laughter from her popped the bubble, and he could breathe again.

"What's going on here?"

He turned toward the voice to find Raf coming from the cold storage barn toward them. Winter's laughs settled into hiccups.

"Hey, Raf. I'd like you to meet someone." He stood and shook Raf's hand with his left one. He was glad to see his friend who was always in his corner. He needed someone on his side too.

"This is Winter. Winter, this is my very good friend, Mr. Alvarez."

"Hey, Winter. You don't have to call me Mr. Alvarez. My name is Rafael, but all my friends call me Raf." Raf shot him a look as if to say he was an idiot—which he was—then held up a hand to high-five Winter, which she returned with earnest.

"Hello, Raf. Do you work here too?"

"I do. I help your dad. He couldn't run this place without me." Raf winked and Winter nodded as if she couldn't agree more.

Winter waved her hand to make Raf come closer. He obliged her. "He can't do math either."

Raf threw his head back and laughed. "*Sí, chica.* He's

terrible at math, but he's a whiz at growing apple trees. Has he taken you around the orchard yet?"

"We just got here. We're waiting for Grandpa."

Raf shot a glance at him. He shrugged. "My dad can be charming when he wants to."

"Unlike you." Raf turned to Winter. "Would you like a tour? I can drive you around on the golf cart while your dad gets some work done in the office."

"Thanks, man, but you don't have to do that." He appreciated Raf stepping in to help him out. Raf was good with kids. He practically raised his three younger brothers. But he would be the one to watch Winter and keep her busy. That was his job for the next few weeks. And with this broken wrist, he didn't have much else to do.

She narrowed her eyes. "He said you have donuts."

"We do. Lots. Do you want one?"

"Yes, please."

Brad's phone vibrated in his jeans pocket. He dug it out and hesitated. He could let the call go to voicemail. He and Winter were having a good time. He didn't want anything to ruin it. She was even taking to Raf. It was as if she might fit into his life. This call would remind her she didn't belong here, belong with him.

But Raf and Winter stared at him with a quizzical expression. He needed to make a move. "This might be for you." He held the phone out to Winter so she could read Nora's name.

Her face lit up and she answered the call. "Hi, Aunt Nora."

Raf raised a brow.

"It's Maggie's sister. She's probably calling to check on Winter."

"How are things going? She seems happy." Raf turned his back and lowered his voice while Winter chirped on with her aunt.

"I don't know. One second she hates me, the next second she asks me serious questions about why I've been out of her life." He never imagined she would show up in his world. He figured Maggie would have her convinced that a biological father was nothing more than a donor.

"And you don't have an answer for her." Raf shoved his hands in his pockets.

"Not one she'd understand. Hell, I don't understand it completely." He had stopped trying to understand just so he wouldn't lose his mind. He didn't know how else to get on with his life. He did the same thing he'd done when his mother left. She hadn't wanted him so he stayed away. Maggie didn't want him in Winter's life, so he stayed away there too.

"Is that why you didn't tell any of us about having a daughter? Because you can't figure out why you didn't have her in your life?"

"I'm sorry about that, man. I am. I just didn't see the point. From the moment Maggie told me she was pregnant, she said she didn't want me around. I figured why say anything until I could get her to change her mind. And when she didn't, I didn't know how to explain."

"Were you there when she was born?"

He glanced over at Winter to make sure she was still deep in conversation. He didn't want a repeat episode of her overhearing him. "Maggie wouldn't allow me to come to the delivery. But she had made the mistake of telling me she was in labor. I tried to get to the hospital, though. I drove all the way to Vermont, but I couldn't see her. She had a guy with her at the time. I had waited for her to come out of the hospital with the baby. But she must have noticed me because the guy came out alone and said Maggie didn't want me there and that he would be the baby's father."

His heart had broken into a million pieces in that moment, and he hadn't known that was even possible. He left then and went back to his car where he tried to drive home, but the unexpected tears made it impossible to drive. He had pulled over at a rest area and parked in the corner. He had never cried before that moment and never since.

"Brad, Aunt Nora wants to talk to you." Winter held out the phone.

He took it with his left hand. "Hey, Nora. How's it going?"

"You let her get hurt? What the hell is the matter with you? You're supposed to be watching her." Nora's loud voice bounced around in his head. He had to pull the phone away from his ear to make it stop.

"Hang on a second. She didn't get hurt. She ran into the path of a plastic Frisbee. She's fine."

"What about the boy she collided with? Or the fact she may have a concussion? Did you take her to the doctor?"

"There didn't seem to be a reason. She was okay. If she had been hurt, I would've taken her to see Doc." Or Riesling River.

"You don't know if she had a concussion. I can't believe how irresponsible you are. What was I thinking leaving her with you? Maggie would kill me if she could."

"Listen, lady, you don't know me at all, so back up. I do know what a concussion looks like, and Winter didn't have one."

"I'm going to change my work schedule. I'll be on a plane to take my niece back."

"No, you won't. She's fine. You have nothing to worry about."

"Nothing to worry about? You are the most arrogant person I have ever met."

"Why, because I can take care of my daughter and don't need you to help me? You're crazy, lady." He clamped his mouth shut a little too late. Winter stared up at him with wide eyes. Even Raf had that brow arching for his hairline.

He moved the phone away from his mouth and looked at Winter. "I'm sorry. I shouldn't have said that. Did you tell your aunt you were hurt?"

"I told her I was fine." Winter lifted her chin.

His chest filled with something that resembled pride. "She told you she wasn't hurt. I have everything under control."

"If you let one little hair on her head get hurt, you'll be sorry. I promise you that."

He was already sorrier than she knew and not because Winter was staying with him because she had gotten hurt in his care. He should never have said that he didn't want a family and made her run away. He wanted to unsay it.

"Your threats are empty. I'm going to let you return to your forest or whatever it is you're doing. Don't hurry back." He ended the call and shoved his phone in his pocket with a shaking hand.

"Wow. She got you riled up," Raf said.

"It's no big deal." His heart raced, making him a liar. He didn't dare risk a glance at Winter. He hadn't been at his best in front of her, and she would probably figure it out. She was smarter than he was even at her age.

She tugged on the sleeve of his good arm. "Brad?"

He shook his head. No way to escape her scrutinizing gaze. He should have left her home. He wouldn't have had to answer Nora's call if Winter hadn't been with him. For a stupid second he thought they were connecting, but Nora reminded him that would never happen. He wasn't really good for Winter. He didn't know how to raise her. What was he going to teach her? How to make apple cider? "Yeah?"

"Will you take me to get a donut? I can eat it while you work. If that's okay." Her smile spread across her face like the sun coming up over the horizon. She turned to Raf. "Would it be okay if we took a tour another day? I want to see where Brad works."

"Whenever you want." He high-fived Winter again and patted him on the shoulder with a nod.

"You didn't answer me. Can I have that donut now?"

He was a sucker for that smile. "Sure, kid. Let's go."

CHAPTER NINE

Lyra pulled out of the school parking lot and turned right. Nothing changed in Candlewood Falls. She had been a fool to think it would. She had left flyers all over town and not one person had called about her cleaning business. And just this morning, when she had dropped Theo off at school, one of the moms tapped on her window before she could pull away.

"Why are you back in town?" Leanne had said.

"I don't believe that is any of your business." She had known Leanne from back in the day. She was in the grade behind her.

"I heard you're starting a business. I can tell you no one who knew you then will hire you. You thought you were all that back in the day. Well, you weren't. And now that your husband is a thief, you're less than that. I feel sorry for your boys. No one will like them."

"That's enough, Leanne."

"I also heard you were dating Brad Wilde." Leanne barked out a laugh. "As if he would want you now. He could have any woman in town and plenty who want him. He's probably just using you." Leanne turned on her sneaker-clad heel and marched back to her mini-van.

Her insides shook. Who was that woman to talk to her that way? Did the whole town have the memory of an elephant? Did no one let the past stay in the past? She banged the steering wheel. She just wanted to be left alone to fix the broken pieces of her life.

Dating Brad Wilde. As if.

She turned onto Sycamore Street. She would not even entertain the idea of dating someone like Brad. He was too sure of himself and expected everyone to bend to his will. Sure, he was being nice by wanting to put up that flyer for her, but it was just like him to think he could come in and save the day. Well, he couldn't. And the likes of women such as Leanne and Phoebe would only undo whatever he had done because they were still mad about a teenage slight.

The houses in this part of town were spread out with big yards and long driveways. The streets were narrow and serpentine. Most of the leaves were gone now, but the open space made her lungs expand. She had needed the greenery and quiet in Candlewood Falls that North Jersey could not provide her, but she was second-guessing her decision to come home.

Some cars were parked along the road, causing her to slow down on the turn. A yellow sign sticking up out of one lawn read, *Save our marriage. Come to our garage sale.*

November was a strange time of year to hold a garage sale because the weather could be so iffy, but if a marriage was at stake, no time like the present. She parked in front of a white German sedan and walked up the driveway.

She loved garage sales. She had never told a soul that

because it would get her strange looks. Her mother would be horrified to go through someone else's old things like a garbage picker and would be doubly horrified to find out her daughter did it. But so many wonderful things could be found at a garage sale. And it gave a person's items a chance at another life, to make new memories in the future. She enjoyed honoring someone else's past by making it part of her everyday life. And now that she was on a tight budget, finding treasures at a garage sale would allow her to make her ugly little rental nicer for the boys and soothe some of the ache in her soul.

A couple browsed the tables, but didn't buy anything. A man with a fishing hat ambled down the driveway toward her, waving as he passed.

"Oh good, another person here to help us, Stu." A woman with short gray hair yelled over her shoulder. She wore jeans with a blue cardigan wrapped tightly over her round figure. Her face was kind, and her brown eyes twinkled.

"Well, praise the lord." Stu limped out of the garage in his flannel shirt and pants hiked up high on his waist. What was left of his hair was white and cut to a half-inch. His shoulders were hunched, but he still had some of his straight posture from his youth left. "Thank you for coming. You saved me divorce lawyer fees." He glanced at his wife with adoration.

Her stomach twisted. No one had ever looked at her that way. "How long have you been married?"

"Too long," Stu said.

"I should have dumped him for Jeffrey Nagy in nineteen sixty-four when I had the chance. He became a pilot." She leaned over and placed a kiss on his weathered cheek.

"He's nothing. I can still take him." Stu flexed a small bicep. His wife grabbed the dish towel beside her and swatted him with it.

Candlewood Falls was a small town where everyone knew everyone else, but she had no idea who these people were, and she liked it that way. For a few minutes she wouldn't be judged by her past and she could enjoy the loving banter of a couple who had learned an ease with each other that only a lifetime together could produce. She stifled an envious sigh. She had dreamed of that very thing.

She moved away from this adorable couple to inspect their wares. Tables were set up along the sides of the driveway and inside the garage. Each filled with things like crystal candlestick holders that caught the gleam of the sun, a jewelry box of costume earrings, lamps, empty photo albums, and boxes of silverware. Inside the garage was a rack of hanging clothes.

"I'm Gertrude. Please pay my husband no mind. He still thinks he's thirty."

"And still as strong," Stu said as he wandered back into the garage and into his house.

"The way you are together is lovely."

"You should see us when he comes into my kitchen with dirty boots. Are you married?"

She glanced at her empty ring finger that once wore a two-carat diamond. "Not anymore. I didn't pick as well as you did."

"I'm sorry. Divorce can be hard. Have a look around. Let me know if you have any questions."

"Are you moving?"

"To Florida. We're tired of the Jersey winters. I can't wait."

"These are nice." She grabbed a round piece of wrought iron that had been twisted into a design. The box it came from had two others.

"Stu made those. He liked to play with rusted fences." Gertrude laughed. "He would melt the iron and bend it to make decorations. I think we're getting rid of six. Our children don't want anymore."

"How much?"

"For all six? Ten dollars."

"For all his hard work."

"Don't let him hear you. He thinks he's Picasso. He wants hundreds for them. I told him to hush up. They aren't coming to Florida with us. If I could, I'd give them away. I must have a dozen in the house."

She fished a ten out of her wallet and handed it over. "I have the perfect place in the house for them. Thank you."

"My pleasure, dear. What did you say your name was?"

She hadn't, and maybe shouldn't. "Lyra."

"It's nice to meet you."

"You too, Gertrude. Say goodbye to Stu for me." She turned and went back to her car. Three other cars pulled up and parked on the road, bringing more people to save Stu and Gertrude's marriage. Lyra snickered. She liked that couple.

Some of the earlier anger had dissipated. Nice people did exist. She shouldn't lose faith. Brad had surprised her with his kindness, if it was genuine. For a therapist, even a former one, she had some real issues. She needed to stop thinking about Brad Wilde.

She put Stu's artwork into her trunk and drove herself home. She knew exactly where she wanted to hang the artwork, and she would get started on it right away. Then

93

she would go back out and pound the pavement for cleaning clients.

She pulled into the driveway and stopped short. Her mother's Lexus was parked in her spot. With a long breath, she pushed out of the car. Her mother jumped out of hers at the same time.

"Lyra, where were you?" Clarisse wore her crisp black trousers with a smart white blouse and matching black cardigan draped over her shoulders. Her heels sunk into the dirt driveway with each step.

"Out, Mother. What brings you here?" She popped the trunk and pulled out her new treasure. Her mouth watered with the possibilities this new find had.

"I wanted to see if you felt like going to the club with me for breakfast. You went out wearing that?"

She glanced down at her clothes, having forgotten what she had on. Her ripped jeans, purple sweater, and dirty white lace-up sneakers stared back at her. "It appears that way."

"My goodness. Did anyone see you in those pants?"

"They came with rips in them." And had been on sale. The sweater was one of her favorites.

"I don't understand why anyone deliberately buys clothes that look like they're ready for the garbage."

"They make me feel young."

"A good facial will do the same thing. And by the way, have you had one?" Her mother stepped closer to scrutinize.

She stepped away and grabbed her box. "I squeezed it in between the full body massage and the fraud investigation."

"Don't sass me. I'm just looking out for you."

"I don't need anyone to look out for me or my skin.

We're both just fine. I'm going to hang up some artwork. Do you want to have a cup of coffee inside?"

"Artwork? What gallery did you get them from? I heard the art gallery over in Clinton is having a fabulous show in two weeks. A new artist who does wonderful things with color. Is it some of his work? William something was his name."

"This is art by Stu. He's an old man madly in love with his wife." She unlocked the door, gave it a good hip check to get it open, and went inside.

"I never heard of him. Where does he show?"

"Mother, Stu is just a guy in town. He's not an artist. He and his wife were having a garage sale. I picked these up from them." She pulled out the first piece of wrought iron all twisted and bent and held it out for her mother to see.

"You're not going to hang that up in this house, are you?" Mom's eyebrows jumped up, cracking her makeup.

"Of course, I am."

"This place is already in disrepair. You can't make it worse by displaying someone's trash."

"Stu makes them by hand and gives them to his children as gifts. His wife has these hanging all over the house. They are beautiful."

"Anything sold at a garage sale is just someone's trash."

"You know what they say about one man's trash." She pulled the second one out and liked it better than the first. This one would go on the wall opposite the front door for everyone to see when they walked in. Everyone being her and the boys.

"Didn't you have expensive art in your house in North Caldwell?"

"I did. And it's all being sold to pay down the money Michael owes."

"I never understood why you married that man."

"You were the one who encouraged me." She threw her hands in the air. "Oh, never mind. I don't want to have this conversation again. I have some errands to run. I have to take a rain check on that coffee after all." She needed her mother to get out of her house before she blew the roof off with the steam coming out of her ears.

Someone knocked on the door. She almost wept with relief. Any distraction was welcome even though she couldn't imagine who was at the door. But with strangers present, her mother would be less likely to cause a scene.

She opened the door to Brad and his adorable daughter. "Hi," she said.

"Hello, Lyra. We brought you apple cider donuts." Winter held out a bag of cinnamon powdered donuts with the Wilde Orchards logo on it. Matching powder coated the corners of her mouth.

Brad looked on as if he was powerless to stop his girl. "She wanted to bring you some. I hope you don't mind."

"We were at the orchard today. All morning. I got a tour on a golf cart. Grandpa and Raf took me so Brad could work."

"Well, if it isn't Brad Wilde. I haven't seen you in years. What, it must be ten at least. How are you?" Her mother swooped in and planted herself directly beside her, nearly knocking her out of the doorway. "Lyra, invite your guests in. Please excuse my daughter. I think she forgot her manners."

"Hello, Mrs. Chambers," Brad said. "We can't stay.

Winter just wanted to bring Lyra and the boys some donuts."

Lyra took the bag from Winter. "Thank you. It was very thoughtful. The boys will enjoy them when they get home from school." Which would come too fast and she still had to try and get a cleaning client or she would have to put in an application at the local stores on Main Street. She really didn't want to work where she would be forced to see everyone from town.

"School?" Clarisse said. "Shouldn't you be in school too, young lady?"

"My name is Winter Reis, not young lady. I am home-schooled. I did all my schoolwork this morning so I could go to work with Brad. He said I couldn't stay home alone. But I'm big enough. I'm ten."

She covered her laugh with her hand. Winter was a handful. And more like her father than Brad probably realized.

"I think ten is too young to be left alone. Brad was right to bring you with him. Why don't you come with me so I can help you clean that donut powder off your face?" Clarisse shot Brad a wilting look and escorted Winter into the kitchen.

"I'm sorry about my mother."

"Don't be. I tried five times to get Winter to use a napkin. She refused. We'll be out of your hair in a second."

"Thank you for these. It was very thoughtful." She did not want to read into this gesture. Two thoughtful incidents from Brad. She may have misjudged him.

"No problem. Winter did think Theo would like them, and I had to agree. I mean they are the best donuts in Hunterdon County." He teased. "Plus, I thought maybe you could use a treat after the last time I saw you. Have you had any luck with getting clients?"

"Actually, no. Do you want to come inside?" She stepped aside.

He brushed past her and left his earthy scent in his wake. She leaned into it and let it wrap around her. She wondered what those strong arms would feel like holding her. She had never been with a man in such good shape. Michael had allowed himself to get doughy, but Brad was pure muscle, hard and edgy. A little like those tattoos and his hair. God help her, she wanted to touch that too.

"I'd like to hire you," he said.

"Excuse me?"

"You heard me. I need some help around my house." He held up his broken hand. "I have several more weeks with this thing, and honestly, it's a pain in my ass. There are a lot of things I can't do well with my left hand. I mean a lot. Now that I have Winter with me, I could use some help. Can you come a few times a week? And are you willing to do anything else besides clean?"

"Like what?" She told her imagination to sit the hell down.

"Food shop. I never liked doing it anyway. When it was just me, I ate on the run, but Winter needs food in the house. She's always asking for something to eat, and I don't have it. Plus, I read online that kids do better with a sched-ule. I thought I'd try to make dinner at the same time every night. You know, like a routine. Do you think that would help?"

"Help with what?"

"Help me connect to her." He lowered his voice. "Sometimes we're getting along like today, but other times, not as much. And if she gets hungry, she's a bit of a beast."

"Sounds like Theo. I need to think about it." He was nicer than she had expected, but she wondered if that was an act or not. If she did work for him, it would probably increase the rumors about her and him. She didn't need that kind of notoriety after what she'd been through with Michael. It might be better just to lay low and not give the people in town something to talk about.

"What's there to think about? You're starting a business, and you don't have any clients. Work for me, and I can spread the word around that everyone should hire you. My word goes pretty far around Candlewood Falls."

She wished she had some of that confidence. "Thanks, but I'm not sure it's a good arrangement."

"You want to make money, don't you? I'm assuming you don't want to clean houses for the fun of it."

She could think of other things that would be far more enjoyable involving the very hot Brad Wilde, but he wasn't offering that, and she wasn't about to go looking for it. Not in the literal sense, anyway.

"I appreciate what you're trying to do, but I'll figure it out. Someone will hire me eventually."

"Hire you for what?" Her mother returned with Winter now clean and spotless, though Winter's scowl had returned. Her mother had such a way with people.

"Nothing."

"Can we go now?" Winter said to Brad.

"Lyra, dear, hire you for what? Is Brad hiring you for something?" Clarisse looked between her and Brad.

"I want to go home," Winter said.

"In a second." Brad glared at Winter, but it didn't seem

to dissuade her. He turned his fiery gaze on her instead. "I want her to hire her to clean my house."

"That's nonsense." Her mouth huffed and puffed. "My daughter is a well-respected therapist. She's not someone's maid."

"Mother, I don't need you to speak for me."

"But this man has the wrong idea about you."

Brad crossed his arms over his massive chest, making room for the brace, and fixed his snarly gaze on her again, this time complete with arched brow. His body language was all dare. He had to be egging her on to tell her mother the whole truth. Well, she wouldn't give him the satisfaction of seeing her and her mother fight.

"He has the wrong idea about a lot of things."

"Like what?" Brad said.

"Like your persuasion skills for one. You assume that the whole world will sit up and listen to you just because you're...well, you. And you seem to think that you have to come to my aid as if I can't take care of myself. I don't need you"—she turned to Clarisse—"or you to take care of me. I made my choices, and I'm willing to live with them. Now, if you'll both excuse me, I have some wrought iron handmade artwork to hang." She yanked open the door and waved them all out.

But she had to make sure of one thing first. "Winter, thank you so much for the donuts and for thinking of us. Theo and Lucas will be thrilled to have them. You are a very nice person. I'm glad you live next door to me."

"Thank you." Winter turned to follow Brad out the door, but she stopped and turned back. "Lyra, I have to tell the truth."

Brad stopped too and stared at Winter. "What's up, kid?"

Winter met Brad's cold gaze with one of her own. "You said I should always say the truth, but be nice. I have truth to say."

"Can this wait?" he said.

"No." Winter turned back to her. "Lyra, the donuts were Brad's idea. He thought of you, but he wanted me to say I did. My mom used to say that I shouldn't take credit for something I didn't do. Like a school project or something. I think she might have meant something like this too."

Her words tangled around her tongue. She didn't know what to say. Heat filled her face.

"If you want the job, I'll see you tomorrow at nine. Let's go, Winter." He turned on his heel and stomped off. Winter raced to keep up.

Her mother brushed past her with her black patent leather purse dangling off her wrist. "You cannot possibly be considering cleaning that man's house. It is beneath you."

She should not even think about showing up at Brad's house with a mop and a bucket. No good could come of it. Except maybe more clients. Because whether she liked it or not, his word did have some clout in town. She'd be risking the rumor mill for sure, but her dignity was so banged up, what was one more ding? Her mother would lose her mind if she started cleaning houses. She shouldn't do that to her. Her mother meant well, loved her in her twisted way, only wanted what was best for her. As long as it fit in with Clarisse's plan.

"Lyra, did you hear me? You need to go back to being a therapist."

"Sorry, Mom, but I can't be a therapist anymore. I need

to start making money my own way. Looks like I have my first client."

Her mother hurried off in a huff. Lyra checked outside the front door.

Nope, still no broom.

CHAPTER TEN

Lyra shoved the last of her cleaning supplies into the trunk of her car. It seemed stupid to drive next to door to Brad's house when she could walk, but she'd have to make several trips to bring everything she wanted. She might have to invest in a collapsible wagon because she still had to get stuff into the house. Hopefully, he had a vacuum.

Tires crunched against the driveway. She turned at the sound of gravel meeting rubber. She wasn't expecting anyone, but maybe Michelle was making a quick stop to wish her well. She had called Michelle to tell her about Brad's offer.

Michelle had said, "Jump on that offer. Then jump him."

She had no intention of jumping a client. Even if he was the sexiest man she had ever seen. What would he want with an almost divorced woman with two boys and a sketchy future? He would want a woman who was put together better. Someone like who she used to be before the rug was yanked out from under her, and she went careening to the floor on her head.

A sleek silver sedan bounced along her pathetic excuse for a driveway. Her stomach hollowed out. This wasn't any expensive foreign car. Oh, no, this car had subtle black leather interior that felt like butter against her skin. A hint of musk always surrounded the inside no matter how many miles the car saw. She had laughed and cried in that vehicle.

Michael jumped out of the car. He must have gotten bail. His black trench coat floated in the wind as he hurried toward her. He waved a large manila envelope in his hand. At least the boys weren't around to witness what was about to go down.

"Hello, Michael."

"Are you kidding me with these divorce papers, Lyra?" Anger strangled his voice like a serial killer with a death grip on his victim's throat. His cheeks were flushed, and his hair was disheveled instead of the slicked back look he preferred.

"I don't believe so." She checked the time on her phone. She didn't want to be late on her first day of work.

"We can't get divorced. How will that look when I go to trial? Are you trying to send me to jail?"

"I believe you've managed that feat all by yourself." She aimed her gaze past Michael, not wanting to look at him. Two big bushes flanked the end of the driveway, making it hard to see the road. She'd have to get them trimmed. She would add it to her list.

"But it won't look good to the jury if you aren't the supportive wife." Spit flew from his mouth as he choked out each word. She almost felt sorry for him. He was out of control and not used to being helpless.

"I guess you should have thought about that before you stole money. Why did you come here? We could have had this conversation on the phone." At least then she could have hung up on him.

"Because I wanted you to tell me to my face that you want a divorce. I don't understand you. Why do you want to put the screws to me too?"

"Michael, I don't want to be married to you anymore. Was that clear enough? Don't drag this out any longer than it has to be. Just sign them, and we can both get on with our lives."

"I'm not signing these papers. I need you."

"You have never needed me or wanted me for that matter. I was a habit. You should be concerned about your relationship with your children now." She checked the time on her phone again. Now she was late. But she was not going to tell Michael where she was going. She would just have to find a way to explain her tardiness to Brad.

"Right now I have to plan my defense. I can't spend time in jail. I won't survive there. Not for five minutes. You can't let me go to jail. I need you sitting behind me in that courtroom. I need every advantage on my side for this fight."

She pounded her thighs. "I don't care anymore what you need. Don't you get it? I'm tired of caring about your needs. It's always been about your needs. You're like an actor on the stage who has to steal the whole show. No one else's needs ever come close to being met as long as your needs are in the way. And they always are. Even now. You don't care one bit how what you've done has affected any of us. You only care about staying out of jail. Well, I hope you go to jail." She squeezed her eyes shut and screeched like a banshee.

"You're out of your ever-loving mind with all that yelling. This isn't over. Not by a long shot." Michael shook the envelope in his fist and hopped back into the car. His car kicked up dirt on the way back to the road.

She bent in half with her hands on her knees and sucked in long breaths. Maybe she was unstable. Maybe she had finally come unhinged.

On many occasions, she told her clients that it was okay to let out the emotions. Scream. Cry. Yell. Whatever it took to get through the pain. Because pushing the pain down would do no good. She had to walk through the discomfort to the other side in order to get on with her life. And she didn't even love Michael. She had stopped loving him a long time ago. She was grieving the idea of losing a husband. Of losing the story she had written in her head.

But she would have to shelve further introspection because she needed to get to Brad's before he fired her.

She got in her car and followed the driveway, finding a spot behind his truck. His house fit him. The deep-red clapboard had a farm feel to it. The swing on the wraparound porch invited her to sit and look out at the trees. He had a pile of cut wood for the fireplace. The front door was wood and tall with a glass window.

Brad came out onto the porch. He stole her breath with his hair hanging over his broad shoulders. His black shirt fit to his muscles, making her fingers want to take a walk across them. He gave a small wave.

"Hi," she said, getting out of the car.

"Are you okay?" He trotted down the steps, his legs bowing slightly at the knees. She was a legs gal, and she liked butts, and arms, and help her god, everything about this man's body.

"Sure. Why?" She hurried to the trunk to give her hands and mind something to do beside ogle him.

"Did I hear you yelling a few minutes ago?" He followed her around the car. Even outside, his presence sucked up the air.

"I don't think so." She grabbed the tote to put some space between them.

"Lyra, give me a break here. I stepped out onto the porch and saw you talking to some guy right through the trees. I might be a farmer, but I'm not stupid. I just want to know you're okay. Do you need me to speak to that guy? Who is he anyway?"

"That was my soon-to-be ex. He wants to contest the divorce. And no, I don't need you saying anything to him. I can take care of it myself."

"Why were you yelling? And don't say it wasn't you." He arched a brow.

"Okay, yes. That was me. Are you happy now? You saw me behaving badly." She might as well come clean. She was too tired to fight him, and if he told the whole damn world, so be it.

He stepped closer and put his hands over hers, holding the tote. "I've done my share of behaving badly. That was not it." His blue eyes darkened like a storm-filled ocean.

She swallowed hard against the lump in her throat. Images of him doing all kinds of bad things played on high speed in her mind. Tugging on the tote, she side-stepped him and headed for the door.

"I do not like fighting with people. In fact, all I've wanted since I've been back was to live my life in peace. But the whole town has held a grudge."

"The whole town?"

"Yes."

"Not me. Can I help you with that?" He hurried after her, cutting her off before she could get to the steps.

"Not with your broken hand. Back up, big guy." She tried to dodge him, but he was too fast. "You're impossible."

He stepped back and choked out a laugh. The laugh ignited the distinguished creases around his eyes. He opened the door for her. She caught a whiff of his earthy scent. This man would be the death of her.

The entryway had white clapboard on the walls, and the floor was a dark hardwood that flowed into the open space which included a living area and a kitchen behind that. A staircase with a wood railing cut into the space in the middle without taking up space. A hallway led off the living area to the right and left.

"Why do you let what other people think bother you?" he said.

"I don't." She did know why she worried about other people's opinions. She had been raised to worry. Her mother drilled into her that a Chambers was always put together. A Chambers never let her slip show. A Chambers was someone everyone else wanted to be. And she had believed it for so long.

But everything had changed when she realized her whole life had been built on a false image. She wasn't this happy, put together person. She was a mess. Even now with her cleaning clothes on, no makeup, and her hair piled on top of her head, half of it spilling around her face like string cheese. She almost laughed at her silly fantasies about Brad. He would never want her.

"Do you really need all those things?" He pointed to the tote she had put down when they walked in.

"I like to be prepared."

"For what? It's one house, and only two people live in it."

"Are you going to let me do my job, or are you planning on micromanaging me?" She hadn't known what she would need or want when she started this job. She preferred to have it all so she would look competent.

"I don't do that. I wouldn't do that."

"Something tells me you might. You're used to running the show and have a lot of people who answer to you. Leave the cleaning to me, okay?"

"It's your party."

"How many bedrooms?" His home was warm with a stone fireplace and built-ins flanking it, but other than some beige curtains on the windows, nothing decorated the walls or the shelf space other than a very large television. She saw no pictures of his family or even of himself anywhere.

"Three. All upstairs. There's an office on this floor to the left and a laundry room and half bath down that hall to the right."

"How many baths?"

"Three upstairs and the half down here. I have a basement, but it isn't finished so you don't need to clean that."

"Good to know." She had no idea how long cleaning his house would take. She could spend hours cleaning her own, but if she planned on making any money at this, she would have to cut corners. She also didn't need to spend any extra time in his personal space.

"This is a lot of house for one guy. How long have you lived here?" Had there been some woman who had occupied this space with him? Where was she? She wanted to know more about the man with a hard exterior and sweet undercurrent.

"About five years. I bought it for the property. I've been fixing the house up the whole time. It's almost done."

"It's lovely." She hoped to give her sorry little rental the illusion of lovely. She couldn't find any more garage sales coming up. She might have to go into town—which she loathed to do—and meander around the antiques store for a find.

"Thanks. I wanted a nice house with some space to move around in. Not a lot. I don't need much, but having a bathroom inside beats having to run out to the outhouse in the cold night." His face beamed.

She had almost forgotten that Brad and Brooklyn grew up with their dad in his cabin up the mountain. Silas was an eccentric guy. She wasn't sure if keeping some of the basics away from his children was a good idea, but Brad didn't seem too worse for wear because of it.

"You'll have to tell me sometime what it was like living in that cabin." She understood now why one guy would want so many bathrooms.

"It wasn't all bad, if that's what you're getting at. It wasn't the house you grew up in, with all the fancy crystal chandeliers and maids running around, but it was home. We did all right there." His words sliced deep.

"I wasn't trying to offend you."

Her parents' home was something out of a magazine—he had that much right—but she had never felt truly comfortable there. Her mother had so many rules about what could be touched and what couldn't. She was never allowed to make a mess because someone might pop over unexpectedly, and her mother never wanted to be caught off guard. She was never allowed to have a friend in her room if it wasn't spotless.

"You didn't offend me. Not possible, actually." The warmth had left his eyes and was replaced with a stark stare. "Do you need Winter and me to leave the house?"

She picked up the box and headed for the remodeled kitchen with its white quartz countertops, white shaker cabinets, and stainless steel appliances. "That's up to you. I can work around you, if you want to stay. Is Winter upstairs doing schoolwork? You don't have to disrupt her."

"She was." He sagged against the island's counter. The fight, it seemed, had drained out of him. "She and I are having a bad morning. She locked herself in her bedroom." He glanced at her from the side.

Her heart knew some of his pain. She wanted to go to him but removed her cleaning supplies from the box instead. "It's not easy being a parent, and you've been thrown into it after the game already started. And the rules change often and fast."

She had counseled many parents over the years who didn't understand their children. They would sit in her office with despondent expressions, wondering where the child they knew went and who was this new unrecognizable creature threatening to cut them out of their lives. She was on the road not far behind those parents with her own two children. Lucas was pulling away more and more every day, especially since they had moved. She needed to do a better job of checking in with him.

"I'm not used to coming in off the bench, that's for sure." A small smile tugged at his lips.

"Ah, yes, you were mister football back in the day." She had cheered at every game for four years, watching all the boys tear up the field. She had never wished Brad would look her way back then. Her mother had told her any young man from the Wilde family was not marriage material. Clarisse believed the worst of Brad's father. Brad's one uncle was a drunk and had died in a brawl. His other uncle had a reputation for being mean. That uncle belonged to a group of men who sat in judgment of others and on occasion tried to run people out of town that were different than they were.

"You remember that I played ball?" That smile spread wider and warmed his eyes.

Wonderful. The man would think she was just another woman hot for him. She could imagine the length of the list of women who have tried to catch him. She needed to change the subject and decided to bring it back around to Winter. A much safer subject.

"Does Winter talk about her mom?"

He regarded her for a moment. "Not much." Moving around the island, he pulled a bottled water from the fridge. He held it up in a gesture to ask if she wanted any. She shook her head.

"You should ask her about how she feels. She's got to be missing her mom terribly. It's hard for a child to lose the only parent she's known. And she's been taken from her home and hoisted on some guy she's never met."

"But I'm her father." He hit the counter with the water bottle. Some spilled out. He reached for a towel, switched hands at the last second, and wiped up the water.

"Yeah...don't take this the wrong way, but you're not her dad in the way it counts. At least not yet. I know you're trying, and that's great. But it takes time to bond and for her to feel safe with you."

"She doesn't feel safe with me?" He pushed away from

the counter and went to the windows on the back wall, looking out onto his property.

His land, like hers, backed up to woods. She loved that about this stretch of road. She could never afford the privacy a large yard would give her and she needed, but the woods behind them gave her the feeling of being protected by green space. He must love the space and the trees as well.

"I don't know for sure if Winter feels unsafe. She might not. But she has to be scared a little. Hell, I'm scared about moving back to a town I knew, and I'm three times her age." She closed the distance between them, no longer able to control herself, and placed a hand on his arm. Touching might be a step too far, she would never touch a client, but the hurt was on his face and she had these feelings swirling inside her she didn't know what to do with.

"Have you thought about family therapy?"

"She isn't staying with me that long."

"What's going to happen after she leaves?"

"What do you mean?"

She wanted to hit him upside that thick head with her duster. "I mean, Brad Wilde, when Winter goes to live with her aunt, do you have plans to stay in her life?"

CHAPTER ELEVEN

Brad walked past the bathroom for the third time. Lyra was scrubbing the heck out of his tub. He had no idea it was that dirty. Or maybe she was still working out her problems with that husband of hers. Ex-husband.

He returned to the kitchen, unsure of what to do with himself. He couldn't chop wood. He couldn't do anything meaningful at work. He wasn't much of a cook, but he could make a mean applesauce. And he couldn't leave the house to go for an easy hike because Winter still hadn't come out of her room.

He hadn't answered Lyra when she asked what his plans were for Winter after she left. He hadn't thought that far ahead. He was trying to get from one day to the next. Next week was Thanksgiving and then Christmas just a few short weeks later. He had no idea how to handle Christmas with a kid. He should probably get a tree. They could cut one down.

He stopped and cursed. He wasn't cutting any damn tree down with his broken hand. He wasn't going to make applesauce or cut apples or wrap presents all that well with this hand. He wanted to rip the brace off and throw it out. But he heard Riesling's words and Raf's warnings. Take care of that hand or he wouldn't be able to prune and plant in February. His orchard was his life. Winter would leave. And she probably wouldn't want him around at all. He saw no point in making future plans.

"I'm all done." Lyra came into the kitchen lugging that huge box of hers. He had to refrain from laughing because the box was half her size. He would have let her use his supplies if she had only asked, but she had wanted to be in complete control. She had even seemed surprised he owned a vacuum. He had no problem with a woman who wanted to be in control. They were usually the best in bed.

"Thanks." He pulled out his wallet and handed over the agreed upon amount in cash. He wanted to pay her more, but she told him no. He didn't want her to struggle. Living in that dump next door could only mean she didn't get much in the divorce and was trying to make it without her family's help. He admired her guts—and her figure.

Even in her black sweatpants and dusty sweatshirt, she was beautiful. Her hair spilled out of the hair tie and around her face. She continued to blow the strands away with a fierce whoosh from the corner of her mouth only to have them float back down in stubborn defiance. Her cheeks were red from all that scrubbing, but her amber eyes glowed. They reminded him of freshly jarred honey, and he wanted a taste.

"I have something for you," he said, trying to ignore the heat in his low belly. Lyra wasn't what he had expected. She was far more down-to-earth than she used to be. Time and life had mellowed her. But she was closed off, not letting him near her. When she had touched his arm earlier, it was so out of character he almost screamed like his cousin Sam.

"You don't have to do anything else for me." She turned her gaze away. He wanted it back.

"It's nothing big." He dug the card out of his wallet too. "Here. You have another client."

"What?" She hesitated but took the card.

"Denise Newfeld wants you to clean for her. I was talking to her at the orchard the other day. You came up in conversation. She jumped on the chance to hire you."

She handed the card back. "Thank you, but no. Denise Newfeld hates me. Well, she hated me in high school. We were huge rivals. She's probably just looking for the opportunity to rub my failures in my face."

"Come on, Lyra. That was twenty years ago. You can't believe Denise still cares about that stuff, can you?" He refused to take the card. She dropped it on the counter.

"I can, and I do. You saw how Phoebe behaved in the Green Bean. And the other morning at parent drop-off, Leanne Jones screamed at me in line. No, thank you. I don't need Denise Newfeld's business."

"How many other clients besides me do you have?"

She rearranged the contents of her box and avoided his gaze.

"Lyra?"

Her head snapped up, and her eyes burned with indignation. "Just you. You can tell everyone that comes to the orchard that Lyra Chambers is a failure. Everyone can say I deserve it, that I had it coming because I was such a stuck-up bitch. Karma and all that." She waved a hand in the air and worked her bottom lip under her teeth.

He came around the counter and stood inches from her.

She smelled of flowers with a hint of bleach tucked in. "Do you really think I enjoy seeing you suffer? I mean, if I did, wouldn't it have been more fun to sit down and watch Phoebe have her way with you than go out of my way to give you a job and find you more? You're mad at the world, but don't be mad at me."

"Why are you being so nice to me? If it's all an act, let's just end it here and now. I've had enough unpleasant surprises in my life recently. I could do without you pulling the rug out from under me too."

"You think I'm pretending to like you?"

"I don't know, Brad. I can't figure out why you're so willing to help when everyone else is so willing to make me pay."

He closed the space between them with half a step. He should stop before he got his face slapped, but he had to make her understand that she had his head turned around. She tilted up her chin to meet his gaze. Her chest expanded faster.

"I never do anything I don't want to." He held her chin between his thumb and finger. He had to use his left hand and hoped he wouldn't look as awkward as it felt. He wanted to be in control right now more than anything because he was pretty sure if he showed any weakness she would misunderstand him and run away.

"But why do you want to help me? Tell me why." Her words were raspy like sandpaper over wood. She ran the tip of her tongue over her lip. He was a goner.

"Because I want to be the one who puts a smile on your face."

The heat between them was thick enough to cut. He slid his hand from her chin to cup her cheek. She stared up at him with wide, expecting eyes. Her skin burned his hand. He leaned in and pressed his lips to hers.

The connection made his body tremble, surprising him. She kissed him back with a fierceness, pushing his lips open with her tongue. She hadn't hesitated, as if she had wanted him to kiss her. His head spun. She was going to knock him on his ass with the power behind that kiss. He hoped his legs wouldn't decide to give out.

Her arms went around his neck. She pressed her soft body against his. He tugged on her hair, tilting her head up more, deepening the kiss. His other hand came up to cup her cheek. He needed to touch her, wanted to touch her everywhere. He wanted to hold her against him, kissing her until they were exhausted.

Her tongue dipped and rolled, taunting him. Her teeth nipped his lip. He bit back a groan and ran his hands down her back. In sudden surprise, the kiss stopped like a record player needle scraping vinyl.

"Ouch." She yanked her head back.

"Oh, shit. I'm sorry." His brace was stuck in her hair. He had forgotten about his wrist and the Velcro because she was blowing his mind with that tongue of hers. "Don't move. I'll get it out."

He leaned closer to get a better look, putting his lips near her ear. His heart raced around in his chest and sent heat to his face. And not in a good way. He had never been in the kind of situation with a woman where he blundered through sex.

She gripped his arm while he worked her hair free. He stole a glance at her, expecting fury to line her face. Her cheeks were spotted pink. She gnawed on that lip again. She met his gaze and smiled. Maybe he'd get another chance to do this the right way.

"Gross. Are you two kissing?" Winter stood in the doorway with her hands on her hips. A scowl plastered across her cute face.

"It's not what it looks like," he said.

"I know what kissing looks like, Dad. Yuck." She turned on her heel and marched out of the room.

Getting caught by Winter was worse than getting caught by his father. He pulled his hand free. Lyra rubbed her head. Winter's words shook him.

"Wait a second. Did she just call me Dad?"

Lyra stared at the card with Denise Newfeld's number on it. She should not call this woman. She would only end up regretting it later.

She walked out of the kitchen into her living area, then back again. Dinner was cleaned up, and the boys were in their room doing homework. The house was quiet for five minutes. Now would be a good time to make a call before Theo or Lucas remembered they needed her to do something.

She stared at the card as if it might jump off the counter and bite her. She grabbed her cell, a cardigan off the hook by the back door, and pushed out into the backyard with the card between her fingers. The lights in Brad's house glowed through the bare trees. Her fingers floated over her lips.

Brad Wilde had kissed her senseless. She wanted to scream again, and this time with fists in the air and joy coming from her

119

throat. That man could kiss. She hadn't doubted it. He was suave and confident. And rugged. A man in a flannel shirt, work boots, and a few tattoos turned her to pudding. Chocolate pudding. Chocolate pudding that she could lick off Brad. She exhaled long and deep. She didn't even care that his brace had snagged her hair. He seemed a little embarrassed by the whole thing, but not as embarrassed as when Winter caught them.

She shoved her arms through the cardigan and plopped down on the step that still wobbled from side to side. She did need to get that fixed.

She stared at Denise's number again. They were never friends. Denise was the girl that everyone liked in school. She had a saccharin smile that Lyra was pretty sure had been glued on with bubble gum. Denise pretended to be everyone's friend, but she had overheard Denise more than once stabbing those girls in the back. No one had ever caught on, and she couldn't figure out why.

Denise went to all the right parties, was on the student council, and was the class treasurer. She was on the yearbook committee and the homecoming committee. Denise volunteered to be a part of the theater's crew. Lyra was pretty sure Denise did all the behind-the-scenes things because it saved her from being cut from any of the activities. Smart, actually. All the reward without any of the risk. She wished she had thought of it herself.

Denise didn't like her because she was the cheer captain, the homecoming queen, the prom queen, voted most popular and most attractive. Lyra's picture was on most of the yearbook pages. Right next to Denise's.

If she was going to make this venture work, she needed more clients. She had bills to pay and boys to raise. She swallowed what was left of her pride and dialed.

Denise picked up on the second ring. "Hello?"

"Hi, Denise, this is Lyra Chambers Ryan. How are you?"

"Oh, Lyra. I'm so glad you called. Brad Wilde said he'd give you my number, but I hadn't heard from you. I figured you had changed your plans." Denise's voice was as she remembered, high pitched and squeaky.

She pushed off the steps and paced her little patio, being careful not to trip over the pavers sticking out of the ground. "Brad mentioned you were looking for a cleaning service." Her stomach twisted into a million mop strings. She should have driven to the next town or two towns over and culminated clients from there.

She imagined Denise getting off the phone and telling everyone of her friends that Lyra Chambers was desperate and begging for work. They would all have a good laugh. Every time she thought she could pull this off in her hometown, all her old anxieties reared their head. She wasn't a child anymore. She had nothing to prove anymore. It didn't matter what these people thought. Brad was right about that, but she struggled to heed his advice.

"I just had to let my last cleaning person go. They scratched up my brand-new stovetop and wouldn't fess up about it. Horrible, really. Anyway, I'd like to have you come by for a trial run. I'll pay you, of course. Afterward, I'll inspect your work, and if we're a fit, it's a go-ahead. What time tomorrow can you come by? I'll text you my address."

Denise wanted to give her an interview. The gall of that woman. She had never heard of anyone interviewing their cleaning person especially if they've come recommended. She glanced over at Brad's house. How much did he have to push Denise for this phone call? She hoped he hadn't tried too hard.

"Lyra, sweetheart, are you still there?"

"Yes. Of course, text me your address. I can come over after I drop Theo off at school."

"See you then." Denise ended the call.

She should be happier that she had her first real client. She would ace Denise's test. So why did she feel as if she was about to walk into the lion's den?

CHAPTER TWELVE

Lyra pulled into Denise's driveway and swallowed the envy stuck in her throat. The house stretched into the cloud covered sky with the rolling hills as a backdrop. The house with its taupe siding, tan stone around the double glass front doors, and three-car garage sat as if it were keeping guard of what had to be over five acres. She had lived like this once. She missed the comfort and security a house like this could bring, mostly at night when she lay awake in her small bedroom wondering what the future held.

Today the future held a cleaning client. She pushed out of the car into the damp November air and straightened her shoulders. She chose to leave Michael and start over. Starting over looked like her wearing her favorite yoga pants she would never clean in for fear of ruining the hundred-dollar fabric and matching racerback tank that flattered her curves underneath her zip-up fleece that she bought on sale at a major department store's seconds outlet.

She had even bothered with makeup that she would probably sweat off.

Starting over also looked like her setting a good example for her boys. She wanted to show them that life wasn't always fair, but hard work and perseverance paid off. She grabbed her tote of supplies and rang the bell.

Denise opened the door in a similar outfit, but Lyra doubted Denise had scoured the racks for a deal. She had expected Denise's overbright smile, but instead Denise's smile wobbled on her lips. Her eyes were red-rimmed and the tip of her nose pink. She clutched a tissue in her hand. "Lyra, you made it. Come on in." Denise sniffled and wiped her nose with the back of her hand instead of the tissue.

"Denise, I don't mean to pry, but if you have a cold, we can reschedule." The last thing she needed was to get sick and bring it back to the boys right before Thanksgiving. She had only planned a small dinner for the three of them. This year would be unlike any other year when they had hosted two dozen people all of whom were connected to Michael in some way.

"No, no, it's fine. I was watching kitten videos. That's all. No need to worry. Put down your box and let me give you a tour." She left the box in the two-story foyer and followed Denise from room to room as she doled out the list of dos and don'ts.

Denise returned to the kitchen while she went upstairs to begin. The house echoed even though it was filled with artwork and beautiful pieces of furniture. Denise didn't really need a cleaning person. The bathrooms were practically spotless. She and her husband didn't have kids to drag their toys, shoes, and dirty underwear around. Denise didn't even have a dog. She wondered for a brief second if the boys would like a puppy for Christmas. As if she needed something else to look after, but it might make Lucas smile again.

She was done with the work inside of an hour and searched for Denise to say goodbye to—and more importantly, get paid. She had expected Denise to pop in and check on her while she worked, but she hadn't seen her. Not even when she was cleaning the kitchen. If Denise always stayed hidden while she worked, then cleaning here might not be so bad. And if Denise ended up happy, she might even refer her to her friends. She owed Brad if this worked out.

She did a lap around the first floor and found Denise sitting on the back patio wrapped in a blanket, clutching a coffee mug—and crying. *Oh, boy.* Did she back out gracefully and return whistling to let Denise know she was there? Or did she run for the front door and forget she ever saw Denise blowing her nose between muffled wails. She could do without the money for now.

Instead, her feet knew what to do before her brain agreed. "Denise, are you okay?" She approached as if Denise was a wounded wild animal, and in some ways she was.

Denise jumped in her chair and dropped the mug on the cement patio. The white porcelain cracked into several large pieces. "Oh, no." She cried harder.

"Stay there. You don't have on any shoes. I'll get something to clean up with." She ran for her tote where there was a dust broom and a pan. Brad had teased her about being overprepared. But she was glad she had thought ahead. She hadn't seen anything like this in Denise's house, and the brooms were in the garage. Too far to run.

She returned to find Denise tiptoeing over the pieces in her bare feet. She shook her head. Denise listened about as well as Theo did.

"Denise, you're going to cut your feet."

"Oh, who cares?"

"You will when you bleed all over your pretty patio." She brushed up the pieces and did an extra sweep to make sure she got everything.

"I don't care about this patio. I hate it. I hate the whole house." Her face crumpled.

She should turn and run. She didn't need to console this woman. They weren't friends. They didn't even like each other. Well, they hadn't. She didn't know Denise at all anymore.

"How about if I make us some tea? It's damp out here." She had seen a silver teakettle under the stovetop.

"He's cheating on me." Denise sniffled, shook her head, and met Lyra's gaze.

"Your husband?" She racked her brain for her husband's name, but couldn't pull it up. Had Denise ever mentioned it?

"Ian is cheating on me with some twenty-five-year-old bimbo in his office. Why is it always the young ones? And what does she see in him? He's in his forties, balding, and he's already paunchy in the middle. She's pretty. She could have anyone her age."

"You saw her?"

"She's on Instagram."

Of course, she was. "Have you talked to him about this?"

"He didn't deny it. He looked me right in the eye and said the bimbo was hot for him. He liked being desired. He said I was a cold fish and boring." She burst into tears again.

She put the dustpan down on the chair. "Let's go inside and have that tea." She ushered Denise to the kitchen island and moved around until she located the tea bags.

"I used to like sex. I did. I keep telling myself I'm too young to not want to do it, but every time Ian comes near me…I don't know…I don't want to touch him. There must be something wrong with me." Denise grabbed a napkin and blew her nose.

She put the water up to boil. "There's nothing wrong with you. Have you and Ian been having trouble for a while now?" She and Michael had started having problems right after Theo was born. Michael had been the one to turn away from her. At first she hadn't noticed being too busy with a newborn. But then somewhere along the way she had reached for her husband, and he didn't reach back. He had one excuse after the other, usually involving work. His excuses had seemed plausible, and she was busy with her boys and her practice. She wasn't paying attention to Michael. And therein lay the problem.

"We haven't had sex in a year. At first I thought it was a rut. Relationships go through those things. We were both busy with work. We both volunteer for different organizations. But last year I brought up kids. That was when things changed."

The teakettle whistled, interrupting the conversation. She poured water into the mugs, milk into Denise's, and took the seat opposite her. She listened while Denise prattled on about the changes in Ian and what had led up to today's breakdown. Ian was moving out. He was in love with his bimbo. And the bimbo was pregnant.

Denise's clock to the jaw was just as bad as hers had been. Michael had affairs, had been with hookers when he was arrested. And there was the little thing of committing a felony and losing everything they, all his employees, and stockholders had worked for.

The next time around with a man, she wanted someone simple. Someone who didn't live a life in the limelight. Someone who didn't care what other people thought, didn't shop for the best clothes, the best cars, the best boats. She wanted a man who was down-to-earth. A man like Brad.

Denise heaved a heavy sigh. "Thank you for listening to me."

"You're going to be okay. You're tough." She eased off the stool and collected her things.

"Will you be back next week? I don't blame you if you never want to speak to me again. We were never friends, and then I make you take care of me while I have my break-down. You're very nice, Lyra. I'm sorry I didn't see that sooner. And if I can be honest for a second, I had planned on making today hard on you. I wanted you to sweat for a little while as payback. I really am a horrible person."

"That was honest. Thank you for saying what's on your mind. More people should try it. I don't mind listening. If I can be honest too, I used to be a therapist, but I closed my practice before moving back."

"You're very good at it. Let me get you a check." Denise ran from the hallway and returned with the money. "Next week. Oh, it's Thanksgiving. Can you come Wednesday?"

She had so much to do to get ready for the holiday, but she had to make this work. "I'll be here."

"Perfect. See you then." Denise gripped her in an unexpected hug and held on tight. "I'm going to send Brad a big box of cookies to thank him for sending you. You're very lucky to be dating him." Denise winked.

"We're not dating."

"Really? The way his face lit up when he spoke about you, I thought for sure you two were a fast and furious thing."

"Nope. Just neighbors." She hoped Denise hadn't pulled out the telephone chain to spread that rumor.

"Too bad. He's hot. Any woman in her right mind would snag him up."

Denise had a point. But she wasn't ready to snag anybody. And Brad had a lot on his plate with Winter. He wasn't ready for a commitment.

"I think he knows that," she said. One look at Brad's swagger and any person would know the man exuded confidence. If he were a pro athlete, women would write their numbers on their bellies and flash him as he passed by.

"It's that arrogance that gets the women every time. It makes a girl wonder what he must be like in bed, all rough and in charge. He wasn't ever my type. I don't like those tattoos or the fact he probably had a string of women in his bed. But he does have a lot to offer. He's worth a ton with that orchard. A real catch, if he could ever settle down. I don't think anyone has the power to hold him."

She said her goodbyes with promises for next week and returned to her car. On the way home, she stopped at Wilde Orchards. She wanted some apples. And nothing more. Nothing like a glimpse at the man who had it all. A man that might kiss like the devil, but could never want her. Not the way she was now. She couldn't offer him anything he didn't already have.

But it didn't stop her from wondering what he was like in bed either.

And wonder was all she would do.

CHAPTER THIRTEEN

Brad threw the pen on the desk. He ran his good hand through his hair. He had papers to sign and could barely hold the pen. Part of his job was to renew contracts with the retailers who sold their apples. They had two new supermarkets who wanted Wilde apples, but he couldn't get them on the truck until both parties had signed. Something that should take him ten seconds took ten minutes and looked like a first grader signed it. He grabbed his phone and sent a text to his cousin Sam with voice command.

Come to my office.

Be right there.

He pushed out of the chair hard enough that it rolled into the wall and left a mark. He glanced out the window that looked onto the parking lot. Lyra's blue Volvo pulled into a spot. She hopped out wearing cute workout clothes that hugged her legs. She had great legs. She also had great lips. Lips that had made his head spin for the whole day. She went inside the store. He'd run over and see if she needed any help.

He turned from the window and almost collided with Sam. Sam was his younger cousin, his uncle SJ's son. SJ had died twelve years ago in a drunken fight. Brooklyn's fiancé Caleb had been accused of killing SJ, but he had been exonerated. No one knew the whole story. His family hoped someday soon the killer would be found and brought to justice.

"What's up?" he growled at Sam.

"You just texted me to come into your office." Sam scratched the top of his red-haired head. He and Sam looked nothing alike. Sam was a good-looking guy, because he was a Wilde, but Sam was thin and lanky even at thirty. They did have the same blue eyes. All the Wildes seemed to have those eyes.

"Oh, yeah. I forgot. I signed the papers for the new supermarkets. Can you get them sent out? And then tell Raf when they are returned and signed by the general managers of the stores. I want the shipment sent out before Thanksgiving. Raf will take care of sending out the apples. We might as well get some money for the extra product we produced this year." He wanted to get out of the office before Lyra had a chance to leave, but Sam was standing in his way, and he wasn't about to even hint to Sam about Lyra. Lyra was his business.

"I'll take care of it. No problem. How's Winter?"

"She's fine. I have an appointment I need to get to." He tried to dodge past Sam, but Sam blocked his path.

"You should take her to the Christmas Victorian House Tour. Winter might like seeing all the houses decorated for Christmas. Lacey plans on doing a big display. It would be nice if we could all support her right now. She's been through a lot." Sam was always looking out for his sister.

He and Sam were similar that way. He would do anything to help Brooklyn, even if it meant shooting someone. He would have shot the guy who had set her barn on fire, if Caleb hadn't come up with a better idea.

"Winter might like that. She's been going on and on about Christmas. I'll suggest it." He could mention it to Lyra too. Her boys might like to go.

"She'll get to ride the school bus. That will be fun for her. Uncle Silas said you were homeschooling her."

"Sam, dude, not everyone thinks it's cool to ride the bus. But yeah, she's doing school from home so she can stay in her regular school and not go here in Candlewood Falls." Maybe getting Winter entrenched in Candlewood Falls was a bad idea. She wasn't going to stay, and he didn't need all the memories of the things they did together blindsiding him after she left.

He grabbed the papers and shoved them at Sam. "I have got to go. Take care of this. Thanks." He tore out of the office before Sam could say anything else. Sam was decent and all, but he never stopped talking.

He took the steps two at a time, ran down the hall, and bulldozed through the employee door to the store where they sold food, gift items, and also pastries from their bakery. He waved to Annabelle behind the bakery counter and turned for the front of the store.

Lyra was nowhere in sight. He went out of the store and searched the garden area but didn't see her. He hurried to the parking lot and found her. The car door was open, and she hitched her leg to slide inside.

He put his fingers to his mouth and whistled. She turned around. Their gazes met and held. Heat ran up his neck. He was pretty sure he was grinning like a fool. The magnet current between her and him pulled him toward her without any effort.

She slid the rest of the way into the car as if his presence did nothing to affect her. He'd see about that. He leaned on the roof of the car with his arm and looked down at her. "What brings you here?"

She held up the bag. "Apples."

"Were you treated nice by my employees?" This close he could see the gold flecks in her brown eyes and a small freckle between her eyebrows.

"Everyone was helpful and courteous."

"How was your appointment with Denise?"

She blinked. "Fine. Thank you for the referral. Denise wants me to come back next week."

He forced his chest not to puff up. So, he had been right about putting those two together. "Glad I could help. Where are you headed?"

"Home." She wasn't giving him a lot to work with, each answer being only one word. He might have to try harder. He wanted a repeat performance of that kiss.

"Do you want to grab some lunch?" He was done with work here. Raf had the orchard covered. Sam could take care of the paperwork. The store was a well-oiled machine. Sticking around made him feel useless anyway.

"Don't you have Winter with you?"

"Actually, she wanted to see my dad's cabin. She rushed through her schoolwork so he could take her. And then they're going for a hike. After that, they're going to carve pumpkins. He had a few leftover from this year's crop. She's in her glory." Unlike how she ever seemed to be with him. He hadn't brought up the fact she'd called him Dad when she busted in on his kiss with Lyra. And Winter hadn't said it since. If she said it again, he'd say something. He liked the sound of it, and that scared the hell out of him.

"Maybe some other time. But thank you. I have work to do around the house before the boys get home from school."

"I might be wrong, but I got the impression you liked kissing me the other day." Before he had stupidly caught his brace in her hair.

She unfolded herself from the front seat, pushing him backward with her flat hands on his chest. He could get used to her hands on him.

She stayed close, and he could smell her sweet scent. "Look." She kept her voice low. "Your place of business isn't the spot for this discussion, but everyone in town thinks we're a thing. I don't want to give them more to chew on, okay? I have enough problems with what Michael did."

"Then let's go out of town." The gossipers had started. That didn't take long, and he and Lyra had barely spent any time together. Well, let them talk. He would gladly give them something worth talking about.

"I don't think so. I'm very grateful for all you've done for me. I truly am. You are very unexpected, but I can't take any more risks. I have my boys to think about. And you have Winter to worry about. She needs all your attention now. Take care of her." She jumped back in the car and slammed the door shut.

She kicked the engine over and indicated he needed to get out of the way. He hesitated, but the determined look in her eye said she might actually run him over. He didn't need a broken foot to match his hand. He moved, and she sped away.

"Someone was in a hurry," Raf said, walking up to him.

"I think I pissed her off."

"What else is new?" Raf laughed.

He shook his head. "I don't understand women."

"Join the club. That's why I stay away from them. My first love is the land."

He had felt that way too. His first love was the orchard. Then Winter walked into his life in the flesh and everything changed. He was a little afraid to admit it, but Lyra had stirred something in him that he had believed was buried deep in the ground.

With Lyra's car gone from sight, he turned to his friend. "Did you ever think about starting your own farm?"

"Why are you asking me that?" Raf took a step back.

"I don't know. Maybe because these past few weeks you've had to step into my role, and you're almost as good as I am at it."

Raf shook his head and laughed. "You are a prick."

"You could, you know. You could do my job with your eyes closed."

"I like being second-in-command. When things get hot and heavy I can send the problems to you because it's your name on the sign. I get all the benefits of working the orchard and hardly any of the headaches. Speaking of headaches, Sam told me the supermarket papers are signed."

"Just waiting on the return signature."

"There's something I do want to talk to you about." Raf kicked the dirt.

"What's that?"

"How would you feel if Tino started working here?"

Raf's younger brother Tino had been in and out of trouble with the law, but he seemed to be trying to get his life together. "What did you want him to do?"

"Plant and prune in February. He can till the dirt. He can fix the tractors and the backhoe when they break down. In the summer he can be a picker. He's a hard worker. Not afraid to get dirty. He needs a little help, that's all. Not too many people want to hire a guy with a record."

"Sure, Raf. But if he screws up, it's on you." He would do anything to help Raf much the way he would do anything for Brooklyn.

"Wouldn't have it any other way. Thanks." Raf stuck out his hand. He had to shake with his left, which made the moment awkward until Raf grabbed him and pulled him into a hug.

"No problem." He patted Raf on the shoulder and eased out of the embrace.

"Now, are you going to go after your woman?"

"She's not my woman."

"Oh yeah, by the looks you two were giving each other, I can't imagine she belongs to anyone else."

"You're full of it."

"No, brother, it's you that's full of it. Go get her. Or I will." Raf barked out a laugh and ambled away.

Raf had a point. He had a few hours to kill before Winter was back. He jumped into his truck and headed home. Maybe, if he was lucky, he could get Lyra to kiss him again.

Lyra pulled into her driveway. After seeing Brad at the orchard, she decided she couldn't go home right away. When he had leaned over her, his strong arm resting on the roof of the car, she could smell his woodsy scent. His hair had floated around his face like a mane, and she wanted to tangle her fingers in it. Her heart had done a dance when he smiled.

She needed to stay focused on her plans. And that was what had her stopping at the side of the road where someone had left stuff at the curb. They had written a sign that read Free. Most of it was junk. Just someone's garbage they were trying to get rid of. But she had found some treasures. A small end table that needed to be refinished and reminded her of something Denise had in her house.

The table's wood was definitely birch. And the top was glass. The wood had been neglected, but with a little love it would look nice next to her sofa. She had also found a couple of wicker baskets that were brand new. They would work in her kitchen on the shelves above the counter.

While she was digging through the garbage, she could have sworn a couple of cars had slowed to get a better look at the woman picking through trash. But right now, she didn't care. She liked discovering valuables in weird places.

She dragged the table out of the trunk and placed it in the garage. She needed a couple of supplies to fix it up and could use some of the money she made today to buy them. Her chest filled with something that resembled pride. All in all, it had been a good day. Even helping Denise deal with some of her problems had made her feel as if she did some good. And maybe she had. She had been a decent therapist once.

Only bumping into Brad had thrown her. She had wanted to see him, but when he was actually there, her tongue had tied in knots. Fear had made her antagonistic.

She left the table in the garage and went around the back. The front door had been sticking more and she couldn't figure out how to jiggle the key without possibly breaking it.

"It's about time you got home." Brad pushed off the back steps and stood his full height. "It's cold out here."

She jumped. "What are you doing here?"

"I didn't like how things ended at the orchard." He shoved his hands in his pockets but winced and pulled away his injured one.

"Brad, please understand. I don't want the whole town talking about me."

"There you go, caring about what other people think. Let them talk, Lyra. That has nothing to do with us. The gossipers are the simple-minded ones. We're two consenting adults. We can do what we want. Or tell me you didn't like that kiss, and I'll walk back to my house without another word."

She wouldn't lie. The kiss had been amazing. "What are you asking me for?"

"I don't know." He ran his good hand through his hair. "My life turned upside recently, but I like how I feel when I'm with you. Being with you is easy. I've never felt like that with a woman before."

"My life turned upside recently too, if you remember. I don't know if I'm in the right mind frame to get involved with a man. And I'm not one for a sex-only relationship."

His eyes narrowed, but he gave her a mischievous smile. "I didn't think a sex-only thing was on the table."

"It's not. Didn't you just hear me? I don't do affairs."

"Neither do I."

She wanted to believe that. But he had always been surrounded by women who wanted him. He could have the pick of the crop. She groaned at her bad pun. "You're telling me that you would turn down a chance to have sex without strings?"

"Are you sure that's not what you're offering?"

"Brad!"

He bellowed a deep, hearty laugh. When he had calmed himself down some, he closed the space between them and took her hands. The warmth from his skin heated up hers like a slow-burning fire.

"There was a time in my life when I would have rather had a relationship that didn't involve any kind of commitment from me. I won't lie to you. But I'm not that man anymore. Having Winter with me has shown me how important something stable is."

Falling for a man who loved his child would be as easy as reading a good book with a hot cup of tea. But she needed to keep both feet planted firmly on the ground and her senses about her. "How will Winter feel about you dating?"

"Honestly, she likes you better than me right now. I think she would enjoy having you around." He rubbed his thumb over her knuckles, sending prickles over her skin.

"It's not fair for her to get attached to me if she's leaving. Or if I do."

"We haven't even begun, and you're already breaking us up." He ran his thumb over her wrist. If he continued to touch her, she would lose all resolve.

"This is serious. People could get hurt if we only think about ourselves."

He dropped his hands and stepped back. "You're right. I'm being selfish. I'm not thinking about how any of this will affect Winter or your kids. I'm sorry. I fell into my old habits because I like you, and I want to spend more time with you. But we can't be anything more than friends. I hope we can at least be that."

She wanted to grab back all her words and think it through further. But the set of his jaw told her his mind was changed. The warmth in his blue eyes froze over.

"Brad,…"

"No, it's okay. You don't have to say anything else. I get it. I always put what I want ahead of what everyone else does. That was why Maggie didn't want me in Winter's life. She was right to throw me out. I'm not doing a good job as a dad, and I was about to make it worse. I'll leave you alone now." He walked past her toward the front yard.

Her heart pounded in her throat, blocking her air. She was afraid to move for fear of choking to death. She hadn't meant to hurt him. She had been afraid to take a chance. He was a good dad. He tried so hard to win Winter over, and he was even succeeding though Winter was making it hard for him to see that.

"Brad, wait." She called after him. She needed to explain how she felt about him. That she liked his kindness and his sense of humor. That his size and confidence actually gave her a sense of comfort she had never experienced before. She had always felt alone, having to take care of herself, even married. But with him, his sense of assuredness wrapped around her, keeping her safe.

He hesitated but turned. His face was grim. "Yeah?"

She didn't know what to say. The words tangled in her mouth, tripping up her tongue. She stood there, mute.

"I'll see you on Tuesday to clean?" he said, saving her from more embarrassment.

"Sure. Take care."

He gave a wave with his braced hand and disappeared around the trees.

She sank onto the rickety steps. He had given her what she wanted. So why did she feel like she'd been run over by a truck?

CHAPTER FOURTEEN

B rad stood off to the side while Winter squealed. He wasn't about to get involved. She was on her own, the way she wanted to be, even at ten. He needed to ask his dad if he was like that at that age.

"They are so cute." Winter hugged Alpacino who hummed in return. "Tell me their names again," Winter said to Brooklyn.

He had brought Winter to the alpaca farm after trying to hide from Lyra while she cleaned his house. He needed to get out and stretch his legs. His hand had him completely useless, and it was driving him crazy.

So was not being able to touch Lyra. But he had to put Winter's needs ahead of his. At least until Nora came for her. He hoped these few weeks together would at least connect Winter to him enough that she would want to keep in touch. Maybe he could set up some kind of visitation schedule.

"You know the one you're hugging. The two-tone tan one is Alistair. He's the resident joker. Keep an eye on that rake. He drops it everywhere. Caleb and I have tripped over it more than once."

Alistair had also helped them take care of Caleb's problems in the fall. For him, Alistair was the man.

"The black one is Chewpaca," Brooklyn said. "Inside the barn on the other side are the ladies, Lucy and Ethel."

"I love them all." Winter turned in circles. "Can I feed them?"

"Sure, but later. I'll let you fill their food bins at dinnertime. Do you want to help rake the hay?" Brooklyn looked at him and raised her brows. He had no idea what his sister wanted or expected him to do. The alpacas were her domain, and Winter was too excited to pay any attention to him.

"Yes. Can I rake? Brad, is that okay with you?" Winter ran over to him and tugged on his flannel shirt. "Did you see Chewpaca put his paws up on that little table? Aunt Brooklyn said she's teaching him to drink out of a straw. Isn't that cool?"

He had heard the whole story not five minutes ago, but he feigned surprise for Winter's sake. "You're shitting me."

"Dad, you can't say that." Winter stamped her feet.

"Bradford, watch your mouth," Brooklyn said the same time as Winter admonished him.

He winked. Today was a good day, after all. Winter could do whatever she wanted or say anything she desired as long as she kept calling him Dad.

Winter motioned for him to squat down beside her. She brushed his hair away from his shoulders. "I'm going to get you a hairbrush for Christmas."

His chest swelled. "My hair needs a good hairbrush, does it?"

"I saw the one you use. It's all broken. Can I ask you something?"

"Always."

"Can we bring Lyra here? I think she would like the alpacas. Did you know their fur is turned into socks?"

He lifted his pant leg and revealed his navy-blue heather alpaca fleece socks. Winter squealed in delight.

"I'm making Christmas stockings for Lacey to hang on her mantel this year. I can make a couple for you two as well," Brooklyn said.

"Yes, please," Winter said, touching the top of his sock and running her fingers down to the edge of his hiking shoe. "They're soft."

"How about if I get you a pair for Christmas?" he said.

"That would be a good present, but you should check with Santa to make sure he isn't bringing me any."

He didn't know ten-year-olds still believed in Santa, but he wasn't about to mention that to Winter. He'd have to do a little research about the whole Santa believing thing. "I'll call him. But to answer your question, I don't know if we can bring Lyra here. She's kind of busy."

"What about Theo? He loves animals."

"Sure. We can ask Theo. And Lucas too."

Winter scrunched up her nose. "Lucas is grumpy."

"He'll get over it." He had to stand and release the cramp in his legs.

"Hey, guys, I thought we could make some applesauce together. What do you think?" Brooklyn broke up their conversation, for which he was glad. He didn't know how to explain they would be seeing less of Lyra and the boys.

"You know how to make applesauce?" Winter's eyebrows climbed into her bangs.

"Sure. It's your dad's recipe. The orchard sells it."

Winter spun around to look at him. "You make apple-sauce? Applesauce is my favorite thing ever."

"I need a little help cutting the apples these days, but yeah, I can make applesauce. Do you want to learn? Then you can make your favorite food anytime you want."

"I can tell my friends at school that my whole family knows how to do it. They'll be jealous."

He couldn't help but laugh a little. She was darn cute with her enthusiasm for everything around her. He had stopped finding the wonder in making applesauce when he had to sit through marketing meetings, sales meetings, and product meetings.

He took the alpacas for granted too. They had been in their family for years. The Sunnyside Up Farm belonged to their grandmother Cordy before Brooklyn bought it. Which reminded him. "Is Cordy coming for Christmas?"

"A few days after. She wants to meet Winter."

"Tell me who Cordy is?" Winter said, looking between the two of them.

Brooklyn placed a hand on her shoulder. "Cordy is our grandmother. That makes her your great-grandmother."

Which he was pretty sure Cordy didn't like to think about. He and Brooklyn weren't allowed to call her any version of grandmother. She had wanted to be called by her name. And that was what they did, but Cordy was the best grandmother anyone could ask for. She was full of life and very spontaneous. Nothing stopped her. He liked to think he had a lot of his maternal grandmother in him.

"Aunt Brooklyn, can I sleep over tonight?"

"Winter, I don't think it's nice to invite ourselves over to someone's house," he said.

Winter dropped her gaze to her shoes. Her face turned red. He wanted to be sick. He had made her upset.

"She can invite herself here anytime she wants," Brooklyn said, then turned to Winter. "What I think your dad means is it isn't polite to invite ourselves over to a friend's house. But with family, you don't need an invitation ever. You are always welcome here. And I know Grandpa Silas feels the same way about his house." Brooklyn wrapped Winter in a hug that she went willingly into.

He mouthed a thank you over Winter's head.

"Let's go make that applesauce." Brooklyn waved them into the house.

Yeah, today was a good day.

The house was too empty. He hated it. Brad wandered from room to room, not knowing what to do with himself. Winter was sleeping at Brooklyn's. Brooklyn had texted that they had dinner and she, Caleb, and Winter were playing board games. Winter had called to tell him she had fed the alpacas their dinner. She had also asked for a very expensive doll that all her friends had but didn't play with anymore because they were too big. She had confessed she still liked the doll because they came with their own stories, and she was never able to get one because her mom couldn't afford it. Brooklyn told him to wait to get such an extravagant gift. He didn't know how she could be so confident. She didn't have kids.

He wanted to ask Lyra and had pulled out his phone several times to text her and ask, but each time he stopped himself. He wasn't going to be happy with just a friendship from her. He needed to keep his distance so he wasn't tempted to ask for more. Maybe when Winter went back to Nora's, they could try again. If it wasn't too late.

He went outside, hoping the vast sky full of stars would give him some space to breathe. The night air was damp and chilly. He zipped up his hoodie. Since that required only the tip of his fingers, he could manage. He was ready to get this stupid brace off and his hand back. An owl hooted in the distance as if to say he agreed. He would give Riesling a call and see if there was any way to get rid of it sooner. It was starting to smell. Not exactly sexy when trying to seduce a woman.

He glanced over at Lyra's. The windows glowed yellow and spilled their light onto the grass. He wasn't trying to seduce her. But after kissing her, he wanted more. Much more.

A fire would be nice out here tonight. He gathered some of the cut wood from the porch and placed it beside the firepit, dropping a few pieces because he was trying to use his left hand more. He needed kindling first and went looking for it. That was easier to carry and assemble. He put one log on top of the base of branches and sticks. He grabbed the long lighter and some paper to burn.

He struggled to light the lighter with his left hand. He couldn't get his fingers to grip and push the safety back at the same time. When he used his right hand, a pain shot up his wrist from his thumb, sending an ache into his elbow.

He tried one more time with his good hand, and the lighter flickered to a flame. He almost jumped with excitement. But his fingers slipped, and the lighter spun out of his hands. "Damn it."

"Brad, are you okay?" Lyra's voice floated through the trees and drifted around him.

He hung his head. He didn't want to be incompetent in front of her. Up until now, he had managed to hide how difficult some things were with this brace. She was doing him a favor by not wanting to have sex with him. He didn't know how he would handle having sex with one hand and not his proficient one.

"All good. Thanks." He dropped down to find the lighter somewhere in the grass.

The rustle of branches moving and twigs breaking came through the trees. He turned in the direction of the noise. A small white light bounced closer to him. Lyra pushed through the remainder of the trees, shining her phone at him.

"You didn't sound good. You yelled pretty loudly. Did you hurt yourself?"

His fingers gripped the lighter, and he stood. "I'm fine. Just dropped the lighter." He held it up in case she might see it.

"Oh. I'm sorry. I heard you and thought the worst. I'll leave you to it." She turned for the trees again.

"Lyra, wait."

She turned back. "Yes?"

"I was going to start a fire. Would you like to sit with me?" He sounded like a desperate fool. She had made her position clear.

"I don't want to intrude. I'm sure Winter would like to enjoy it with you."

"She's sleeping at Brooklyn's. I didn't want to be inside anymore. The house is too quiet without her. I thought a fire might help me relax. I'd like the company, but I understand if you don't want to."

She hesitated. The waiting killed him, but he didn't have any other way to protect himself.

"I'd like that. Theo and Lucas are out with Michelle. She took them to the movies. They won't be back for a few hours."

"You're still friends with Michelle."

"She's always been a good friend. And the only person in Candlewood Falls who likes me." Lyra came the rest of the way and took the lighter out of his hand.

Her touch scorched him. He wouldn't need the fire with her so close. The light from his back windows gave him enough light to see her dark eyes that reminded him of melted chocolate. Which he wouldn't mind tasting from her lips. She had a fleece jacket zipped up to her neck. He wanted to take his time dragging that zipper down to reveal what was underneath.

"She's not the only one who likes you." His voice came out lower and hoarse, as if his throat was squeezing each word with its bare hands.

Lyra met his gaze. The current between them scalded. He wouldn't make a move. She would have to be the one who came to him. But if she did, he would drink her in, kiss her everywhere, and show her how she affected him.

"Yes, of course. You too."

"Please tell me I'm not the only one who feels the connection here." So much for not making a move. He hadn't budged, but his big mouth couldn't shut up.

"It's not just you." She licked her lips.

He didn't want to spook her. She seemed so small at the moment, standing in front of him in the dark. If he said or did the wrong thing, she would take off for the trees. "Would you mind lighting the fire? I might miss with this hand and set something else up in flames."

She leaned over and put the lighter to the paper. The flame bit into the paper and sizzled. His skin sizzled right along with it.

"It's chilly tonight." She rubbed her arms.

"Would you like me to get a blanket?"

"No, thank you. Once the fire gets going, I'll warm up."

He would be happy to be the thing that warmed her up. He stood while she took one of the Adirondack chairs near the firepit. With her so close, the fire did nothing to relax him.

"I'm sorry about what I said the other day," Lyra said.

"What was that?" He had a pretty good idea what she had said. He'd replayed their last conversation in his head a hundred times since then. She had been right. He needed to focus his attention on Winter. But when Lyra was around, his attention jumped around a bit.

"I didn't mean to imply you weren't a good father. You are." She leaned forward, rubbing her hands together.

"You were right to remind me to think about Winter. I took her to see the alpacas today. She fell in love with them. Her whole face lit up. That was better than anything else I've ever done. Just some dumb farm animal made her go crazy. That's why she's sleeping at Brooklyn's. She wants to feed them breakfast. I think Alpacino is her favorite."

"Alpacino?" Lyra's laugh burst bright enough to leave stars in the sky. The lines around her eyes creased, making her more beautiful.

"Yeah." He wanted to laugh too or at least get covered in

hers. "They all have goofy names. My grandmother has a real sense of humor."

"I never met Cordy. I wish I had."

"She'll be in town after Christmas. I'll introduce you. You can meet the animals too."

"That would be nice."

"Winter thought you and the boys would like the alpacas." He shoved his hands in his pockets to keep from touching her. His brace made that nearly impossible. He had to settle for letting that hand dangle, useless.

"She did? She's adorable. She reminds me so much of you." Lyra held her hands up to the fire.

"You think I'm adorable?" He knew that wasn't what she meant, but he couldn't let her get away with the comment. He had to tease her a little.

She dropped her gaze to the grass. "Um, you are very charming. But I meant that she seems to really enjoy the outdoors and all it has to offer. Like you."

"I don't know about her being like me. I can see she has my eyes because she looks so much like Brooklyn. But everything else is because of her mother."

She stood and faced him. "May I be so bold for a second?"

He turned to her. He hoped as hell that she wanted to forget this whole conversation and their last one and go inside and make out.

"Sure. Go ahead."

"I know this isn't my place, and as a former therapist I should never say this, especially about someone who has passed away, but that woman was out of her mind to keep you away from Winter." She placed a hand on his arm and squeezed.

The air got caught in his throat. He had to swallow just to breathe. She might not have asked that he scoop her up and lick her creamy skin, but she still knocked him for a loop.

"Thank you."

"There's one more thing." She pushed her hair away from her face and blew a breath over her lips.

She could be so confident and sure of herself, and in the next moment she seemed as if a good breeze might blow her away. Like she couldn't keep herself grounded.

"Oh yeah? What's that?" He wanted to rouse her so she'd tilt that chin at him and show him his place.

But she didn't do any of that. Instead, she put her hands on either side of his face. Her touch froze him to the spot. She stood on tiptoe and kissed him.

Now, that was more like it.

CHAPTER FIFTEEN

She had lost her mind. But, dear god, she couldn't help herself. She could blame it on the fire that crackled and danced in the breeze. Fires were erotic for her. Or she could blame her aggressiveness on how endearing Brad looked when he recanted the story of Winter and the alpacas. Or she could simply and honestly admit she wanted him.

He tangled his good hand into her hair and rested his injured hand on her low back. Every nerve ending was on hypersensitivity. The Velcro of the brace scratched at her skin where her jacket had ridden up. The hand in her hair tugged, sending delicious shivers down her body.

Her mouth fell open, and he skillfully took her kisses. But it wasn't enough. The kissing made her brain foggy, but she needed more of him. She needed all the clothes gone. She needed to feel alive and desired because she couldn't remember when she had felt that way.

She had spent so much time worrying about looking the part, she had forgotten to look where she was going. And though she was still trying to find out who she was, Brad seemed to see her as her. He didn't judge her ripped and dirty clothes. He didn't think anything of her wanting to clean houses. He was nice to her when so many others had been anything but.

He ran his hands over her sides and up her back. She reached under his sweatshirt. His skin burned against her palms. His muscles were solid and thick. Her fingers played in the down of chest hair in his center, then traced the line to the top of his jeans.

He moved his mouth to the soft spot below her ear. His tongue tickled and caressed a line down to her jacket and then back up. She tilted her head back and allowed the cool breeze to tantalize her wet skin.

She gripped his face again and brought his mouth back to hers. She wanted to drown in his expert kissing. His beard scruff pricked her fingertips, making her squirm. She wouldn't be able to stand much longer.

He fumbled with her jacket zipper. She eased out of the kiss.

"Let me." Her voice croaked against the mounting desire. The light from the fire showed the burning intensity in his blue eyes.

"Is this really happening?" He pushed the jacket off her shoulders.

"Unless you don't want to."

"Oh, no. That's up to you. I absolutely want to and will go all the way if you give me the go ahead. But just a couple of days ago you wanted to be only friends. This is more than that. I don't want you to regret anything once it's over."

He would not take advantage of her vulnerabilities and that made her heart open wide to him. This could be the most foolish thing she had ever done—or the smartest. "I won't regret anything."

"Lyra, no matter what you think you know about me, I'm not a guy who sleeps around. I don't like one-night stands."

"You've never had a one-night stand?"

"I never said that." He toyed with the collar of her jacket, keeping his gaze on her breasts. "I've changed."

She wanted him to drag that lustful gaze all over her body, and she wanted to see him without anything blocking her view. "If we do this, our friendship is over. You go your way, and I go mine."

"Hang on a second, lady. Are you telling me if we sleep together now, you don't want anything to do with me?" He stepped back, almost tripping over the leg of the chair.

"Well, no...I don't know." The electric connection slipped away. She wanted it back. She just wanted to take care of her needs for a change. She had accused Brad of not putting Winter first, but she was tired of putting everyone else's needs above hers. Michael had drained the last of her emotional well when he destroyed their already imbalanced lives. Even her job forced her to listen to other people's issues all day long. She only wanted a man to make her feel as if she was the most beautiful, most desired person around. If only for a little while.

"I didn't come over here planning on any of this. I wanted to kiss you, and you kissed me back. I hadn't thought any further ahead than that." Not thinking was her problem. She had packed up the boys and moved back to Candlewood Falls without a whole lot of thought and landed them in that dump of a rental.

She hadn't thought about a career until she got here.

Being a cleaning person wasn't exactly what she had dreamed about in college. And she had never planned to get involved with Candlewood Falls' most eligible bachelor. But here she was, making a mess of everything.

"I kissed you because I've wanted to kiss you since the first time. You're all I think about. I want to know we're starting something, and we'll see where it goes. We don't have to make promises, but I don't need any more bed buddies. I've had more than my fair share." He grabbed a thick stick and moved the fire around, extinguishing it.

"Brad, I'm sorry. I wasn't thinking. I don't think I can give you more right now."

"We seem to continually find ourselves in this space. We like each other. Now you need to decide what has you so afraid. I'm not going anywhere. This town is my home. My family is here. And if by some miracle, I get to continue to spend time with Winter, that will be here too. You're the one who's running. Now you need to figure out where. Good night, Lyra." He walked off and went inside.

She stayed a few minutes longer, unable to make her feet move. The rest of the fire burned down, leaving her cold and in the dark. The lights in his house went out, swallowing up the rest of her sight.

She should march right up to his door and throw herself at him. Tell him exactly what he wanted to hear because she wanted to be with him. She wanted to make love with him, and hold him all night. Or at least until her boys returned home.

But he was right. She was afraid. Afraid to lose herself to a man again. Afraid that she was jumping too fast. Afraid to fall in love for real this time. Because real love meant she had to be the real Lyra. And she didn't know who that was.

He was such an ass. He had walked away from the sexiest woman he had ever been with. She was her true self with him. She didn't put on airs. She didn't pretend to be anything other than the complete mess that she was.

Brad had expected her to be a total stuck-up bitch when he realized she had moved in next door. He thought within minutes bulldozers would show up and demolish that awful house, and a huge modern cement box would go in its place, completely wrong for the area. He had expected glass and glitz from her. But she had decorated that house with secondhand stuff as if it were worth millions. And every time she cleaned his house, she commented on the warmth of the space.

He had figured she had bought the land because it was a great piece of property when actually she was just a renter with no place else to go at the moment. But at every turn she had surprised him. She was nothing like the way she was in the old days. And she wanted him.

That woman could kiss. He paced from one room to the next on the first floor. His hand ached from all the overuse he'd done today. He hated that he couldn't completely feel her skin when he had touched her back. If they had gone further, he would have ripped the brace off. But she had put the brakes on fast and hard.

He returned to the kitchen and grabbed a beer out of the fridge. He didn't want to drink in front of Winter in case it set a bad example. But he needed a drink now to cool his jets. Next would be a cold shower. Lyra had riled him up good. He downed half the beer in one gulp.

He glanced out the window. She was gone now. She had

stuck around for a few minutes after he came inside. He had looked out the window to find her standing by the fire, staring into the red embers. He had debated going back out to her, but she had to come to him. If she had knocked on his door, he would have lifted her up and carried her to his bed.

Or he could go to her. They still had some time before her kids returned. He tossed the beer bottle in the recycling hard enough it bounced out. He cursed. No way. He meant what he had said. He didn't do friends with benefits. That never worked out. He would not want to see her with another man if they were sleeping together. He might be a bit old-fashioned that way, but he was a one-woman guy.

They didn't have to make a commitment this early on, but he needed to know she wasn't looking for anyone else while she had him. And he was pretty sure he could satisfy her in bed. He looked at his hand. Well, he could have before this stupid thing happened.

He picked up his phone and found Raf's number. He hit call before he could stop himself. Raf would probably give him a hard time for being turned around by Lyra. Raf didn't make commitments to women.

"What's going on?" Raf said.

"Can you explain to me why women are so confusing?" He checked the doors and went upstairs.

"This again? You two just need to do it and get it over with."

"How many women have asked you for a friends with benefits situation?" He peeked in Winter's room even though she wasn't home. The space smelled like strawberries and bubble gum. He didn't dare touch a thing, including the pile of clothes on the floor. He missed her, that was all.

159

"How many women ask me for sex without a commitment?" Raf burst out laughing. "Not a one, bro. I might take a girl up on that, if she meant it. All the perks without any of the hassle."

He dropped down on the chair in his room and put the call on speaker. The room was dark except for the light coming in from his bathroom. He closed his eyes. "Not me. If she's in my bed, then that's the only bed I want her to be in. I don't want to find out she's getting it on with some other dude."

"I'm sorry. What did you do with my good friend Brad Wilde?"

"Shut up, Raf."

"You got it bad, bro. I feel sorry for you."

"Why?" His head snapped up.

"'Cause you ain't ever going to be happy until she decides she wants a commitment. I never thought I'd see the day this happened. But I'm glad I have. You need more in your life than the orchard."

"This coming from you? Your life is the orchard too."

"I don't have time for a relationship. I have three brothers who always need me to look out for them."

"Your brothers are old enough to look after themselves." Each of Raf's brothers had a story that included jail, foster care, or addiction. They all had lived a hard life. Raf had been the one who came out of it with the least amount of scars.

"It's my job to keep an eye on them. They don't have anyone else. We didn't get a dad like Silas. Hell, I might even take Huck as a replacement father. He's better than my father any day."

His uncle Huck was a royal pain in the ass, always

causing trouble. He couldn't understand how his aunt Ruby stayed with him. He had run off all three of his daughters years ago. He never saw or spoke to those cousins because of it. Huck would be a terrible father for Raf and his brothers.

"Stay away from Huck. You know Silas would do anything for you, if you asked him. You practically moved into our cabin when you walked onto the orchard back then."

"Your home was a good home for me. I owe you."

"Not this again," he said echoing Raf moments before. "I'm sorry I called if you're going to get all sad and sappy on me."

"The man who hates emotions."

"We can't all be like you Spanish guys, in touch with your feminine side."

Raf choked out another laugh. "Any time you want a lesson, you let me know. Women dig that sensitive side. Men of Spanish descent make great lovers. See ya." Raf ended the call.

He pushed off the couch and went back to the window. A car bounced down Lyra's driveway, if it could even be called that. It was more like two ruts in the ground. The slam of car doors echoed. Michelle must have returned with the boys early. He guessed there would be no more chances tonight.

He went back downstairs, too unsettled to stay in his room, and turned on the TV. He propped his feet on the coffee table. Winter's notebook slipped off onto the floor. The pages had fluttered open. She had drawn a picture of a man and woman holding hands. The man was tall and wide, with long hair and squiggles to represent his tattoos on his arm. He had to laugh at that one. She had given him blue eyes too.

The woman resembled Lyra with her curves and wavy black hair. Sitting on the ground in front of the man and woman were three kids. Two boys and a girl. Written below the foot of the girl in small letters was the word family. His stomach hollowed out.

He closed the book and put it back on the table. He would not hurt Winter. If Lyra was not interested in being with him as anything more than screw buddies, then they couldn't be together. He had to protect Winter from anymore hurt because in a few short weeks, Nora would return and rip Winter away. Based on that drawing, she might actually like him.

He had no power to fight Nora or Maggie's last wishes. He wasn't Winter's guardian. He wasn't anything more than a glorified babysitter at the moment. But his heart was in it two hundred percent. He wanted his daughter. He wanted her to live with him and be a permanent part of his family. Nora could be the one who had visitation rights.

And if that meant he had to let Lyra go, then he would. He didn't want to give Nora any reasons to keep Winter from him. And if that picture in the notebook was telling the truth, Winter wanted to be with him too. He only hoped she didn't want a package deal.

CHAPTER SIXTEEN

L yra grabbed her cleaning tote and dragged herself to Denise's front door, working her way around the red Jeep Grand Cherokee in the driveway. She didn't recognize the vehicle.

Last night, she had barely slept, and her body ached from head to toe. She couldn't get Brad's kiss and the hurt look on his face out of her mind. She had barely straightened out the complications in her life, then walked smack into more as if they were a plate glass window.

But she had been lonely for so long. Brad woke up a part of her she had ignored. She would have been fine with a little uncomplicated sex. She had never imagined that Brad Wilde of all people didn't do flings. It appeared Winter's presence had grounded him some. She was glad he had Winter and she had her dad, but Lyra would have liked to have found Brad while he was still sewing some oats.

She rang the bell. Denise threw the door open before the bell could stop. "Wonderful. You're here. We've been waiting. Come in." Denise grabbed the tote and hurried toward the kitchen.

"Denise, who's we?"

But Denise didn't stop. Without many choices, she followed. Sitting at the island with an oversized dark-blue ceramic mug between two manicured hands was a woman with light-brown skin, dark eyes, cork-screw hair, and a boho chic top Lyra would have guessed cost above a hundred dollars.

"Lyra, this is my good friend Josie. We take yoga together. Josie is an artist. She paints. She needs your help."

"Hi." Josie put the mug down and came around to shake her hand with a firm grip. "I hope you don't mind. Denise said you'd be completely into me being here."

She looked between the two women. "I don't understand."

Denise put her hands on her shoulders, directed her to the kitchen table, and plopped her into the chair. "Lyra, sweetheart, Josie is in need of a therapist."

She jumped up. "Oh, no. I don't counsel people any longer. I'm sorry."

"You sat with me just last week and helped me work through my marital problems. You gave me the courage to tell Ian to get the hell out of the house if he wanted that young chickee to knock uglies with. He moved out and said he wouldn't fight me on anything I wanted in the divorce." Denise nodded with enthusiasm.

She suspected Ian's agreement to Denise's demands had more to do with the fact he committed adultery than anything she had said. She doubted very much one chat with Denise while she was upset would have given her the courage to stand up to her husband.

"Denise, you did that all by yourself. It wasn't because of anything I had said."

"Don't be silly. You found me a blubbering mess in the kitchen. By the time you left I felt like I could take on the world. Sit down. I'll make coffee, and you two can get chatting."

"But what about the cleaning?"

Denise waved a hand in the air. "Forget the cleaning. Ian's money will pay you to counsel Josie. Fuck him. He can pay to counsel all my friends."

She was afraid that might be true. "Josie, I'm not practicing any longer. I'm not taking clients. Wouldn't you be happier with someone who had an open practice?"

"Do you have your license?" Josie grabbed her mug and sat at the table, tucking a jean-clad leg under her.

"Well, yes, but—"

"But nothing." Josie shook her head. "You helped Denise. I need some of that too. It's my mother."

They spent the better part of two hours talking about Josie and her problems with her mother. Many of which Lyra could relate to. By the end, Josie was hugging her and asking for her number to grab a coffee with. On her.

"And could I hire you to clean my art studio?" Josie said.

"That would be nice."

"Great. I'm also going to tell my sister about you. She's a stay-at-home mom with four little kids. She needs a lot of help." Josie hugged her goodbye and excused herself to answer a text.

She grabbed her tote and asked Denise to join her on the porch. "I can't keep giving your friends advice. Please don't put me in that position again." Though getting another cleaning client didn't hurt.

"This is just like getting together for drinks with a couple of gals and gabbing. What's wrong with that?"

"The money you paid me for starters."

"Don't be silly. You earned it. And you helped Josie so much. Isn't that the best part?"

She couldn't argue with that totally. She did like seeing the light go on in Josie's eyes when she realized she had more power in the relationship than she thought. "I don't feel right taking your money if I'm not cleaning."

"So next time you clean." Denise waved to her neighbor walking her dog.

"Just clean. No more friends."

"I promise." Denise's hand went behind her back.

She shook her head, already regretting this.

Lyra drove around Candlewood Falls after leaving Denise's. She didn't have much of a destination in mind, but the idea of going home didn't sit well with her. The house was too small. She couldn't spread her wings in there. And she couldn't risk the possibility that Brad would be outside. She didn't have the energy to fight her lustful desire at the moment. All he would have to do was move his hair away from his face, and she'd jump him like a desperate thief.

She turned down Main Street and brought the car to a crawl. So many of the shops were the same like the book-store, Knit for Your Life—the yarn store, and the hair salon. But some new ones were in place. She had never seen Witchy Woman. She would have to stop in there and see what that was all about. There was also an antique store on the street. She turned at the corner and drove down a side street that ran along the parking lot behind the stores.

She should really go home and get ready for Thanksgiving tomorrow, but that antique store had called her like a talisman. She was cooking for her and the boys, and then they were going to her parents' house for dessert. She was dreading having to listen to her mother prattle on about the gossip in town and her disappointments in Lyra's choices. The antique store would give her a pick-me-up she needed. And maybe she could find something cute for the house. Or... no, she wouldn't finish that thought. She wouldn't finish the thought that she might find something cute for Brad's house.

The afternoon air was damp and chilly. She shuddered inside her puffed vest as she followed the walkway to Main Street. The pedestrian traffic was light. And it would be on the day before Thanksgiving. Most people were either at the grocery store or home cooking and baking. She wondered what Brad and Winter would be doing tomorrow. He was probably spending it with his large family. She envied their numbers.

She pulled on the door to the antique store. The small space was filled with objects all the way to the back and in some places three or four tall. The smell of wood and time and a life lived met her inside the door and welcomed her to explore. The burgundy carpet had faded where the sun washed over it and had been worn from miles of footprints.

"Well, hello." A tall bald man with kind eyes came through a curtain separating the show area from the back. He wore cargo pants tucked into boots and a plaid shirt hanging out.

"Hi. You have a nice place."

"Take a look around. I'm just opening up a couple of boxes in the back. My shipment came in late. The name's Allen. Just give a holler if you need anything."

"Thanks." Allen left her alone while she wandered the store. The antique jewelry caught her attention. All those gold pieces with stones in deep reds, dark blues, and mysterious greens. Each one held a story like a secret. She imagined elegant women in long black dresses with pearls around their necks at cocktail parties where people dined at intricate wood tables a mile long and servants that stood to the side waiting to refill a plate or a glass.

That seemed like the kind of life she had once wanted. It was certainly the kind of life her mother tried desperately to have, and came close. But her mother was from the wrong era. She had needed to be alive in the late eighteen hundreds and probably from England.

Lyra moved around the store, admiring the pieces, but not finding anything in her price range or quite what she had in mind. Allen pushed through the curtain and wiped his glasses on the hem of his shirt, then plopped them on his face. He blinked a few times before a smile settled on his lips.

"Still here," he said.

"It's a lovely store. I could look at antiques all day."

"A woman I understand."

She approached the counter. "How was your new shipment?"

"Junk. I hate to say it. But sometimes I'm ordering things without knowing what I'm getting. I thought I had a find from an estate sale, but it wasn't worth it. I sent it all to the dumpster."

An idea tickled the back of her brain, but she needed to shake that loose. She was out of her mind for even considering such a thing. "What time are you open until?"

"Six. Most of Main Street closes up then except for Murphy's and the hair salon some evenings. I guess a few others too. We're all closed tomorrow, but everyone will be in full swing for Black Friday. Us small town folks still hope people will do shopping in person instead of the computer."

"There's something to be said for old traditions. I hope you sell a lot. Have a nice day, Allen. I'm sure I'll be back soon." Sooner than later.

She returned to the damp day with a new breeze kicking up and blowing her hair around. She tilted her chin, letting the wind caress her, and wondered what Brad's touch would do to her skin.

She groaned. "Get it together, Lyra," she said under her breath.

She decided a hot chocolate would top off the day before she went home. The boys wouldn't be there for a while. Michelle was picking them up again. Michelle had taken the week off from work. She was a freelance editor for some major publishing houses and needed a break from her screen. She was more than happy to escort her boys for a few days. They all had comics and cosplay in common, which Lyra was grateful for because she didn't have the guts to don one of those wild costumes.

Her phone rang, and she dug it out of her purse. Her mother's name was on the screen. She debated on answering but decided she had better, or Clarisse would just keep calling.

"Hi, Mom."

"Lyra, dear, I hate to do this, but I have to cancel

Thanksgiving dessert. Your father is under the weather. I think it's the flu. He says it's just a cold, but that stubborn man is running a fever and coughing up a lung. I'm taking him to the doctor soon, but you and the boys shouldn't come tomorrow. I don't want you getting sick. I doubt that house of yours has the proper insulation. It's probably freezing. You'll never be able to fight off what he has."

"That's too bad. I hope he feels better. The boys were looking forward to seeing him."

"Let's try for next week. I'll pick up some good pies from Wilde Orchards. Kiss the boys for me." And her mother was gone like that.

She returned her phone to her bag and crossed the street. Her mother had a tendency to exaggerate. She'd check in with her father later. Looked as if she and the boys would be alone for the holiday.

Even the Green Bean was quiet. A barista was behind the counter, wiping it down. The seats were empty except for one. She should turn and run before he saw her. She didn't need that hot chocolate. In fact, she could stop at the grocery store on the way home and buy a box for what one would cost here. She needed to be better with her money anyway.

As she turned to go, a vicelike grip caught her around the waist and squeezed her hard enough to knock her off-balance. She stumbled into the table that hit the chair. Wood smacked and crashed together like the percussion section of a marching band. At least she and Winter didn't collapse in a heap on the floor.

Brad jumped to his feet. The barista dropped her cloth. Winter smiled up at her as if they'd been on an adventure.

"Hi, Lyra. I didn't know you were meeting us here."

Winter untangled herself as if nothing happened and fixed Brad with a glare. "Brad, why didn't you tell me Lyra was coming too? I would have saved half my cookie for her." Winter turned back to her. "Are Theo and Lucas still at school? I finished all my work last night so I didn't have to have schooltime today. Brad said that was okay. He checked my folder. He still can't do fifth-grade math. Can you?"

"Winter, come back and sit down." Brad's voice was stern. He pointed to the chair beside him.

"You're sitting with us too, right?" Winter said, ignoring Brad.

"I don't think so. I'm sorry. I just came in for a drink to take back to my house. I have to get home to cook." And pick up some dessert along the way—and not from the orchard.

"Oh. Could you sit with us while your drink is cooking?"

She glanced over at Brad for some help, but he sat back down with his face in his phone. So much for that. "Okay. Come help me order."

Winter stood beside her while she asked for a hot chocolate for her and another cookie for Winter. "You have to save it for later. When your dad says it's okay."

"Okay."

They returned to the table. A green flyer was under Brad's hands. She could only make out some of the words with his big arms covering most of it. The Victorian House Christmas Tour was scheduled for the week before Christmas. She always loved seeing the houses all decorated for Christmas each year.

"Hello, Brad," she said.

He finally looked up. His face was cross with no sign of

that smile she was beginning to dream about. "Hello, Lyra. Nice to see you again." He pushed out of the chair. "Grab your coat, Winter. We need to get going. I have to stop at work on the way home."

"But Lyra just got here."

"It's okay, sweetie. Your dad didn't know I was coming. I was just on the street doing a little window shopping and decided to stop in. You should do as he says." She couldn't meet Brad's watchful eye so she busied herself with helping Winter slip her arms into her coat. She doubted a ten-year-old would appreciate the assistance, but she needed to keep her hands and her gaze on something other than that man.

It seemed as if everything had changed between them. And wasn't that what she wanted? She had been the one to push him away. A man like him couldn't be used to being rejected, and she had done it in a harsh way. He would have rather she said she didn't find him sexually attractive than say she didn't want to date him.

"Please, Dad. Just a few minutes more. I'm still drinking my hot chocolate." Winter brought her cup to her lips and simulated taking a sip.

The cup was probably empty by the smirk on Brad's face. "Two minutes." He lowered himself into the chair.

No one spoke. The tension around them brewed like bad coffee. The barista brought over her hot chocolate and Winter's cookie. Lyra fiddled with the cozy on her cup, but she didn't want the drink any longer. If it weren't for Winter, she would run from the Green Bean as fast as her legs would carry her.

"Are you thinking about attending the Christmas Victorian House Tour this year?" She couldn't think of another thing to say to this man who had her head on backwards.

"What?" he grunted.

She huffed and pointed at the flyer. "The annual house tour. Are you thinking of going this year?"

He glanced down as if he were seeing the flyer for the first time. "This? Oh. Maybe. My cousin's bed and breakfast is on the tour this year. Brooklyn said we should show a united family front for Lacey. She's had a lot going on, lately."

"That's nice of her family to support her." She wished she had a little of that.

"I want to go," Winter said.

"You do?" Brad handed Winter a napkin to wipe her chocolate-covered mouth.

"I want to see all the houses lit up for Christmas. My mom and I would drive around the neighborhoods to look at houses every year." Winter's face fell. She kept her gaze on the table. "I won't be able to do that this year." Her head snapped up. "Please, Dad. Can we go?"

The color had drained from Brad's face. The poor man really didn't know how to handle the situation he had been thrown into, but he was trying. She knew that much.

"Sure. Yeah. We can go. I'll get the tickets."

"Lyra, will you and Lucas and Theo come too?" Winter bounced in her seat.

Before she could open her mouth to protest—tagging along was not a good idea based on the wide-eyed glare Brad shot her—a woman with long reddish-brown hair and pretty features approached the table.

"Hey, Brad. How's the hand?"

"Hey, Riesling. It's okay. Thanks." He fiddled with his cup, ignoring her and not making eye contact with Riesling.

The woman turned to her and stuck out her hand. "Hi,

I'm Riesling River. Brad doesn't have enough manners to introduce us." Riesling turned back to Brad. "You're such a barbarian."

Winter snickered behind her hand.

"Hey," he protested, but didn't seem committed to the fight.

Without much choice, Lyra shook and wondered why Brad hadn't introduced them. He couldn't be embarrassed by her, could he? She did look a bit of a mess without any makeup and she was wearing sweats, but she had just come from Denise's house. She didn't exactly clean in her best wares.

But she did recognize the name River. The River family owned the winery in town. Riesling was one of seven kids, but much younger than she was. They weren't in school together so their paths hadn't crossed. She ran in circles with Riesling's brothers Malbec and Merlot. "Nice to meet you. I'm Lyra Chambers." She preferred to be Chambers over Ryan. Michael could have his name back. She still hadn't received the divorce papers yet. She might have to think of something creative to do to get a fire under him.

"Chambers. Did you grow up here?"

"I did. I was a few years ahead of you. I went to school with Brad and Malbec."

Riesling rolled her eyes. "Lucky you. And who is this cutie?" Riesling addressed Winter.

"My name is Winter Reis. Kind of like your name. But we're not related. I don't think. Brad, is she related to us?"

"Nope." He picked at the lid of his cup.

Riesling snatched it out of his hand. "You're behaving like a child today. What gives with you?"

"When can I get this thing off?"

"About a month." She rescued the flyer from under his forearms. "Hey, are you guys going to this?"

"Yes," Winter said.

"Cool. I think I'm going to go this year with my daughter Ashling. She's six. A little younger than you."

"I'm ten." Winter held up ten fingers.

"You're very grown-up for ten. Looks like my mobile order is up. See you guys." And just like that Riesling whisked away.

"I'd better get going too." She pushed out of the chair. The legs scraped against the hard floor. "Take care, Brad. Winter, it was lovely to see you again. Have a happy Thanksgiving." She forced a smile on her face and returned to the damp and gray day outside.

The clock had ticked past lunchtime, and even though sunset was still a few hours away, the day had taken on the start of darkness like a shade being drawn shut. She zipped up her vest and shook thoughts of lonely holidays and lonelier nights away. When darkness did finally fall and Main Street had closed up tightly, she would come back. She needed to see something, but only when she could be certain no one was watching.

Brad did not want to remain friends. And she didn't know how to tell him she wanted more but was too afraid to reach for it. Funny how one's life falling apart could shake even the most confident of esteems.

"Lyra, can you hang on a second?" Brad stood outside the coffee shop in just his button-down flannel shirt. The breeze pushed his hair around. He tied the sides back with some effort.

"That looks like it's difficult with the brace."

"A lot of things are tough with the brace. Can I talk to

175

you a minute?" He shoved his good hand into his jean pocket and hunched his shoulders against the cold.

"You should go inside. You don't have your coat."

"I'm good. I can handle November weather. Winter and I were wondering what you and the boys were doing for Thanksgiving. It's last minute, I know, but we'd like you to come over. Some of my family is going to be there. If you don't have any other plans, that is."

She wasn't expecting an invitation. It would be nice to have a houseful of people around to fill the empty spaces in her world. The boys would enjoy some male company and of course

Winter. But she could be setting herself up for heartbreak. Being around him for a holiday might be more than she could handle. It would give her a glimpse into the possibilities with him. Possibilities that couldn't become a reality.

"We were supposed to see my parents for dessert, but my dad's under the weather. My mother called to cancel that." She glanced behind Brad to find Winter waiting just outside the door with an expectant look on her face. This little girl must be the orchestrator behind the invite.

"Well, you should come then, if it's only the three of you." His face lit up with that bright smile that ignited a fire in her.

"I don't want to impose on your family's day."

"You aren't. I came out here to ask you."

"Are you coming? Please, Lyra. You have to come. It won't be fun without you." Winter ran over and stood beside Brad.

"She's right. It won't be fun without you and the boys."

She didn't have the heart to tell Winter no. "Okay, we'll be there."

"Yay." Winter jumped up and down, clapping her hands. "Hey, kid, wait for me at the truck, okay?"

Winter glared at Brad, but said goodbye to her and stood by the truck parked a couple of spots down.

He turned to her. "This is just a friend asking another friend over. You don't have to worry that I have some ulterior motive to convince you to get involved with me."

She wished he had a plan to seduce her and not just for them to be friends, but that was on her. She had to own her decision to reject the possibility of a relationship with him.

She took in his navy sweater that clung to his pec muscles, making her hands want to feel how soft the fabric was in contrast to his hard muscles and the jeans that were tight enough to give her an idea of how thin his waist was, but loose enough to hide his thighs from her.

Which only made her want to find out what was underneath.

"I wasn't worried. I know you'll be the perfect gentleman."

He leaned in and she got a whiff of his woodsy scent. "Is that how you think of me?"

"Of course, how else would I think of you?" She would rather think of him as the rugged earth man who knew how to use his hands to coax a tree to life. Brad wasn't afraid to get dirty, and he wasn't afraid to take control.

He placed a kiss on her cheek near her ear and sent a tingle over her skin. She shivered.

"You should get into your car, it appears you might be cold. We'll see you tomorrow."

He brushed past her and helped Winter get into the truck without looking back. Her fingers traced the spot where he left the kiss. She expected her skin to burn there, but it was her insides burning up. The truck drove away and still, she didn't move.

"Lyra, what are you doing here?"

She spun around to see Michelle's perfect smile that always lit up her hazel eyes like the afternoon sun. In true Michelle fashion, she wore leggings with blocks of Swiss cheese all over them and a black quilted jacket. Her straight dark hair was streaked with burgundy.

"Finishing my daily caffeine fix." She had left her hot chocolate behind inside the Green Bean, but didn't need it anymore. Brad's kiss revved her blood flow just fine.

"That's too bad. I was stopping for coffee. When I saw you, I thought what good luck. I was just coming from yoga. Where are you headed?"

"Um…" She couldn't remember where she was headed next.

"Are you okay?" Michelle stepped closer and put a hand to her forehead.

"Yes. Yes. I'm fine. I just got invited to Thanksgiving at Brad Wilde's house."

"That's great."

"I can't go." She couldn't believe she had said okay. She had no willpower where he was concerned. She would have more luck turning down a pumpkin pie.

"Why not?"

"Because I can't get involved with him."

"Who says involved? Maybe you could take him around the block a few times." Michelle giggled.

"And that's the problem. I would actually consider a quick fling with him. I can't handle much more than that at the moment. But he doesn't want to do friends with benefits. He wants the possibility of a future."

"Wowza." Michelle fanned herself. "Brad Wilde is telling you he's considering a commitment, and you want to tell him no? There are at least a hundred women in line for that spot and would probably take you out for it."

"That's insane. He's a catch, but he's arrogant and can be selfish at times. Work is his number one priority. There are plenty of men just as good as Brad Wilde." She wasn't sure who she was trying to convince, Michelle or herself.

"She who protests too much…" Michelle gave her a long glance.

"Be quiet, please."

"You might as well face the truth. Brad has not been interested in anything serious since he dated some woman years ago. There were whispers of marriage, but she was all high-and-mighty. She wasn't from town and stuck her nose up at everything. Including his orchard. She broke his heart from what I heard. You must mean something to him if he wants to try with you."

"Honestly, Michelle, I doubt I mean much. We hardly know each other."

"You're being kind of tough on yourself. You always do that. You're worth it, Lyra. Believe that for once." Michelle kissed her on the cheek and pranced into the coffee shop.

Once again she was standing on the sidewalk by herself more confused than ever.

CHAPTER SEVENTEEN

Lyra couldn't sleep. She threw the covers back and padded out of the room. She quietly checked on the boys. Theo was on his back with the blankets tangled around his legs. Lucas was curled on his side with his hand under his cheek like he did when he was a baby. She watched them for a moment, allowing memories of small boys that smelled like vanilla and playing pretend in the backyard skip across her mind like an old movie reel. She missed snuggling with them on the couch as they ate popcorn and watched their favorite animated films. Time had come along and stolen them from her before she had a chance to fill her memory box. Had she done enough for them? Had they spent enough time together? How much had she failed them?

She closed the door and went into the living and kitchen area. With the light from the microwave, she put water in the teakettle.

The house was starting to feel homey with the touches she had added, but her boys deserved better than a tired old rental. She should have moved into her parents' house. At least then Lucas wouldn't be embarrassed by his house. He hadn't said as much, but she could tell he wished they lived somewhere else. He hadn't invited one friend over these weeks. Back at their old house, he was always asking if someone could come over. And when she had suggested it, he had only shrugged and went into his bedroom. Theo had told her Lucas was making plenty of friends. Everyone liked him. So no friends wasn't the problem. It was the house.

Before the kettle could whistle and wake the boys, she lifted it off the stove and poured the water over the tea bag, but didn't drink it.

Her hands itched to remodel the kitchen and put in new counters and cabinets. She wanted the new brass fixtures that were making the rounds in the house magazines and all over the internet. The floors needed a good sanding and a buffing. The appliances had debuted some four decades earlier. But nothing could change. She didn't have the money for remodels. And the place wasn't even hers.

But she did love finding a good bargain or a steal at a flea market. She had wanted to rush out to the back of the antique store when Allen had said he had trashed most of his shipment. She could make use of just about anything. The idea stuck in her head, and she couldn't shake it loose.

But it was late and the boys were asleep. What if one of them woke up in the middle of the night, and she was gone? They were old enough to stay alone, and they each had a phone. They could call her if they didn't see the car. She could also leave a note.

She ran for paper and jotted a few words down to tell them not to worry. She had gone for a ride. She'd be back soon. To call if there was an emergency.

She grabbed her coat and locked the door behind her. The cold air bit into her skin as if to hold her in place, but she pushed forward. She would just drive by the dumpster and look. She didn't even have to get out of the car. No one would have to know. And if she found something…her skin tingled. Allen didn't want it. He had thrown it out. She didn't have to feel guilty for taking it.

She stole a glance at Brad's house, but could barely see anything through the trees. The slice of moon didn't do much to offer light. All his windows were dark. The only light on was the front porch that spilled some soft white onto the porch. She wanted to know what he would say about her weird new obsession. Maybe he would understand.

Michelle's words stuck in her mind. Brad had been in a relationship with someone like who she had been once. He must think she wasn't like that any longer, but deep down she was. She was about to climb into a dumpster just to create the illusion of prosperity, if only to herself.

Candlewood Falls' streets were quiet. She got to town in no time at all. All the shops were closed and even some of the apartments above them were dark. She was the only fool out on a cold night. The night before Thanksgiving. When she should be home cooking. That would have been a better way to deal with her insomnia than getting in the car and parking behind the antique store.

She climbed out of the car and looked around. The backs of the stores were beige brick with gray metal doors. The parking lot was empty except for one stranded car up on cinder blocks in the far corner.

The antique store had a sign over their door and another on the dumpster. She had assumed multiple stores would share the dumpsters, but there were two other dumpsters that others must use. Maybe Allen liked the idea of being able to change his mind about what he tossed and didn't want to find shredded lettuce covered in mayonnaise all over his stuff.

Her short stature prevented her from seeing inside the dumpster. She dragged over two milk crates left by one of the metal doors and stacked them. Holding the edge of the dumpster, she said a silent prayer she wouldn't fall on her backside, then stepped up.

The smell of damp cardboard made her nose wrinkle. The parking lot didn't have enough light to help her see inside. She turned on the flashlight feature of her phone and shoved boxes around.

Most of the stuff was junk. Broken drinking glasses or plates made from stoneware. A velvet picture of Elvis. She chuckled at that one. Closer to the bottom was a vintage mission style dining chair. She held her phone between her teeth, then leaned in and gripped the chair with both hands. She yanked, almost fell off the crates, but righted herself and placed the chair on the ground. She checked her teeth to make sure nothing had come loose. She couldn't afford a trip to the dentist.

The chair might have a vintage look, but she guessed it wasn't valuable or Allen would have kept it. She ran the flashlight over it quickly. It didn't seem to be in bad shape. She could always paint it. The boys could use it in their room. Maybe she could buy a cheap corner desk, and they could do their homework in that spot instead of at the kitchen table or on their beds.

Another sweep through the dumpster didn't reveal anything worthwhile. She would consider her chair find a gold mine. She promised herself she'd come back to the dumpster next week. She could find other dumpsters even out of town and search for more treasures. She negotiated the chair into the backseat and headed for home.

As she pulled onto Main Street, a car turned the corner behind her. She startled as the headlights caught her rearview mirror, blinding her. Someone else must have insomnia. She turned right at the stop sign and so did the car. Her heart picked up speed, but she reprimanded herself for panicking.

Or had the police seen her on camera taking from the dumpster? Was there some law in town that forbade diving into a dumpster? Her parents would be horrified if she got arrested for stealing garbage of all things.

She held her breath as she made another turn at the last second and let it loose when the car went straight. With shaking hands, she zig-zagged her way back to her house, almost certain the car had not followed her. She slowed as she passed Brad's place.

A single light was on toward the back of the house. Her heart gave a sigh of relief knowing he was nearby. He would be the kind of man who would protect his woman. He would never jeopardize their lives and their life savings for greed. He would fight for them and fight anyone who tried to hurt them. She sure hoped he would fight to keep Winter. They deserved to be together.

She would leave the chair in the car for now. Tonight's escapade had worn her out. She was ready to climb into bed and pull the covers up to her neck. She only wished she had a strong man with long hair and tattoos to curl up against. And if she was willing to take the risk, she could have him.

So, then why didn't she?

"Hurry up, boys." Lyra yelled through the open front door. She waited on the front porch holding a covered plate. She was up early this morning even after the night she had and decided to bake a cake to bring to Brad's for dessert.

She had texted to ask what kind of cake he liked, but he said not to bring anything. That they had pies from the orchard, but she would never show up empty-handed and doubted he wanted flowers. She also didn't know if he drank wine or what beer he might like. So, he was getting a homemade carrot cake whether he liked it or not.

"Boys. For the hundredth time, let's get a move on." She stamped the cold from her feet.

"Sorry." Theo bounced out the front door, nearly knocking into her. His collar was twisted and his shirt tail wasn't tucked in. But his smile was in place. She didn't have the heart to tell him to fix his clothes when he beamed at her that way. Her little boy—who wasn't so little anymore—was the joy of her life. She adored her children.

Lucas trudged after him in his typical Eeyore style. His steps were slow and his gate long as if he had all day to get where he was going, and it was the world's job to wait for him. His face was firmly planted in his phone.

She gripped his shoulder as he crossed the threshold outside. His head snapped up and a scowl painted lines on his young face. "What?"

"First up, drop the snarl. We're going to a friend's house. I don't care how much you don't want to be there. You will act like a gentleman and be polite. Second, pull out those earbuds and either shove them in your pocket or give them to me. When someone speaks to you, I want you to be able to hear them." She held out her hand.

With an exasperated huff, he yanked out the earbuds and shoved them into the front pockets of his jeans. He brushed past her and walked beside Theo as they followed the driveway to the street. There was no point in driving the car next door. The sun hadn't completely set yet so she didn't have to worry her heel would catch a rogue branch or rock, but on the way home she'd need her phone to light the path.

She locked the door and prayed for strength. Teenagers would be the death of her no matter how much she loved them. She was secretly glad she never got into teen counseling. They were a difficult bunch.

She hoped this evening went well. She could use a relaxing night.

A car parked perpendicular to the end of the driveway. The boys stopped in their tracks and glanced back at her. The familiar sleek silver sedan blocked their path. Her stomach sank to her knees.

"It's Dad." Theo ran to the car.

Lucas looked back at her with wide eyes. "I don't want to talk to him."

"You don't have to." She would not force her son to speak to his father until Lucas was ready. Michael would have to put in the hard work to fix what he broke with his child. That wasn't her job.

"What do I do?"

"Take the cake. Go through the trees to Brad's. Tell him Theo and I will be there soon."

Michael struggled out of the car because Theo wouldn't back away from the door. When he found his footing, Theo threw himself into Michael's arms, but Michael didn't stay that way long. He was never much for displays of affection with his boys.

The two exchanged words she could not hear, but from the hurt expression on Theo's face, Michael had said something upsetting.

"Theo, come here now." Her voice held enough force he hurried to her without argument. "What did Dad say to you?"

"He said he wasn't here to spend Thanksgiving with us, and I can't come visit him anytime soon. He says he's too busy getting ready for his trial. He also said he has something for you." Tears filled Theo's eyes.

"I'm so sorry, buddy. When your dad gets his life in order, he'll come around." She could only hope for her children's sakes. "Why don't you go next door to Brad's? Lucas went through the trees. Go that way instead of around the front. I'll be along soon." She pulled Theo into a hug and kissed his head. Her heart ached for him, and she wanted to scratch Michael's eyes out.

"Michael, what in the world are you doing here today?"

"I needed to see you. Since it's a holiday I thought you would be home. But it looks like you and the boys were going out. Where to?" Michael stood before her in his black ski jacket and jeans. Dark half-circles bruised the skin under his eyes.

"None of your business."

"My children are my business." She was glad she wasn't still holding the cake because she would have smashed it right in his indignant face.

"Not when you don't ever call them or ask about them. Not when you tell Theo you aren't even here to see him or that he can't visit with you. I don't care what you think of me. We're through, but those boys will always be your children. You owe them the best version of you. Not this entitled spoiled brat you've become."

"Listen here." He stepped closer, but she didn't budge. "My life is a sinking ship at the moment. It would do those boys some good to sit quietly while I figure out what to do. They have no idea how bad things are for me."

"It's always about you." She fought the urge to scream at him.

"The boys would understand if you didn't coddle them so much. Theo was practically crying just now. My boys aren't criers."

"You have no idea who your boys are. Since you're here, interrupting my Thanksgiving, I want to ask you something."

"What, Lyra?" he said with malice.

"When did you begin stealing? Was it after that business trip to Costa Rica? Or was it after our vacation to Europe? Did stealing become a game between you and your friends?"

"I don't have the time or the energy for your questions, and even if I did, I won't answer you anymore. Here." He pulled out of his jacket the manila envelope that had been sent to him by her lawyers. "I signed the papers."

She waited for the punch line.

"Take it." He waved the envelope at her. "You wanted a divorce. You have it. I need to get on with life and plan my defense. We're going to take a different tactic that doesn't require the supportive wife. I don't need you."

"Is everything okay here?" Brad's voice washed a wave of relief over her.

"I'm fine. You should go back inside." She didn't need him to save her, but the joy of seeing his broad shoulders, menacing grimace, and urgent pace coming toward her nearly knocked her over. She was tired of feeling like a victim after what Michael did to her and their family, but Brad standing beside her gave her a sense of comfort that she wouldn't have to fight this battle alone.

Michael glared at Brad. "Who are you?"

"That's kind of my question, pal. I know you're Lyra's ex. Theo and Lucas told me that much. What I want to know is what you're doing here bothering her today?" Brad took another step forward, closing some of the space between him and Michael.

"I'm talking with my wife." Michael took a step back.

"Lyra, do you want to talk to this man?" Brad held her gaze, but the tension rolled off him.

She had never seen this side of him, the side where his eyes were ice cold and his jaw clenched enough the muscle bulged through his skin. He fisted his hands, even the one in the brace. She wasn't surprised that he could take on this role. He was a man's man and not accustomed to being bullied. And not by someone who he could probably snap like a twig.

"I have what I need. Please go, Michael." She fisted the envelope in her hand. She was free.

"Is he why you wanted a divorce? How long have you been fucking him?" Michael's face screwed up in an ugly snarl.

She lunged for him, dropping the envelope. She wanted to dig her fingers into his eyes and scratch them out. "How dare you?" She had suffered through his affairs. She had lost her lifestyle because of his selfishness. He had humiliated her with his choices.

Brad gripped her around the waist and pulled her back. "Easy there." He dropped her behind him in one swoop. "Assaulting him won't help. Can I take care of this for you?"

She couldn't find the strength to speak. She nodded instead.

"The lady asked you to go. Now get in that car and get the hell out of here before I put you in the car myself."

"You just said I shouldn't assault him," she said.

"You. Not me. I'll wipe the road with him. Now, Ryan, get the hell out of here before I call the police and tell them I have an armed intruder on my property."

"I'm not armed."

"No shit. But they don't know that."

"You're insane like she is. I'm going. Lyra, tell the boys I'll be in touch when I can." Michael jumped in his car and sped away.

When the car was out of sight, her legs gave out. Brad caught her before she could hit the ground.

CHAPTER EIGHTEEN

Brad scooped up Lyra and carried her through the trees and onto his front porch. She was light in his arms and resting her head against his shoulder. His wrist didn't seem to mind the added weight.

She smelled like wild orange and soap, and he wanted that scent all over him. He had wanted to protect her when Lucas had told him what was going on. His blood had burned enough to blur his vision. He placed her on the porch swing and sat beside her. "Are you okay?"

She nodded. "Thank you for helping me. I don't know what happened. One second I was fighting mad and the next the ground shifted from under me."

"The adrenaline rush was probably over and relief set in. I'm glad I was there to catch you." He would have beat the crap out of Michael Ryan if he had to, but she had it under control. She was smart and savvy. She didn't need him, and someone like her might not want him. Deep down he was nothing more than a farmer. He had been surprised to see her crumple into his arms, not that he minded her being there.

"I hate it that someone my size can't intimidate the way you can. Michael has never backed off so quickly when it was just the two of us fighting. He always found a way to twist my words. Why is that? Why do people bully?"

He laced his fingers through hers. Her hand was cold and small against his. "I'm sorry to say this, but your ex-husband is a weasel. If he were a real man, he wouldn't have stolen all that money."

"Not a man like you. You would never hurt anyone." She placed her other hand on his cheek. The pressure of her palm on his skin sliced opened his desire for more.

"Not on purpose." His emotions for this woman strangled his words as if they were impossible to say. But what was quickly becoming impossible was keeping his hands off her.

He turned his face and placed a kiss on her palm. She let out a little gasp. He wanted to devour her in that instance. He wanted to know what she would feel like under him, all soft and small pressed against his bigger body. He would never hurt her, only protect her, if she would let him.

She leaned in and kissed him. Her hands tangled in the ends of his hair and she tugged, opening his mouth. Hot spikes pierced his body when their tongues collided. His control snapped, and he drew her onto his lap because he couldn't stand any space between them. He didn't care if she could tell what she was doing to him through his jeans. He would gladly show her the effect she had on him. Attraction drove him at top speed, careening into an abyss that would swallow him up and creating a need he didn't even know was there.

She must feel it too because she pushed her breasts against his chest, rubbing their bodies together and making his head spin. He ran his good hand over the side of one mound, and she moaned. If he died now, he'd be pissed off that he couldn't know what it felt like to have her wrapped around him with nothing between them except sweat.

Her sweater was in his way, and his brace was keeping his other hand on her back because it throbbed at the moment. He wasn't sure if he would fumble with that hand, and he didn't want to ruin the mood. She pulled at his shirt, struggling with the buttons. One popped off. He'd need a new shirt when they went inside—he broke the kiss.

"I have a houseful of people." The realization was as bright as the sun coming out from behind a cloud.

She stared up at him with glassy eyes as if he had spoken in a foreign language. Her lips were wet and red. Her chest heaved as if she were trying to get air. He was turned on all over again.

"I...um...what?" She blinked a few times.

"I have a houseful of people. I'd like to keep this going, but someone might come looking for us." Like her kids. Or Winter. How did parents have sex when kids were around? He wasn't about to ask his dad, and he didn't have any friends with children. They must lock doors or rent hotel rooms. Or worse, they never had any.

She moved away from him and tugged her top into place. "I don't know what got into me. I'm sorry. You said you didn't want to do this, and I just threw myself at you."

"It wasn't exactly like that. And I never said I didn't want to make out. I'd like to do that and a whole lot more, but I don't want this to be a one-night thing. That's done for me." With a whole lot of regret, he stood and held out a hand to her.

"I'm afraid, Brad." She slipped her hand into his and held his gaze as she rose from the bench.

"There have been very few things that scare me in life. Now there are two. Being a dad and how I'm feeling for you."

Lyra's heart clamored around in her chest as if it were looking for a way out. If she had to guess, it wanted to jump out of her and right at Brad. This man was rough and rugged on the outside like the bark of an oak tree that would snag and scratch, leaving a scar. But on the inside, he was melted butter, warm and soft and dripping with delicious goodness. Or maybe a little badness and she wanted to run her tongue all over it.

She needed to pull herself together because he led her into the house. His hand was still clasped with hers. The feel of his calluses against her skin sent shivers from her head to her toes. And not just that, but when her legs had given out and he caught her, she couldn't think of one other person she would have wanted by her side in that moment. The fear that he had put in Michael's eyes all for her benefit made her heart just clamor more. Here she was a woman in the middle of an ugly divorce with nothing to her name except a few mops and some trash she had hunted for, and she was falling for Brad Wilde like an avalanche on the loose.

The house smelled of cooking turkey, cranberries, and spice. Laughter punctuated the air as people milled around the kitchen, plucking puffed pastries from trays and pouring wine and beer.

The three kids were at the table with their heads bent, looking at someone's phone. Lucas pointed at the screen and tilted the phone so Winter could get a better look. Her mommy pride swelled. She recognized Brad's father, Silas, standing by the window talking with a man she didn't know. Brad resembled his father with the same stature, jawline, and blue eyes.

Brad continued to hold her hand as he brought her around the room. "Lyra, this is my good friend Raf and his brother Tino."

Two very attractive men with shiny black hair and dark eyes smiled at her. The one named Tino held up his beer can. But the resemblances between the two men stopped there. Brad said they were brothers, but they didn't look like it.

"Brooklyn, you remember Lyra, don't you?"

"It's nice to see you again." She held out a hand to Brooklyn who hesitated.

Brooklyn studied Brad, for a second then turned her gaze back and gripped her hand. "Hi, Lyra. Welcome back to Candlewood Falls. If you'll excuse me." She eased away and went to stand by the man speaking with Silas. The man put an arm around Brooklyn's shoulders and pulled her against him.

"I don't think she likes me."

"Sure she does. She's just weird around new people."

She wasn't sure if he meant that or if he was just trying to make her feel better, but she appreciated what he said. The rest of the night played out without incident. They ate and laughed. Silas was a stoic man, but kind. They spoke a little about the town and how it had changed and how so much had stayed the same. Raf was the life of the party, but his brother said little. Even the children got along.

Lyra stood in the corner and took in the whole scene. This was what holidays were supposed to be about. Everyone being themselves, enjoying the food, and finding comfort in each other's company. She had never had this before. Her mother wanted events to be perfect as if the whole night should be scripted with the right plates, perfect food, and artful conversation. Clarisse would have been outraged at the game of tossing the bread rolls that had played out between Brad, his friends, his dad, and the man who ended up being Brooklyn's fiancé Caleb. And her holidays with Michael were quiet, just the four of them, no friends or family to bolster the room full of loud joy. She had longed for a house full of love like this one was.

Brooklyn had avoided her most of the night. She didn't know why, or what she had done to insult her, but she would give Brooklyn the space she seemed to need. She was getting used to some of the people of this town not wanting her around. Brooklyn might be one of them, but she hoped that wasn't so. Brad would want his sister to approve of the woman in his life.

"Why are you standing over here?" Winter stood beside her with a soda in a red cup.

"I like watching." Observing was what she did. It was how she was able to help people quickly in her practice.

"Yeah? Me too. My mom used to say I was staring, and it was rude."

"I guess it can be if you stare at one person long enough. But I like watching a room full of people. It's like I'm at the theater. Have you ever seen a play?"

"You mean like on Broadway?"

"Sure."

"No. We could never afford to go. I asked once for tickets as a birthday present, but my mom said I had to ask for something else."

Her heart broke for Winter and her mother. She knew the awful feeling of failure that wrapped around her neck every time she had to tell the boys no because she couldn't afford to get them something. No mother wanted to deny her child. But Maggie Reis had denied Winter time with her father, and that was a shame. Whatever Maggie thought of Brad, she had been mistaken. Probably consumed by terror and allowed that fear to dictate her choices. Oh, the mistakes made under the thumb of dread.

"Maybe your dad can take you sometime." She would suggest it to Brad when they had a minute alone.

"I'm leaving in a few weeks. He can't take me. Vermont is too far away."

"I think he might. He could come and get you." She wondered how Brad would manage a long-distance relationship with Winter. But knowing him, he'd figure something out.

"Aunt Nora won't let me go with Brad."

"And why is that, do you think?"

"She doesn't like Brad." Winter slurped from her cup.

"How do you feel about that?" She might find herself pulling Auntie Nora over to the side and having an honest discussion about who Brad actually was.

Winter ran her fingernail over the ridges on the cup. "It hurts my feelings. I think he's nice. And he's kind of funny. And he lets me brush his hair."

If she wasn't in love with this man before, she just fell

head over heels and flat on her face. She put a hand on Winter's shoulder. "Sweetie, there is nothing wrong with disagreeing with your aunt. She's trying to do what she thinks is best, but sometimes grown-ups get confused because they're scared. If you want to spend more time with your dad after you leave, you can tell him that. He wants to hear it."

Her head snapped up. "He does?"

"Of course he does. He loves you."

"But he doesn't really know me. And sometimes his face gets all scrunched up when he talks to me like he ate something he hates. Like when I eat Brussels sprouts. They are the worst. I thought he might think of me the way I think of Brussels sprouts."

She bit back her laugh. "He doesn't think of you like Brussels sprouts. I promise. Tell him how you feel about him. Do you think you can do that? Do you need someone to help you tell him?" It wasn't her place to get involved, and she had no business counseling Winter, but this girl needed a little guidance, and the therapist in her would not allow a child to flap in the wind and deal with her emotional turmoil alone.

"I can tell him myself." Winter gave a firm nod. "I'm going to get more soda. Brad said I could have two cups today." She skipped off.

Raf's brother Tino approached her with a wicked smile on his face and a swagger that shouted bad boy, and he knew it. That along with the dark jeans and black button-down shirt that had several of the top buttons open, revealing the tops of his pecs, said this man was confident or imperious. Only time in his company would tell which, but something about him made her think the last thing she would want is time in his company. Let some other woman try to tame him.

"What is a beautiful woman like you doing over here in the corner alone? Doesn't our host know how to treat his lady?" He leaned against the wall and crossed his ankles. His smile was sinful. She'd seen this kind of man before. And didn't much care for him. She preferred her man rugged and honest. Unapologetic for himself and the fact he was a man of the earth. Strong. Solid. Dependable. That kind of man was Brad Wilde.

She tried not to roll her eyes at Tino's ridiculous line. "You're Tino, right?" No point in allowing him to think she knew who he was. "You won the roll tossing game earlier." Many of the rolls had landed on the floor, unconsumable. At least for her. Brad had wiped a few on his shirt and dug in. He had offered one to Winter, but she had scrunched up her nose in that way she shared with Brad and told him in no uncertain terms that bread was dirty.

"That's right. I'm Tino. Short for Santino. My brother and I are very competitive."

"Siblings can be like that." Not that she knew from experience, but she had plenty of clients who came to her to discuss that very thing. "Are you enjoying yourself?" She scanned the group for Brad, but he wasn't around.

"I'm not big on holidays. They weren't much fun growing up."

"That's too bad. I love this time of year. Would you excuse me?" She needed some air and stepped outside on the front porch. The sun had set, and the sky had burst open, revealing a thousand stars across its black velvet surface. She could almost reach up and touch them. The cold night air settled against her. She shivered and rubbed her arms.

Living in the country with all its space was better than living in her overcrowded town with houses on top of each other. Too many had crammed into North Jersey to be near the city and all its white noise, but she was over that. She was tired of the noise around her.

"Hey, I was looking for you." Brad closed the door behind him.

She couldn't fight the smile that hijacked her lips. "I needed some space."

"Raf told me he saw Tino talking to you. Did he bother you? I'll put a stop to it."

"He was just talking. Pretty sure of himself, that one, huh?"

"That's the least of it. I was wondering if you'd be okay with Brooklyn and Caleb taking the boys back to the alpaca farm? Winter was asking Brooklyn if she could show Theo and Lucas Alpacino and the others."

"That's sweet, but she doesn't have to do that."

"She wants to. She asked me to clear the way for her by asking you. I think you two got off on the wrong foot."

"It was nothing. It's not like we were friends."

"I hope you two can be. What do you say? They're heading out now to feed them. She can bring them back in a few hours. Caleb said he'd light a fire, and they could roast marshmallows. Lucas seemed into it."

"He did?" And when was that conversation going on? She had missed it somehow. She had been distracted the whole evening by Brad, watching his every move and wondering when he would slide his hand into hers again. The boys had not come looking for her once, and she had enjoyed a little time of no one tugging on her, asking for something.

"Looked like it to me just now. What do you say? It would give us a few hours alone. To pick up where we left off." He ran a finger down her arm. Just that soft touch was enough to shake her to the core. She would probably disintegrate under more.

"But the others are still inside."

"My dad is putting on his coat as we speak. He's going to Brooklyn's too because Winter asked her grandpa if he would join them. My dad got some goofy grin on his face and agreed. I've never seen him this happy. It's weird. And I will throw Raf and Tino out on their asses if they don't follow the others out the door. Tell me it's okay for your sons to go with my sister. I promise you that they're safe."

Her heart danced in her chest. Heat rushed over her, making her forget about the chill in the night air. This was the moment of no return. If she told him yes, they would go into his home and make love. And if she told him no, then she would have a way out and he wouldn't hate her for it. He would understand that she wasn't ready. That she may never be ready. That getting involved with a man now could be the worst mistake of her life. She wasn't a risk taker. But maybe she should have been.

"Lyra, are you saying no?" Even in the porch light she could see his blue eyes turn to the color of rain.

She stepped closer and inhaled his earthy scent. Her fingers traced the spot where his button popped off. He sucked in his breath, and the power that sound gave her filled in every insecure thought and pushed them away.

"I'm saying yes, Brad. Yes to it all."

CHAPTER NINETEEN

Lyra waited with anticipation as Brad walked Raf and Tino out. She moved her wineglass around on the counter, needing to give her hands something to do or she might start taking apart the fridge and cleaning the shelves. The dinner had been cleaned up and put away. She couldn't even clean the kitchen which she would have liked to do so the nerves flapping around in her stomach wouldn't distract her.

She was about to have sex with Brad Wilde. She hadn't pictured it this way, so planned out like something they had put on the calendar. But knowing what was coming and waiting for it made the desire for him hum like an engine.

He was sexy with his hair pulled back at the sides the way he had worn it tonight. And those eyes shone like a bright sky. His smile was as lovely as the sun. And his strength stole her breath over and over again. But it was his love for his daughter and his honesty that made him more attractive than any of those muscles did. Not that she was complaining. She couldn't wait to get her hands on him.

He returned, shutting the door with a quiet click. He stared at her, saying nothing, but the silence filled a thousand journals. She wanted him in a way like no other. He put his hands in his back pockets, but dropped his right hand to his side as if it occurred to him he still had on the brace. He smiled then, and her legs trembled.

"They're gone." He hitched his chin in the direction of the door.

"I'm glad. Well, not in a I didn't like them way, but in a I'm glad we're alone way." She was already ruining the mood with her nerves. She grabbed the wine and took a sip before she stuck her foot in her mouth a second time.

He crossed the living room to the built-ins and put on some soft music. A woman's sultry voice filled the room with sweet words accompanied by a soulful piano. He took the wine out of her hand and placed it on the counter. Without a word, he led her into the open space in the living area.

He placed a hand on her low back and held her other hand in his. She didn't even mind the brace. He held her close, never taking his gaze away from hers. He swayed to the music, matching its rhythm.

She was helpless but to follow him. Her body wanted to move with his, to go anywhere he asked. He tucked her against him like a flower petal, and she snuggled close with her cheek against his chest. This was the place she had longed to be. The arms of a man who brought her comfort.

"Is this okay?" His words were a whisper as he continued the slow sway of his hips against hers.

"Perfect." It was as if he knew that she needed time before they began. The song switched to a slow country song. She hummed along, listening to the beat of his heart.

"Do you like this song?" His words were low and deep.

"I like dancing with you." She looked up to meet his alluring gaze.

He took her mouth then, devouring it. She leaned into him and enjoyed the way he tasted her with an urgency as if he were hungry and she was the only way he could be satiated. She felt that need too. The kissing wasn't enough to hold off her hunger any longer.

Kissing had never been like this before with any man. She didn't have a lot to compare, but there had been a few extra kissers than those she had gone to bed with. No kissing had her toes curling like this did.

He moved his lips from her mouth to the soft spot below her ear. He kept her close, one hand on her neck, the other on the middle of her back, which she was glad for because she was pretty sure if he let go of her, she would puddle to the floor. His tongue made hot circles on her sensitive skin. Every part of her was on high alert wondering when he would touch it.

She needed to memorize his body. Her hands went under his shirt because she didn't want to waste time with those damn buttons. She already needed to buy him a new one because of her earlier haste. Heat bloomed in her face just thinking about how she had behaved on his front porch only feet from her children.

Her fingers explored the ripples of his abdomen. Searching higher, she ran her hands over his soft chest hair that spread out in a small triangle over his glorious pec muscles. He was solid as stone. She placed her hands flat against his chest, and he rewarded her with a rumbling moan that gave her courage to keep going.

He had ideas of his own, it seemed, because he brought

his mouth back to hers and shifted so he could cup her breast through her sweater. He kneaded it through the fabric with expert care. The sensitive spot between her legs ached for some of that touch.

She wrapped her arms around his neck so she could press herself against him. With wild abandon she rubbed against the erection straining his jeans. She had never been so bold before and liked it.

In fact, she had never slept with a man so soon in the relationship before, if this could be called a relationship at all. She had made Michael wait several months because they were still in college. And before him had been her high school boyfriend. It had taken them four years to sleep together.

Brad eased out of the kiss and looked at her. "Are you okay?"

"Of course. Why?" She was more than okay. She was damn good and really didn't need to have a conversation. But she wondered if her thoughts of other men had slipped into her actions.

"This is moving pretty fast. I just want to make sure you're comfortable. Tell me if you don't like anything. Or if you want to stop."

"You can do the same." She had no intention of stopping unless he asked her to.

"Babe, I'm liking everything just fine."

"Me too."

He took her hand and led her upstairs to the end of the hallway and his bedroom. The lights off, but the shades were up, letting in enough moonlight to cast the room in shadows. She remembered the colors from cleaning his house a few times. He had decorated in navys and browns. The bed was king-size with a headboard made of wood. His earthy scent was here too. She hadn't wanted to scrub that out the last time she was here with her bleach. He had one tall dresser in the corner and a large rocking chair by the window that he liked to leave clothes on. A small nook was off the room where the bathroom and closet were. The space complemented him, simple but strong.

"May I?" He lifted the hem of her sweater over her head and tossed it to the ground. He took her in.

She enjoyed his lingering gaze. "I'd like to have a good view too. Your shirt, sir." She held out her hand.

He choked out a laugh and undid those awful buttons. "You owe me a new shirt." He balled it up and threw it to the side.

"I had been thinking the same thing." She went to him and wrapped her arms around his neck again because she needed to clear the space between them and feel his warmth mingle with hers.

He took her mouth again. This time her head spun. Her hands were on him, touching, learning, enticing. His skin was hot to her touch. And her skin was on fire from the places he ravished with his hands.

He stopped and stepped back abruptly. She forced a slow breath through her nose.

"What's the matter? Did you hear a car?" Had the children returned already? She might explode if she couldn't feel him inside her tonight, but she knew they would have to wait if the children had changed their minds and come home.

"I'm taking the brace off. I can't feel your skin, and it's

driving me mad. Plus it's the hand I'm better with." He pulled at the straps. The Velcro ripped in protest.

"Are you sure that's a good idea?"

"It's been three weeks. I can have it off for a few hours."

"Hours? Do you think we'll be doing this for hours?" The ache between her legs deepened at the thought of making love for hours.

"You bet we will. Come here."

She went willingly. He scooped her up and placed her on the soft mattress. He undid the button of her pants and slid them over her hips. She had discarded her shoes ages ago. He removed his jeans, revealing an erection that stretched his boxer briefs. Everything about him was big. She smiled to herself. If she were a girl who kissed and told, she would be calling Michelle later tonight to report the good news.

He lay beside her, covering half her body with his. She relished the warmth because she was only in her bra and undies. But that didn't last long. He unhinged that bra in one fast movement, then hooked a finger into her panties and dragged them off in record speed.

He was very experienced at this. His mouth took her breast, sucking until she wanted to beg him to take her. But she didn't want it to end just yet. His hand found the other breast and teased her nipple until she found herself begging him to end the torture.

She reached for his briefs and struggled to get them past his erection.

"Let me help you." He pushed the fabric away.

Her hand ran the length of him. But he stilled her. "Not yet."

"Well, that's not fair. You're touching."

"You can touch all you please, but not yet. I want this to last for as long as possible. But your hands on me will make me look like an eighteen-year-old doing it for the first time."

"I doubt that. I don't mean this in a bad way, but something tells me you've had some practice in this arena."

He dropped his mouth to her ear and whispered, "Babe, there isn't a woman on the planet that could have me as aroused as you do. I can't wait to come inside you, but I'm trying to take my time because I want you to enjoy it."

She was a hopeless case for this man. His hand traced a line down the center of her belly until it reached the spot that had been waiting for him all night, but he didn't touch. His fingers went to her inner thigh. His mouth followed the trail his fingers left.

He kissed the inside of her thighs while his hands returned to her breasts. She wasn't going to be able to last either. How could he remain so in control? If his mouth went anywhere else, she would shatter into a galaxy of stars like the ones in tonight's sky. That wasn't how she wanted the end to happen. She wanted to feel him fill her up. She wanted to rock with him so that together they could reach the atmosphere.

"Brad…" She gripped his shoulder.

"Hmm?" His mouth continued to play with her thighs as his fingers found the heat between her legs.

The words disappeared from her brain with a flash. She could only focus on the impatient pleasure his hand created as his fingers took her to a height she had never been to. Without shame, she pressed her hand to his because the pressure was delicious. She was swimming in a heated pool as the waves of desire crested, but never crashed.

He shifted again and kissed her with a new hunger. A

desperate man who needed water to drink, because his mouth was furious as his tongue ran over her lips and her teeth. She matched him because his hands were driving her crazy.

She needed more and couldn't wait. She didn't care if he was ready to explode. So was she. And she wanted nothing more than to tumble head over heels into the abyss.

She reached for him again. He groaned but didn't tell her to stop this time. She pushed him on his back and kissed a long line over his chest hair that thinned below his waist. She ran her tongue over each hip bone, tasting his salty skin.

"Lyra, you're driving me nuts." He pulled her to him and spun them so he was on top of her.

He pushed her legs apart with his strong thigh. She opened to him, making space for his body. He settled between her legs, and she wrapped her legs around his waist because she wanted to feel all of him inside her.

He waited at her entrance for just a moment, holding her gaze with his intense one. A devilish smile tugged on his lips. Then with one thrust he was inside her and she was soaring.

The need heightened. She wanted to satisfy the longing, but she also wanted it to keep going. They moved in a slow rhythm at first as she adjusted to his size, but then desire took hold and they were moving with enough urgency to slick their bodies with sweat.

Each thrust drove her to the brink, but he brought her back before she could go over. As if he knew—and he probably did—what she needed, he touched her where their bodies joined, and she shot to the stars.

Her body was nothing more than burning flames as she fell over the edge and tumbled in a glorious rush to the end.

He gripped her hips and drove into her. He tensed until he tumbled to his own end, calling out her name.

He gathered her in his arms. She curled into him until her heart slowed, and she drifted back to earth.

CHAPTER TWENTY

B rad held Lyra close as the hum of their lovemaking
settled over him. Sex had never been so good, and he
had had some pretty decent sex in his day. But not this
mind-blowing, skull-crushing kind. Never that.

The pain in his hand had turned up the volume to max,
but he didn't care. He wasn't moving even if the house was
on fire.

She cuddled against him, wrapping her leg over both of
his. Her heat made him hard again. He had promised her
hours of satisfying sex, and he would be happy to oblige.

"I didn't know sex could be like this," she said. Her
breath was warm against his chest where she laid her head.

She fit against him perfectly even though she was small.
It was as if she filled in his empty spaces. He had thought he
might hurt her while they made love, but those cries were of
pleasure. Oh, yeah, he was going to be ready for round two
soon.

"Like what?" He shifted so he could see her face, but he
could only make out her outline.

He turned on the reading light he had attached to the top of the headboard. His old girlfriend, Beth, had laughed when he told her he added the light. She thought a farmer wouldn't be interested in reading. He told her he only read almanacs. She hadn't found the humor in it.

"That's a great light. I noticed it the first time I cleaned in here. I'm always looking for a book light when I'm reading a print book."

"I'll get you one for Christmas. You said you didn't know sex could be like this. Like what?" He had asked her to be around in a month when she had specifically said she didn't want to get involved with him. And he had said he didn't want a friends with benefits scenario. Yet here he was naked in bed with this beautiful woman.

She kept her gaze away from his and ran her fingers over his tattoo on his bicep. "Amazing. Special."

He tilted her chin so she would look at him because he couldn't stand the idea that she didn't want to or worse might be afraid to. "It was special for me too. We have good chemistry." And he hoped a whole lot more.

"Tell me about your tattoo," she said, changing the subject.

He would let it go for now. He didn't want to spoil the night with a deep conversation. "Not much to tell. Those are apple trees."

"They look like badass apple trees with thick, tangled branches and no leaves or apples. More like a haunted forest." She traced the trees with her fingers, doing a damn good job of getting him hot all over again.

"I couldn't exactly have a cutesy apple tree on my arm, now could I?" He loved his orchard and making the trees grow and bloom from nothing more than a grafting branch.

Hell, he even liked making applesauce. But for his arm he had wanted something that felt like him. He had the tattoo artist render a forest with apple trees surrounded by oaks and pines without their leaves. The tree roots snaked down below his elbow into an intricate band with geometric designs.

Lyra's hand stopped its caress. "Brad, is this…?" Her gaze met his, her eyes wide with discovery.

She was the first person to ever notice. "Yes, it's a *W*."

"You had a *W* hidden in the branches of one of the trees. Has anyone ever asked you about that?"

"Never. You're the only one who paid attention to the details."

She placed a hand on his face. "You are the most endearing man I have ever met. Your heart is three times your size. And you let everyone miss it. Why?"

What was he going to say? He guarded his heart because his mother left him when he was a kid? Or that he had fallen in love with a woman once and she had stomped on his heart because he wasn't good enough for her? Or his heart had been desecrated when Maggie took Winter from him? No. He wouldn't say any of it. Not now. Not when Lyra had the power to do it to him again.

"I'm an open book. What you see is what you get."

"Are you saying that for your benefit or mine?" She pulled away from him and sat up, pulling the sheets around her.

"Hey, don't go away." He wanted her next to him, making him think about things like bodies tangled together and not about his past. "What do you want me to say? That deep down I'm a big softy? I am who I am, Lyra. I don't pretend to be anyone else."

"I think you do. I think you don't want anyone to see that soft underside of yours." She slipped from the bed and threw his shirt on. It hung to her knees and swallowed her up. She looked good in his shirt.

"I think that's you. I'm the one who asked for more than a friendship with you. You're the one afraid to let anyone see the real you."

"This is me." She held her arms wide. "I'm a complete mess. I'm not the prom queen anymore. And everyone reminds me of that. So, if that's what you're looking for, you're going to be sorely disappointed."

He jumped out of bed too, just to close the space between them. "Is that what you think I'm looking for? You think I want some perfect woman who puts on appearances? Where the hell did you get that idea?"

"Look at you. You're the guy who has it all. A good job. A family that loves you. A beautiful home. And please, put on some pants. I can't have this conversation with you while you're naked. You're distracting me."

"Is that a bad thing?" He grabbed his underwear and shoved his legs in. If the lady wanted him dressed, then he would do as she asked.

"Right now it is. I can't give you what you want. I can't be the arm candy who makes everything look nice. I'm cleaning houses for a living. I'm living in a rental that should probably be condemned. I'm a lousy mother and a bad therapist."

He took a tentative step so she wouldn't go fleeing from the room on him. When she didn't move, he tried again until he was close enough to take her hands.

"I don't want…what did you say? Arm candy? Yeah, I don't want arm candy. In fact, I don't even like candy all that much. It sticks to my fillings. I don't give a shit what you do for a living. I come home from work every day covered in dirt. You haven't seen that yet because I can only sit at my desk like a jerk signing forms. I agree your rental is pretty bad, but that's temporary because you don't let any grass grow under your very sexy feet. You're a great mom. As for a therapist, I have no idea. But I'm guessing you're not as bad as you think."

A small smile spread over her lips. She looked up at him through her lashes. His heart pounded in his chest. This woman was having her way with him. All he wanted was to erase that crease from her brow and have her smile at him. Every damn day.

"I think we're both hiding from the truth," she said.

"I'm not hiding from anything. I want us to be together."

"What about Winter?" She pulled her hands away and looked out the window.

"She doesn't have anything to do with us." He followed her as if he were powerless to stop. He pulled her against him so her back was to his front. He rested his chin on her shoulder, and she placed a cool hand on his heated cheek.

"She has everything to do with us, if there is going to be an us. You have to start facing the fact that you want her here with you."

"I do want her. I've never denied that."

She stepped out of his hold, leaving him cold, and crossed the room. "Then why won't you fight for her?"

Because if he fought and he lost, he wouldn't know how to go on. "Her mother didn't want her with me. I'm honoring her wishes."

"What about what Winter wants?"

"How do you know what she wants?" He certainly

didn't. He didn't know how to bring up the subject with her. Every time he had tried, he found himself in the strange position of not knowing what to say.

"She told me tonight that she wants to stay here with you."

"She does?" Winter had never said a thing to him about that.

"Wow, you are thickheaded sometimes. Of course, she does. She loves you. What are you going to do to make that happen?"

"What did she say to you? How did I miss her telling me she wanted to live with me?"

"Brad, she's ten. She isn't going to say it the way you or I would. She likes the time you spend with her. You made her part of your life. Look how much she enjoys being with your dad. You made her feel safe when her whole world was ripped out from under her."

He dropped onto the corner of the bed. This was a whole new door opening up. Winter wanted to stay with him. Lyra sat beside him and took his hand. She rested her head on his shoulder.

"What if I can't make it happen?" Nora would know how to fight him. She would have ammunition he didn't.

"You'll find a way." Her fingers traced his tattoo again. His blood heated up.

"What if I fail?" He wasn't any good at failure. He'd been lucky most of his life. And the few times things that hadn't gone his way, he had survived through work. Work got him over the hurt. With this stupid hand, he wouldn't be able to do that if he lost Winter.

"You won't fail. It's not an option." She kissed his shoulder, sending electric currents over his skin. She was driving him crazy again.

"And what about us?" He had to know where he stood. His heart was balancing on a ledge, and she could push it over. Or she could save him.

"Do you really come home from work covered in dirt?" Her lips left hot kisses on his neck.

"Most days, yeah." His throat was dry.

"How do you feel about shower sex?"

"Let's go find out."

CHAPTER TWENTY-ONE

L yra hummed as she pulled into Denise's driveway. Denise had called with a last-minute request to clean her house. She was hardly in a position to say no since she needed the money. But it was the day after Thanksgiving and she had wanted to spend it with the boys. And if she were lucky, maybe sneak away for an hour or two with Brad. She had left the boys with her parents. Her father had made a miraculous recovery. She couldn't help but wonder if the cancellation had been legitimate or just her mother's way of trying to manipulate the situation. But her mother had done her a favor because if she hadn't been home, she wouldn't have had that encounter with Michael that led to Brad coming outside and then to the best sex of her life.

She grabbed her tote of cleaning supplies from the trunk and navigated the front walk. The shower sex had been as wonderful as making love in bed. She about had an orgasm when the water beaded up on his taut muscles and ran rivulets over his abdomen and across his thighs. His hair had curled some from the steam, making it thick and wavy.

That man could roar. He was the most gorgeous man she had ever seen.

He had kept the brace off his hand, which had turned out to be a mistake because he hurt himself when he had lifted her up and pressed her back against the shower wall. She had wrapped her legs around his waist, so he could enter her slowly with deliberation that had made her call out his name more than once. She gave a shiver just thinking about the way he moved his hips, impaling her to the wall. And the whole time not even breaking a sweat.

He had said no friends with benefits, but friendship with Brad Wilde definitely had benefits. If she were going to be honest with herself, he was more than a friend to her. He was quickly becoming someone she could rely on.

She raised her hand to ring the bell, but before she could the door swung open.

"Finally, you're here." Denise grabbed her and dragged her inside, almost knocking the tote to the ground.

Denise wore her typical high-end activewear that matched and molded to her body. She may have had a recent round of wrinkle filler because her eyebrows were higher than the last time she saw Denise.

"Come inside. We've been waiting for you." The chatter of voices drifted from the kitchen into the hallway.

"I'm right on time, and who is we?" The calm that had settled over her since the hours spent in Brad's arms last night took a back seat to the huge knot forming in her stomach. "Denise, what did you do?"

"Put down that silly tote. Don't you know yet that when I call you to clean that's code for come over and help my friends?"

"Um...no. In my language, cleaning means cleaning."

"I invited over a few of the girls. After I told them how you helped me and Josie, everyone wants to meet you." Denise tucked her arm through hers and practically skipped into the kitchen. She didn't have much choice except to follow or trip over her own feet.

She stopped in her tracks inside the kitchen entryway. In addition to Josie who sat at the island with orange juice in a champagne glass, three other women were there. Two she didn't know, but the last one was Leanne Jones—the woman from the school drop-off line who hated her.

She turned to go. Denise gripped her arm tighter and shot her a strange look. Denise couldn't possibly understand her need to flee, to be anywhere but the place the woman who disliked her most was. Her mind tried to piece together why Leanne would even be there except to make this time difficult.

"Lyra, I'm sure you remember Rebecca, Trisha, and Leanne. Ladies, this is the amazing Dr. Lyra."

"I'm not a doctor. I'm a licensed therapist that isn't practicing at the moment."

Denise waved a hand through the air. "You're so modest."

"Seriously, you can't go around telling people I have my PhD or a medical degree." She had never been cut out for medical school. She fainted at the sight of blood and would welcome some now just to make this nightmare end.

The women gave her cheery greetings and plopped her down at the kitchen table, then surrounded her. Leanne stood in the corner near the window with a ceramic mug cradled between her hands. She didn't say much except to huff. Lyra desperately wanted to know what she was doing here.

Denise refilled champagne glasses with the orange juice from a crystal pitcher. She guessed orange juice wasn't the only thing being poured, so she declined a glass to keep her wits about her.

"Now, Lyra, Rebecca here is having man problems. Go ahead, Becks, tell Lyra all about it," Denise said.

"She doesn't...Rebecca, you don't have to do that, if you aren't comfortable."

"She's comfortable," Denise said with an emphatic nod. Rebecca nodded right along with Denise.

She needed a way out of this. She didn't want to counsel anyone. She wasn't any good at it. "I would love to sit and chat, but if you don't need me to clean for you, I'll just get back to my boys." She pushed back the chair, but Theresa put a hand on her leg, stopping her mid-rise.

"Please don't go. Denise said you helped her and so did Josie. I could use some advice too, and I'm going to pay you. Tell me your price." Theresa reached for her purse on the back of the chair.

"I planned on paying too," Rebecca said.

"Why are you cleaning houses?" Leanne piped up from the corner. The scowl was a permanent part of her face.

"Because I'm good at it." She resisted the still burning urge to ask Leanne why she had come today.

"And what's it like sleeping with Brad Wilde? All the women in town want to know since you've seemed to take the most eligible bachelor off the market." Leanne crossed her arms over her chest. Her small eyes narrowed, almost daring Lyra to challenge what she had said.

And she would challenge her because what was going on with Brad was no one's business. "I'm sorry, Leanne, I don't know what you mean." But that didn't stop her heart from pounding with a fury and making sweat pop out on her skin. She hoped her face wasn't as red as a bad hair dye job.

"Leanne, stop being so difficult." Denise placed a champagne glass into Leanne's hand and took the mug away. "I invited you because I thought you could use a little guidance too. Now drink up."

Before Leanne could say another word, Rebecca sprung into her story about her husband, for which she was eternally grateful because Leanne retreated to her corner.

The women soaked up everything she said as if they had found water after years of drought. They asked her questions. Rebecca took notes. They laughed and held hands.

Before she knew it, two hours had passed. They had moved from the kitchen to the family room and sunk back into the oversize cushions on the couch. Even Leanne had moved in closer and perched on the edge of a chair.

She doled out suggestions, but mostly she just talked as if they'd been old friends. She had never been friends with these women in her childhood. She hadn't even remembered Theresa or Rebecca, but they had both been in the grade behind her.

Glancing at her phone, she noted the time. "Wow, I have to be going. It's been lovely, ladies."

They all rose with her. The women shoved cash in her hands. She tried to push them off, but they insisted. Theresa even went so far as to tuck the bills right inside her purse.

"Next week same time?" Denise put an arm around her shoulders.

"I don't know. This was fun, but I'm not really practicing at the moment." Having a so-called practice in a friend's family room seemed unethical.

"Looks to me like you are, honey. I'll see you next

week." Theresa gripped her in a hug before sashaying out the front door.

"Lyra, I have to say, you really have yourself altogether." Rebecca squeezed her hand. "I saw on the news what happened with your husband. You are so brave, coming home and starting over. If it were me, I'd be in a million pieces. Please come back next week. This was a lot of fun."

She couldn't say no to Rebecca and the sweet smile on her face or correct her for that matter. She was in a million pieces, but she had found a way to hide the cracks. The morning had been enjoyable, and the idea of having friends lured her like a siren. Maybe she could finally be herself around these women.

"What about you, Leanne? Will you be here too?" She couldn't resist the question even though she might not want to hear the answer.

"Oh, you bet I'll be back. I wouldn't miss it for the world."

CHAPTER TWENTY-TWO

Lyra crossed off another day on the calendar. She couldn't believe how time flew and Christmas was right around the corner. She had never guessed when she pulled into the driveway of her sad little rental that life would finally be good to her. But it was. Even Michael had left her alone.

She lit some candles around the house. The place looked better in softer light because no matter how many dumpsters she dove in to find the perfect pieces to make this house a home for her and the boys, there were still cracks in the plaster, hardwood in need of being replaced, and pink and black tiles in the bathroom. All things she couldn't change here, but if her little group of women continued to grow, she might actually be able to buy something that belonged to her. For the first time in her life, she would have something that was only hers.

Nerves with a thousand legs crawled over her stomach. Brad was due any second. They had planned a rendezvous for this evening. Planning was the only way they could find alone time with three kids to juggle. She wasn't complaining. She loved that they had started having pizza night together. The boys liked Brad, and Winter liked her. They were a good fit.

She went into the bedroom and swapped her gray sweater for the burgundy one with the low neck that accented her cleavage. She doubted they would make it past dinner before she took him to bed so switching the sweater was a moot point, but she liked the way his eyes widened with lust when he saw her. It was all she could do to keep her hands off him in those moments.

A powerful knock startled away her sex-crazed thoughts. Her nerves picked up speed. Over the past three weeks, she and Brad had made love as often as they could. She was very grateful for extended families at those times because he still wasn't comfortable fooling around when the kids were home. He had said it was worse than trying to sneak around his grandmother Cordy's house where he had to take dates because most girls didn't like his one-room cabin. She couldn't wait to see the place where he grew up.

She ran to the door and threw it open. Brad turned toward her. His slow smile made her knees weak. Honestly, she was behaving like a groupie. At least she had refrained from throwing herself at him and wrapping her legs around him. And that was only because she didn't want to hurt his hand.

"Hey, beautiful." He crossed the threshold and caught her mouth in a ravenous kiss that made her think of nothing but the expertise of that tongue and all the places it had been on her.

"Hey, yourself." She eased back.

"I brought wine." He held up the bottle she hadn't noticed until then.

"Are you hungry?"

"Starving." He shrugged out of his leather jacket and tossed it on the back of a chair.

Well, so much for skipping dinner and going straight to bed. His dark-green sweater molded to his chest. Even the brace couldn't distract from how he looked. His jeans were faded and led to his scuffed work boots. He didn't care about fancy clothes or what anyone thought about how he lived his life. And yet she was still worried if he saw her for herself, he would turn and run.

"The food will be ready soon." They had four hours before her parents returned the boys. Winter was sleeping at Brooklyn's because she wanted to help out with the alpacas.

"Your Christmas tree looks nice." He opened the wine and poured two glasses, but she put hers on the end table. Her stomach was so twisted up she didn't think she could get even a sip down. She berated herself for being nervous. But each time with Brad was like the first.

"It isn't much. Not like yours." Her tree was only three feet, the top of a full-size tree cut down. She had found some white lights thrown out in someone's garbage. They only needed a new fuse which had been in the box. She had bought some red velvet ribbon to make bows for the branches. She hadn't packed any of their Christmas decorations when she hurried from her home with Michael. The house was sold two weeks ago in auction. That included everything inside it. Even the decorations.

"You wouldn't let me cut you a bigger one."

"You shouldn't have been cutting down any trees with

that hand." They had gone as a family to cut down trees. She didn't like to think too long or hard about them being a family. She was still trying to hold hard to her friends with benefits scenario until she had her act together.

"My dad did most of the work." He took in the rest of the room. "Lyra, where did all this stuff come from? I know we're usually at my place, but I would have noticed this much furniture."

She had been sneaking out in the middle of the night almost every night to scour dumpsters and garbage cans. She had branched out from Candlewood Falls to some of the nearby towns too. She was obsessed with finding trea-sures in the trash. And no one knew—exactly. She played it off when one of the boys asked, and her mother hadn't been inside the house in weeks. She always met her out or at the door.

"I've picked up a few things here and there."

"I see that."

"Let's eat." She didn't want him to focus on the objects in the room. When she was ready, she would tell him about her little nightly excursions. After the holidays, maybe. Certainly by then, this obsession would pass.

He zigzagged around the rocking chair, coffee table and ottoman she had found in front of someone's house and had reupholstered with some fabric and a staple gun.

He cupped her face. "Would you mind if we let dinner sit for a little while? I have something else I'd like to do first."

And he kissed her.

~

Brad could think of nothing except getting Lyra out of her clothes. He had been thinking about it all day, in fact. This woman had possessed him. When he wasn't with her, he wanted to be and when he was, he wanted her underneath him or on top of him or pressed against the front of him. He didn't know he could feel this way about someone. He had thought he had been in love before—his thoughts screeched to a halt.

"What's the matter?" Lyra's chest heaved from their intense kissing.

"I...I..." He couldn't tell her what he had been thinking. She still hadn't said anything more about a relationship with him and here he was thinking about being in love. They were supposed to be just spending time together. And each day that time grew. He had let nature take its course, the way he did with his trees sometimes, and his heart was in over his head. He wouldn't tell her how he felt. There was no rush.

"Brad, why did you stop kissing me?"

"I don't want to sneak around anymore." So much for wanting to take his time.

"We're hardly sneaking right now."

"No one knows we're actually together. Winter is starting to figure it out because she asks me if we go on dates. Which I always say no to because when we're alone we don't go anywhere."

"I thought you liked the fact the kids weren't around. It's our chance to make love." She pressed her lips to his neck and left a trail of hot kisses to his shoulder. She was distracting him, and he was about to let her.

"I'm not complaining about our time in the bedroom. In fact, I want more of it. And if Winter stays with me permanently, I'm sending her to public school so we can have the whole day to stay in bed if we want to."

"Don't you have an orchard to run?" Her hands slid under his sweater. Her touch made him want to touch her too.

"Don't change the subject. I mean it, Lyra. I don't want to hide. I want to hold your hand when we're out. You won't get within six inches of me when we're in public."

She held his shoulders and his gaze with her fierce one. "Because I don't want to give the gossips anything to talk about. I've only been divorced about five minutes. I don't know how to explain to the boys about us."

He cupped the back of her head so he could get a better look at those dark eyes. "Babe, are you embarrassed by me? Tell me."

"That's crazy. You're the whole package. You're successful, gorgeous, sweet."

"I'll admit that my orchard does well, but it's not mine alone. My dad and three uncles are involved. My grandfather is the president and the overseer of the whole place. I think he's going to retire soon, though. If I walked away, that place would still run. I've taught Raf everything I know. He'd take my spot in a second."

"Are you walking away?" She narrowed her eyes.

"Never. I'll be there till I'm dead. Does that bother you?"

"Why would it bother me?"

"Because I'm not the guy in a tuxedo. I'm the guy in work boots. I'm the guy that gets dirty. And I can't figure out any other reason why you don't want the world to know about us as a couple."

"That's not it."

Lyra was a woman used to nice things and fancy parties. He was happy at home on a Friday night. "Is it because of my dad? I know your mom thinks he's out of his mind, but he's not crazy. He's just eccentric. I can't ask him to be any other way."

"Your dad is adorable. I admit, the idea that you had to grow up in a house without a bathroom is weird to me, but I'm not judging him. You and Brooklyn turned out to be amazing people."

"So, what is it?"

She turned around and went to the window. The candle-light caught her reflection in the glass. His heart braced for the impact of the end of this thing they were doing.

"I don't want to define us to the town." Her words left a cloud of steam on the window.

He cleared the space between them in seconds. He wanted her in his arms where she belonged but didn't reach for her. "No, you don't want to define us at all."

"Why do you want to get involved in my messy life?" She turned to him.

"You're forgetting I can handle a mess."

"This isn't dirt on the floor. People will make up stories about us because they have nothing better to do. I'm sick and tired of being the front-page news."

Tears filled her eyes. He wanted to take her pain away. "Hey, I don't care about anyone except us. And the kids. I actually can't even believe I'm saying that—kids. It still blows my mind, but the five of us are all that matter to me."

Her face softened. "How did I get so lucky to move next door to you? I could've rented a house anywhere." She put a hand on his cheek.

Her touch scorched him. "I'm the lucky one. Will you go

on a date with me? Next week is the annual Victorian House Christmas Tour. I thought we could check it out. Brooklyn and Caleb are going too."

"My parents' house is on that tour." Her eyes widened with what looked like horror.

"Is that a no then?" She was embarrassed by him. She didn't want her family to know they were together. This had nothing to do with the town.

"No, it's just…well, my mother will have questions."

"And you don't want to answer them. I get it." He stepped away from her, needing space to breathe. He had managed to get himself all twisted up over another woman who couldn't accept him. When would he learn? Beth had wanted to shop, decorate, and attend high society events where she demanded he wear a tuxedo. Beth would never have liked his long hair or the tattoos he had accumulated. But maybe the reasons why Lyra was attracted to him were the same reasons why she wouldn't stay with him.

She slid her hands around his waist from behind and rested her cheek against his back. Her breath was warm through the fabric of his shirt.

"I'm sorry. I didn't mean that the way it sounded. I don't like my mother in my business. That's all."

"You came back to Candlewood Falls. Everyone is in everyone else's business. You need to get used to that."

"I'm not used to my mother being around the corner. Would you mind if we brought the kids on the house tour?"

He undid her hold on him and turned to face her. "If you want to, that's fine with me. I'm not sure it's Lucas's thing, though."

"He'll hate it."

"You could leave him home. Or my dad could come

231

hang with him. Lucas wants Silas to teach him how to play chess." That had been something else that put that goofy smile on his father's face. All at once, Silas had a slew of grandkids. He swore he'd heard him asking Brooklyn and Caleb when they would start a family.

"He does? Lucas never mentioned it."

"Babe, us Wilde men are pretty cool to hang out with. And don't sweat Lucas not talking. I barely spoke at his age. It drove Cordy crazy especially because Brooklyn never stopped talking."

"I want to meet your grandmother."

"Consider it done. Now, yes or no to my question."

She hesitated. "Yes. I will go on a proper date with you. Now take me to bed, Brad Wilde, before another minute passes."

"Oh, hell yes."

CHAPTER TWENTY-THREE

Lyra stepped onto the school bus and for a quick second transported back to high school. Staring at the faces of the other people on the bus reminded her she had been pretending each and every day for four years to be the cool girl. She had been anything but.

"You're holding up the line," Brad whispered in her ear from behind her. His soft chuckle and deep voice gave her legs the ability to move forward. She had nothing to fear with him beside her. That's all she had to keep telling herself. It didn't matter what anyone on this bus thought. She and Brad had a right to be together.

Leanne Jones sat in the front seat. "Hello, Lyra," she said with a smirk as she took in Brad as well.

"Good evening, Leanne. It's lovely to see you." She didn't wait for Leanne's reply and headed toward the middle of the bus where Brooklyn and Caleb sat.

Caleb spoke with a man in the seat across the aisle. She swallowed a groan. Malbec River. And seated next to Malbec was a pretty woman, probably his new fiancée she had heard about. In front of them was Riesling and the new doctor, Trey.

"No way," Brad shouted as they came upon his friends. "Caleb, man, you didn't tell me Malbec was going to be here." Brad high-fived Malbec, then punched Caleb who punched him back. Malbec got into the tussle too.

Yup, she was back in high school.

The kids took seats closer to the front.

The bus drove them from house to house where they could get out and file inside to take in the beautiful decorations. Each house was charming and elegant and made her wish for a nicer place to live than her rental. The bus' brakes gave a high-pitched cry before stopping at the end of a long driveway.

"Okay, folks, this is the Candlelight Inn on the Wilde Orchards' property," the bus driver said.

Brad and his friends hooted at the announcement of the orchard. She couldn't help but give a small shout too. He really had helped create a successful business. She didn't care what he had said about it not being completely his. It was.

"Watch your step." The bus driver opened the door, and the people started to spill out.

Brad stepped into the aisle to allow her to get in front of him. He gave her a wink, then slipped his hand into hers. He hadn't gone more than a few minutes without sliding his hand into hers or draping an arm over her shoulders. She had worried she would fear the attention he would draw, but instead she liked people knowing they were together. She had been the one woman who could capture him.

The kids ran ahead and found a spot at the front of the line inside the house. The old Victorian that would become the bed and breakfast soon was decorated with soft white lights along its columns and banisters. The glow dressed up the porch that had been damaged on the side near the gazebo and welcomed them in.

"What happened to the porch?" She turned to Brad.

"Tree. I'd tell Lacey to hire you to fix her porch, but you haven't done such a great job with those back steps of yours. They still swing when I walk on them." He busted out a laugh.

She smacked him. "You are truly impossible."

"Lyra, is my dumb brother bothering you?" Brooklyn slid in step beside her. They linked arms like old friends.

"Hey. I'm not dumb." Brad shoved Brooklyn.

"Hands off my woman, Wilde." Caleb shoved Brad.

"Riesling, we don't act like them, do we?" Malbec held the door open for them all.

"You're a dumb brother too." Riesling patted Malbec on the cheek as she went by.

The six of them followed the tour into the house. Lacey ran over and hugged Brad and Brooklyn. Brad introduced them.

"It's nice to meet you, Lyra," Lacey said. "I would love to stick around and chat with you all, but the town requires every host to greet the guests. I have to follow the rules. Rules are important. Please excuse me a second."

The living area was decorated for an old-fashioned Christmas. The smell of gingerbread drifted toward her. Evergreens twinkling with candlelight hung from the fireplace mantel. What had to be handmade stockings waited to be filled. In the Victorian times they would have been brimmed with candies and fruit. The whole room was something out of a Charles Dickens novel.

"My stockings." Brooklyn beamed as she admired one. "They aren't so bad."

Caleb kissed her on the cheek. "They're great."

"You're getting better, Brooks. I'll give you that," Brad said. "Winter loves hers, but she would; she's only ten."

Brooklyn groaned. "How are we related?"

Lyra took a step closer to the mantel. "These are real apples. Clever."

"They're from the orchard." Brad grabbed one and took a bite.

"I don't think you're supposed to eat them," Trey said.

"I don't think we were properly introduced. I'm Lyra Chambers." She held her hand out to Trey, deliberately using her maiden name. The taste felt good on her tongue.

"I've heard a lot about you." Trey shook her hand with his firm one. Riesling gave him a nudge. "Malbec mentioned Brad was dating. That's all."

"That better be all." Brad put a protective arm around her. She leaned into him and allowed his strength to comfort her. She could get used to the idea no one would hurt her when he was around.

"Brad, you won't be needing to see Trey, will you?" Riesling grabbed Brad by the elbow of his injured hand and laughed.

"She's never going to let you live that down." Malbec brushed past Brad with Eliza Jane and followed some of the guests into the dining room.

"I don't understand," Lyra said.

"It's not important. Riesling thinks she's a comedian." Brad glared at Riesling and took another bite of the apple.

"I am pretty damn funny," Riesling said with a cheesy smile. "Come on, Trey. Let's go see what Malbec and

Eliza are up to." They followed in the other couple's path.

"Who's the guy in the corner?" Brooklyn leaned closer to her and Brad.

"I don't know," she said. For such a small town, she didn't know everyone any longer. That was as fresh as pine scent on the wind.

The man Brooklyn referred to stood in the corner raking Lacey in with his stare. He studied Lacey with curiosity. Lyra's therapist antennae went up. He held his tall frame straight with perfect posture. His hair was cut close, as if he might be military. His gaze never left Lacey as she talked to guests. Lyra might be worried except for the gentle look in his eyes and the easy smile on his attractive face.

"Beats me, but he's staring at Lacey. Maybe an old friend," Brad said. "Do you want me to go over and find out? I'll ask him."

"That is the last thing you should do," Brooklyn said with a shake of her head and gripping Brad's arm.

"Whoever he is, I think he's digging her," she said. The man blew out a low whistle as Lacey bent over to grab dishes out of the sideboard.

Brooklyn turned to her with wide eyes. "I was thinking the same thing. Caleb, what do you think?"

"It's none of my business." Caleb held his hands up. The sleeves of his biker's jacket rode up. "I'm going to get some cookies."

"Me too," Brooklyn said.

Brad grabbed Lyra around the waist and turned her to face him. "Finally, all alone." He placed a kiss on her nose.

Heat flushed her face. "We're hardly alone. This house is packed full of people mingling."

"I don't care. I've been dying to kiss you all night. If I try, will you let me?" He ran his thumb over her jaw.

"Wouldn't you rather tour the rest of the house?" Everyone would see them. The kids could come around the corner any second. The town would explode with tales of the two of them making a public spectacle.

"I know where Lacey keeps her spare key. We can come back anytime. I want the whole town to see me kissing you." The white Christmas lights danced in his blue eyes. He smiled and ignited the desire inside her.

"We could start a scandal." She swiped the apple from him and took a bite.

"My favorite thing." He pulled her closer.

When she was in his arms, anything seemed possible. Even a future with him. She had made some friends in Brooklyn and Caleb. Maybe someday that circle could include Riesling and Eliza Jane.

"Lyra, what are you thinking?" he said, bringing her back to the idyllic bed and breakfast. A place hoping for a new beginning.

Like her.

"Kiss me."

CHAPTER TWENTY-FOUR

"Did you really brush your teeth?" Brad leaned against the bathroom doorjamb while Winter rinsed off her toothbrush, then plopped it into the pink plastic cup. The whole bathroom had drowned in pink. The shower had pink rubber flowers stuck on the wall. The rug on the floor and all the towels were now pink. Even Winter's toothbrush was pink. He used to hate pink.

"Yes, Brad, I did." She fisted her hands on her little hips and glared at him.

He shook his head. "Okay, queen bee, but I know how to check."

"You do not." Her eyebrows shot to her hairline. He bit the inside of his cheek to keep from laughing. He had learned if he laughed when she said something funny, it only encouraged her to keep doing it—even when he didn't want her to. That piece of information was nowhere to be found when he went looking. He must be searching the wrong places for how to be a parent.

"Let's get into bed." Which was also pink along with the

ten stuffed animals he had acquired for her since her arrival, though she still favored the lamb she had brought with her.

Winter jumped onto her bed and bounced a few times before crawling under the covers. "Will you sit with me for a little while? I don't think I can fall asleep just yet."

"That's because you had way too many cookies at Lacey's house." His wrist was throbbing tonight. What he really wanted to do was open a beer, turn on the TV and zone out for a few hours. Instead, he rearranged some of the pillows behind his head and propped his feet on the bed. The beer would have to wait.

"I keep picturing those twinkly lights all over the houses. There were so many. I tried to count them, but they went on forever." She stared up at the ceiling with a huge smile on her face as if she were picturing the houses all over again.

Joy filled his throat, stealing all his air. "They were pretty nice." He had had more fun on the tour than he had imagined. It had started off just as a way to help Lacey out, but being with Lyra out in public like a real couple had his head in the clouds. He especially enjoyed grabbing her hand in front of her mother. Clarisse Chambers had turned three different shades of purple.

"Can we put up lights outside our house?"

"Sure, kiddo. I'll pick up some this week. Before Santa gets here so he can find you." He tried not to hang on to the fact she referred to his house as *ours*. But he wanted to grip on to it with both hands. He'd gladly break his wrist a second time if it could mean the house would be their home.

"Santa already knows I'm here. He knows everything." She shook her head as if he had said the dumbest thing. Which he probably had.

"Does he know what I want for Christmas?" All he

wanted was his little girl to live with him permanently. If Santa could wrap that up with a bow, he'd be eternally grateful.

"Did you write him a letter? It's not too late. I have a letter for him too."

He didn't know that. "What did you put in your letter?"

"I told him the toys I wanted. The ones I told you about." She smoothed out the sheet over her legs. "I asked him to stop in and say hi to my mom."

"He'll stop by and check on your mom. He'll even bring her cookies. Santa is good like that." He hoped Maggie had known what a great job she did with Winter. Even though Maggie had hurt him in an unimaginable way, he could tell that she had loved Winter and had given her a great start.

Winter curled up against his side with her head on his chest. Her tiny body gave off a lot of heat, but he wrapped a protective arm around her and pulled her close. He was certain he'd kill someone who ever tried to hurt her.

Without thinking, he placed a kiss on the top of her head. He waited for her to shove him away, but she snuggled closer and yawned. He had loved before, but he had no idea how the love for his child could feel. The love expanded inside every cell in his body until it threatened to burst. Tears would sometimes pool in his eyes for no reason other than Winter had drawn him a picture or shared her snack with him.

"Do you want to read, or I can tuck you in?"

"No reading tonight." She jumped to her knees, facing him. Her small hands brushed his hair off his shoulders. She took one piece and curled it around her finger. "Your hair is soft like mine," she said.

"You like playing with my hair." He took a piece of her hair and stuck it in his mouth, pretending to chew on it.

She threw herself back and burst out laughing. "That's gross, Daddy."

The beating of his heart seized like an old car engine. He had to cough to get it started again. She had only used the name dad maybe three or four times since she'd been there. He had devoured it up each time but too afraid to make mention of it to her. He didn't want her to stop if he did, which she had anyway.

He waited until her laughs were merely a few hiccups. "Can I talk to you for a second about something important?"

"Okay." Her face contorted into a serious mask as if she were in deep thought. She wore every emotion out loud every second she had one. He had no idea what she would be like as a teenager, but he wanted a front row seat for it.

"What do you think about living with me full-time instead of moving in with your aunt Nora?"

"You mean not go back with her when she comes?"

"That's what I mean. You could stay right in this room and see Grandpa Silas all the time." It couldn't hurt to throw his dad into the mix since the two were like apples and honey.

"Would he live with us too?"

He couldn't help but laugh. "I'm afraid not. Grandpa likes his cabin a lot."

"But you have to go outside to pee," she said with her hand over her mouth.

"I know. I grew up there, remember?"

"But he'll come visit, right?"

"Probably all the time." He wouldn't be able to keep his dad away if he wanted to, which he didn't. He needed and appreciated the support system his family offered him. He would have to figure out how to juggle Winter and the orchard's schedule once he was back at work. She could come there after school until he was ready to go home, like he had as a kid. It was those afternoons watching his dad that made him fall in love with the trees.

"And I can see the alpacas?"

"Whenever you want." He didn't want to hope too hard for this chance, but he couldn't help himself.

"Will Lyra come over?"

"I sure hope so. You like her, right?"

"She's fun. I think she really likes you. Like a boyfriend because she's always smiling so big at you. My friend Rachel is dating Luke. They went to the movies."

He had no idea kids dated at ten. He hoped he could avoid that drama at least until high school. He might not survive Winter dating. "I like Lyra too. So, what do you say? Do you want to stay with me?"

"Will you adopt me?"

"I guess technically that's how it works. I'll figure that part out, if you say yes." He had no idea what the legalities were since he was her father, but he could sit down with Carter River and find out. Carter was the best lawyer in a twenty-mile radius of Candlewood Falls.

"Will my last name become Wilde?"

She asked some grown-up questions for her age. "If you want to change your name to Wilde, you can. Or you can still use your mom's last name if that makes you feel closer to her." He would be proud to have her be a Wilde, but he understood if she needed to stay connected to her mom. He would never take that from her.

She scrunched up her face. "Can I use both names?"

"We can make that happen." He would give her the world if she asked.

"Okay, then. I want to stay. Can we call Aunt Nora now and tell her?"

"How about if I call her first to break the news to her? Then you can talk to her next time."

She slid under the covers and pulled them up to her chin. A lioness-size yawn escaped her mouth. "Okay. You call her first. I'm tired. I want to go to sleep."

"You got it." He slid from the bed and turned off the light. "Good night, Winter."

"Good night, Daddy."

He stepped out onto the front porch with Winter's sleepy good night still holding his heart hostage. He let the cold air cool his heated skin. He would make the call to Nora out here so there wasn't a chance Winter could over-hear in case the conversation went sideways and he lost his temper. He would do his best to stay in control, for Winter's sake, but he wanted his daughter so much he couldn't breathe with the thought of losing her. And when he wanted something, he went for it—and got it.

He tapped at the phone screen until Nora's contact information came up and he could hit call. The phone rang and rang. Voicemail would pick up soon. He tried to form the words he would leave behind when the beep went off.

"Nora, it's Brad. Winter is okay. But call me when you get this. I have something I want to discuss with you." He ended the call and shoved his phone in his pocket.

His daughter would stay where she belongs—with him. And nothing—including Nora—would stop that from happening.

CHAPTER TWENTY-FIVE

Lyra jumped out of the car and hurried to Denise's front door. She looked forward to these cleaning sessions with the ladies. Last week ten women had sat in a circle in Denise's living room. They talked about their husbands, and one woman's wife. They spoke about children, the joy and the heartbreak. They shared stories about aging parents and lives not fulfilled. Without knowing how it even happened, she was conducting group therapy. And loving every minute of it. So much so, that she actually thought maybe she could open up her practice right here in Candlewood Falls.

Denise flung the door open before she could even ring the bell. "Just a fair warning, but Leanne is in a mood today. I was thinking about asking her to leave."

She stepped inside the door and closed it. Conversation voices punctuated with some laughs and gasps played like an orchestra in the other room. Still, she lowered her voice when she spoke so as not to be accidentally overheard.

"I'm sure it's nothing more than her neighbor's dog

again. Leave her for now. If she gives any of the women a hard time, I'll pull her aside." She had learned that Leanne was a lot more bark than bite. She huffed and puffed, but deep down she only wanted to be heard. Like everyone.

"Okay, if you say so. But if you want me to toss her on her butt, just give me a sign." Denise linked her arm through hers and escorted her into the living room.

The session began with the usual hellos and hugs for her. They found their seats on anything from the sofa to chairs brought in from the dining room to the floor.

She pulled her notebook out of her tote bag and settled into one of the oversized comfy chairs. "Who would like to begin?"

"I would." Leanne jumped up and raised her hand. "I think everyone should hear what I have to say before we get started. It affects every member of this group."

She couldn't imagine what Leanne was about to say and looked over at Denise for some information, but Denise only shrugged. She doubted Leanne's proclamation had to do with the dog she had been complaining about for weeks, but with Leanne one could never tell.

"Okay, Leanne. Why don't you go first." She arranged a smile on her face and hoped it looked genuine because the nerves in her stomach were crawling at top speed.

Leanne pulled her knit top into place. "I recently found out something very important. Our fearless leader here, Lyra Chambers Ryan, is not a licensed therapist. She's been coming here week after week, taking our money, pretending to have a license to help us. She's a fraud and a liar like her husband."

A laugh burst out of her as if she were a cannon. "Leanne, that's ridiculous. I've been a licensed therapist for

over ten years. Why would you say something like that?"
She may have been reluctant at first to counsel these
women, but their time together had shown her maybe she
could have another go at a personal practice. She would
never have deliberately misled them or lied to them. That
would make her like Michael.

"Because it's true. My sister-in-law works for the state.
She lives in Edison with my husband's good-for-nothing
brother. Anyway, I asked her to check up on you. I couldn't
figure out why a woman who supposedly was a great therapist would suddenly want to clean houses. It's because you
never amounted to anything after you left town. You came
back lying to each of us."

"Leanne, that's crazy. Your sister-in-law must have
looked in the wrong database," she said.

"Lyra, why is she saying that?" Theresa gaped at her
with wide eyes and a trembling lip. Theresa and Rebecca
had been the first women to trust her with their pain. And
Theresa was so fragile.

She searched the faces of the other women. They all
looked on in either confusion or alarm. After all this time
together, they didn't believe her. That thought cut her in
half.

"I don't know why. Is it because you dislike me?" She
pointed her gaze straight at Leanne.

"It's no secret I don't like you, but that's not why I'm
bringing this up now. You're offering advice to these women
when you aren't qualified to do anything more than scrub
toilets." Leanne crossed her arms over her chest.

"Leanne, maybe you should leave." She had tried to give
this woman the benefit of the doubt their whole time
together, but it appeared she had only wanted to make a fool

of her in front of these people. She fought the nausea in her throat. She would not allow this woman to humiliate her.

"What if Leanne is right?" Sue said, standing and wringing her hands.

Sue lived down the street from Denise and had only shown up for the first time last week. She was a gaunt woman who looked as if she hadn't washed her hair in a while. Denise had shared that Sue's youngest had been sick with a strange infection, but was fine now. She suspected that Sue was still reeling from the trauma based on her unkempt appearance and nervous hand gestures.

"Sue, Leanne is wrong." Denise stood too.

The tension in the room grew like a storm cloud. The other women broke out into conversations. Most of the words went right past her, but she did catch a few doubts as they raced by.

"Hang on a second." She put her hand up. "I can show you my license and put this all to rest. Denise, may I use your computer? It will be easier for everyone to see than on my phone."

"Of course. Let me get the laptop." Denise ran from the room and returned in seconds. "Here you go. The search engine is already open."

She typed in the state's database and punched in her login information. Once on the right page, she typed her name in the search bar.

Nothing came up.

"That can't be…" She tried again. And again. And still her name was nowhere on the page. It was as if she had been erased. "There must be some mistake. I'll make a call and get it fixed."

"There's no mistake," Leanne said. "You've sat in this

room and accepted payment for counseling these women. You're operating without a license. Plain and simple. I could have you arrested for that. But I won't, of course. I'm not that kind of vindictive person. I only want what's best for our little trusting group."

All the women stared at her. Their faces were contorted into different versions of angry and unwelcoming. How quickly the tides had turned.

"I'm telling you all this is a mistake. I have a copy of my license at home." Actually, she had left her paper license at the house in North Jersey. She hadn't bothered to clean out the desk properly when she had left in such a hurry all those weeks ago. Now that desk belonged to someone else, they had most likely discarded the useless contents.

"It doesn't make any sense." Sarah, another woman who had recently joined, grabbed her purse and slung it over her shoulder. "Why lie to us, Lyra? I thought you had changed." Sarah brushed past the other woman and went out the door.

Her departure was a signal for the other women who all filed out with mumbles of agreements and threats of suing until only she and Denise were left.

"I don't understand what happened or why I'm not in the database. How could I have logged in if I hadn't had an account?"

"I don't know, sweetie. But you need to fix this and fast before Leanne tells the whole town."

"And before our session next week."

"I'm afraid we can't have any more sessions. I'm sorry. The last thing I need right now is any kind of scandal that Ian can use against me. The divorce isn't finalized. I think we should hold off on the cleaning until after the holidays as

249

well. You know, just to play it safe. I'm sure you understand."

"No, actually I don't. What did I ever do to that woman that she hates me so much?"

"For some people, the pain of high school never goes away."

"Was I that awful?" And she would always be paying the price for not knowing any better.

"Not any worse than I was. But for Leanne, she had wanted to run with the popular crowd badly. Don't you remember how she would try to dress like you and act like you?"

"I don't."

"She would always show up in outfits that copied one of yours, but hers were never quite right. She tried to like the same music as you did and be a part of the same clubs. But the harder she tried, the worse she made it for herself.

"She tripped in the hallway one day, running after you. I'll never forget it because when she fell, she collided with me and we went down hard on the floor. Her books flew everywhere. The kids laughed at her and pointed. No one helped her up. Not even me, I'm sad to say. But I was embarrassed and a teenager. Not my best time."

"Not anyone's best time, really. I do have a license, Denise. I swear to you."

"Well, honey, at least you did. I'll walk you out."

Lyra slid into her car and rested her head on the steering wheel. These women that she had grown to like thought she was a fraud, a liar. The very things she thought about Michael. For the first time in ages, she wondered if he had been innocent in any of the things he had been accused of doing. Or maybe like Michael, she too was a fraud. She had been pretending to have it all together for so long she had finally started to believe the lie.

She drove away, not looking back. Her cleaning business would suffer as well, she was sure of it. Not that it had gotten off the ground much. She had gladly swapped her broom for a chance to help people and had neglected cultivating any more cleaning clients.

She had nothing to show for her life. Her career was in the toilet and somehow her license had been revoked. She didn't think Michael had the power to take her license away, but maybe he had because she refused to stand by him. She lived in a shanty. And her boys would be out in the world soon, living their own lives. She didn't really have Brad because she had been the one too afraid to commit.

She didn't want to go home. She asked her Bluetooth to dial Michelle. She needed a friend who wouldn't judge her, wouldn't say she told her so, wouldn't expect anything from her, and would hold her hand while she fell apart.

CHAPTER TWENTY-SIX

The phone startled Brad out of his sleep, its screen bathing the dark bedroom in enough light to hurt his eyes. It was midnight. He had gone to bed only an hour ago. With a groan, he rolled over and slapped at the phone to make it shut up. Raf was calling.

"Raf, what's up?" His voice scraped against his dry throat. He had turned up the heat when Winter took her shower, and he had forgotten to turn it down. He roasted under his covers.

Loud voices and music echoed in the background. "Sorry to bother you so late, but I need your help. It's Tino. He's drunk. I can't get him out of Murphy's. They're ready to call the cops because he's trying to start a fight. I can't let him go to jail."

"Maybe a night in jail would do him some good." He swung his legs over the side of the bed and wiped a hand over his face.

"He's my kid brother. I can't let him go to jail. Will you come?"

"Are you sure you don't want to call one of your brothers?" He shoved his legs into his jeans.

"Tino respects you. He listens to you. He also likes working at the orchard. He won't jeopardize that. Can you be here soon?"

"I'm going to have to wake up my daughter for this. And I have to see if someone can take her. You owe me, man. And so does Tino. And I plan on getting payment."

"Thanks. I swear I'll make it up to you."

"You bet your ass you will." He ended the call. He would do anything to help Raf even if that meant dealing with Tino. But things would have to change if Tino expected to stick around. He couldn't keep running out in the middle of the night now that Winter would be living with him. He didn't want her to wake up and find him gone.

He couldn't call his father to come over because more than likely his dad's cell phone was turned off or not charged. He could call Brooklyn to come over, but he didn't want to disturb her. She'd have to be up early to deal with the alpacas.

He threw on a sweatshirt and yanked the sleeve over his brace. Man, he couldn't wait to have his hand back. This thing had become a nuisance and was dirtier than even he liked.

He grabbed the phone and called Lyra. He didn't want to wake her either, but at least she was next door and he wouldn't have to go out of his way to drop off Winter.

"Hey, Brad. You're up late." Her voice was soft and settled against his heart. He hadn't seen her all day, and he missed her.

"So are you." At least he didn't wake her up.

"I can't sleep."

"I need some help."

"Right now?"

"Raf is having a problem with his brother. He needs me to come help him. I don't want to bring Winter or leave her here alone. Can I bring her to your house?" He put on his boots, but didn't bother with the laces.

"Isn't she sleeping?"

"Well, yeah, but what if she wakes up and I'm gone?"

"Leave her a note by her bed. She'll most likely sleep until morning and won't even notice you're gone."

He didn't expect her to advise him to leave Winter home alone, but maybe leaving Winter sleeping wasn't a big deal, and he was overreacting. "I don't know, Lyra. I don't feel right doing that. I wouldn't ask if it wasn't important."

She hesitated long enough he checked his phone to make sure the call was still live.

"Lyra?"

"Okay, okay. Bring her over."

"Thanks. You're the best."

Lyra put the phone down and took off her jacket. So much for treasure hunting tonight. She had caught a break when the boys asked to sleep at her parents' house. After the day she had had with losing her group, she had relished the idea of some alone time and a trip into town to check out the antique store's dumpster. With Christmas only days away, the shipments were coming in fast and furious. Allen had thrown away tons of stuff that she had fallen for. Many of the pieces were in the garage just waiting for her love and attention.

But with Winter coming over, she would have to wait and hopefully wouldn't lose out on some great finds. She needed the trip to decompress. She hadn't lied when she told Brad she couldn't sleep. She had been pacing the floors for hours, all twisted up about the loss of her license. She hadn't been able to get anyone on the phone all afternoon to help her figure out what happened to her name on the database. How had she lost her license?

The knock on the door was swift, and she didn't hesitate to answer it.

"Hey, guys."

Brad's lips were pressed into a thin line. He wore a knit cap with the orchard's logo on it, and the bags under his eyes said he hadn't slept much either. Winter leaned against him in her pink puffer jacket and pink boots. Her hair cascaded in waves over her shoulders. She clutched a pink blanket and rubbed her eyes.

"Thanks for this." He turned to Winter. "I'm sorry about waking you up."

"You'll come back, right?" She straightened Brad's hat.

"Promise."

Winter nodded and kissed his nose. He gave Winter a hug before turning to her with a smile, then he was off before she could say anything more. She hoped Raf appreciated Brad's loyalty.

"Okay, miss, let's get you inside." She closed the door. "You can sleep in my bed. The boys are at their grandparents'. I'll sleep out here on the couch."

"I can't sleep. I want to wait for Brad to come back." Winter plopped on the couch and took off her coat.

"He could be a while." She suspected whatever Brad

went to help Raf with at this hour could take until sunup or when the bail bondsman opened.

"But what if something happens to him?" Winter's eyes filled with tears.

"Nothing will happen to him." She sat beside Winter and squeezed her shoulder. "Would you like a hug?"

Winter slipped her arms around her waist and hugged. "You don't know that. Something happened to my mom. She said she'd be right back too. And she got in a car accident. What if my dad gets in a car accident?"

"Your dad has left you here before, and you weren't worried." Though grief showed up at strange times in all kinds of ways. Simply having her sleep disturbed could have set Winter off to worry about Brad.

"Tonight feels different. I want to stay up until he comes back."

She doubted any kind of bribery would work. Winter had her mind made up. They could watch movies until she drifted off, or they could read a book. Theo had a few good series Winter might like. "I have an idea. Why don't we go for a ride?"

CHAPTER TWENTY-SEVEN

Lyra drove in circles, hoping Winter would fall asleep in the backseat, but no such luck. A light mist had begun to fall, coating the road and the treetops. If the temperatures dropped any more all that mist would turn to ice. She needed to turn back soon.

She hadn't heard from Brad and didn't know if that was a good or bad thing. She should have asked exactly what kind of help Raf needed. Hopefully, he didn't find himself in trouble because of this brother. If she were a betting woman, she'd put money on the brother being Tino.

She drove down Main Street and the call of Allen's dumpster beckoned her. Stopping for a few minutes wouldn't hurt anything. Plenty of people dove in dumpsters for treasures. There were tons of shows about it all over the internet. Winter could stay in the car.

"Where are we going?" Winter sat up and looked out the window.

The mist continued to fall. She parked behind the

antique shop out of the range of any of the cameras. Turning in her seat, she said, "I'm a bit of a treasure hunter these days. I'm looking for something special that other people think is garbage, but that I can turn into magic."

"I love magic." Winter sat up straighter.

"Well, it's like magic. I have to do some work to the treasures first."

"I don't mind work. Brad showed me how to pick the ugliest apples to make applesauce and cider with. Can I help you look for treasure?" Winter unbuckled her seat belt.

"Wouldn't you rather stay in the car?" She should have thought this through better. Brad would not want Winter climbing into the dumpster with her.

"No. I want to come with you." Winter was out of the car before she could stop her.

"Okay, wait up." She guided Winter to the dumpster and pulled over the crates. "You can stand on here with me. But don't try to grab for anything. Let me do that."

"Is this stealing?"

"Everything in here is being thrown out. It's not stealing. We're dumpster diving. It's a hobby." She had just turned Brad's daughter into a criminal. She should really be ashamed of herself.

They shared the space on the crates, but not very well. One of her feet hung off so Winter could have firm footing. The mist slicked the sides of the dumpster and numbed her hands until the feeling in her fingers was gone.

"Does my dad do this too?" Winter reached for a box.

"No, honey. Just me. I haven't even told your dad about this. Remember, tell me if you see something, and I'll pull it out."

"Is what we're doing a secret?" Her face lit up. *Oh boy.*

"Do you like secrets?" She would never ask Winter to keep something from Brad. She would just have to tell him before Winter did.

"My mom said I shouldn't keep secrets from her. She would want me to tell my dad. I'm going to live with him from now on. Secrets would be bad."

So, Brad had had the talk with Winter. Her heart swelled. He was going to be a great father. He already was. Winter was lucky to have found him. "Then we'll tell him." She hoped he wouldn't be too mad about this.

She used the flashlight app to shine inside the dumpster while she moved boxes around. The dumpster was full of boxes. Like she suspected, Allen must have had a big shipment.

Something pink got caught in the glare of the flashlight. "What's that?" Winter pressed her hands on the edge of the dumpster and leaned over.

"Winter, don't." She lunged, but it was too late.

Winter let out a scream and tumbled head over heels into the dumpster. She landed with a thump.

"Are you okay?" Her heart reverberated, threatening to come clean out of her chest.

"My hand hurts." Winter wailed.

"I'm coming." She threw a leg over the side of the slick and wet dumpster and prayed she didn't hurt herself too or they might get stuck. She had dropped her phone and wouldn't be able to call for help.

She fought to move the boxes and stepped on something that crunched under her boots. Winter jumped on her, clinging to her neck.

259

"I've got you." She held Winter close for a second, inhaling her strawberry scent. "Honey, you're going to have to let go of me so we can climb out."

"No. My hand hurts."

She couldn't see well enough to inspect her hand. She hoped it was only a bruise.

Without time to debate and cajole, she peeled Winter off her neck. "I'm going to climb out first. Stay here."

She fumbled over the side of the slippery dumpster, but landed without too much fuss. She helped Winter out and retrieved her phone from the ground. With the light again, she checked over Winter.

Winter held out her hand. A gash in the shape of a half-moon ran from her palm to her wrist. Blood pooled inside her hand. Lyra wiped at her neck and found blood on her hand too.

"This hurts." Tears spilled from her eyes. "I want my daddy." Winter was going to need stitches. At least the doctor's office wasn't far.

"I'll call him. He can meet us at Doc's."

And then he would kill her.

Brad came back into the kitchen after he tucked Winter into her bed. The lines around his mouth had deepened. And those blue eyes were hooded with fatigue. When she had called him about Winter, he had just wrestled a wasted Tino into bed at Raf's house. The night had worn on him, and she had made it worse. All the pain on his face was her fault. The guilt twisted her stomach into knots.

"Is she asleep?" She could not meet his gaze. Her heart had been in her throat all night, choking her. She would regret taking Winter to that dumpster for the rest of her life.

"She is now." He wiped his good hand over his face. "How could you take her to scavenge inside a dumpster?"

"She couldn't sleep. I thought a drive would help out." The excuse sounded hollow even to her.

"A drive maybe. But rummaging through the garbage like a raccoon is something else. Why were you doing that?" He slumped into the chair. She wished he would yell at her or hit something. His calm demeanor only made the guilt worse.

She blew out a long breath. "It's become a kind of hobby. I find cool things there."

"All that stuff in your house? All of it came from the garbage? Do you need money? I could give you money." He pulled his wallet out of his jeans and tossed it on the table. "Take all of it. I must have a couple hundred in there."

Offering her money was a slap across the face. "I don't need your money."

"Then please make me understand why you thought it was a good idea to take my daughter in the middle of the night climbing inside a dumpster? Are you out of your mind? I'm trying to get custody of her. Now I have to call her aunt and tell her she got hurt again on my watch."

"I'm sorry. I wasn't thinking."

"Well, you have that much right. Can you please go? I need to make a call to Nora before I can't reach her." He turned his gaze from her, freezing her out.

She wished she could make him understand that she hadn't meant any harm. That she had become transfixed by the need to collect things. But she could have taken from him the one thing he wanted most in the world. He would never forgive her. And she didn't blame him. Once again, she wasn't thinking and had messed up.

"I'm sorry, Brad. More than you'll ever know." She let herself out into the cold rain.

CHAPTER TWENTY-EIGHT

He wasn't a good father. Brad stared out the window. Snow had begun to fall in big flakes and coated the ground like powdered sugar. He had allowed his daughter to get hurt because he trusted someone else to watch her. He should have stayed home. What if something worse had happened than just a few stitches?

He hadn't slept much since Winter's accident the other night. He found himself getting up in the middle of the night to check on her. Then he'd stand in front of the window in the living room until the sky faded from black to gray, like now, berating himself for trying to keep a little girl safe. He understood apples and his orchard. He didn't know the first thing about being a parent. Maggie had been right all along.

Winter would be better with Nora. She knew how to take care of Winter in ways he didn't. And what would happen when she was older and had women issues that he couldn't help her with? The pain in his chest was unbearable, and he didn't know if he would ever be able to breathe again, but he had decided. Winter should go back with Nora after the first of the year.

He suspected Winter would be up soon. She had already warned him that she didn't like to sleep late on Christmas morning. She didn't want Santa to think all his hard work was for nothing by sleeping in. He hadn't wanted to miss seeing her face when she saw the presents under the tree since this would be their only Christmas together.

He had eaten the cookies and poured the milk into the sink about an hour ago. He wondered if she really still believed at ten, but he couldn't risk asking her. And if this year she needed to believe in Santa, he could get behind that.

Nora had read him the riot act in spades when he had called about the accident. She had been right too. He had screwed up royally. If the cut had been any longer, Winter's vein in her wrist could have been cut on a vertical. A vertical cut on her wrist...he couldn't think about it. There had been a broken mirror in that dumpster. He still couldn't get his head around what Lyra was doing. When would she figure out she didn't need to impress anyone—ever?

He put a pod into his coffee maker and hit the biggest ounce button. He was going to need a lot of caffeine today. His father, Brooklyn, and Caleb would be there soon. His mother would also make her annual Christmas call to him.

He brought his coffee back to the window and glanced in the direction of Lyra's house. He couldn't see it from where he stood, but he assumed she was there. He hadn't seen her since he threw her out of the house. The anger and fear still shook him.

"Wow." Winter bounced on her toes. Her eyes were wide with joy as she took in the tower of presents around the tree. Brooklyn had said he went overboard. "There's even presents in the stockings Aunt Brooklyn made."

Which was a bit of a miracle since Brooklyn was a lousy knitter. The tops were smaller than the bottoms. He had hung them because she had been proud of her attempt. And Winter liked their misshapenness.

"Santa was busy." And so had he been. He had never wrapped so many presents in his life. And with only one good hand, he had done a lousy job, but he wanted Winter to remember this Christmas forever.

"Can I open them?" She bounced more.

"Sure, kiddo. That's why they're here."

She ran full speed at the presents, knocking into them. Some of the boxes toppled over. The tree swayed in its stand. "I never got so many presents before. Mom always said that Santa didn't have a lot of room on his sled so each kid could only get two or maybe three presents." She tore through the paper, tossing it in the air. It floated around her like the snowflakes outside.

He swallowed the knot in his throat with his coffee. All Maggie had to do was tell him Winter wanted something and he would have had it delivered. He pushed away the resentment. He was here for now. "Santa got a bigger sled this year."

Before Winter could finish opening all the presents, the doorbell rang bringing in his sister, father, and Caleb. They sat around the living room opening gifts. Winter showed each of them everything she opened, then directed them to open their presents. She worked her way around the room, sitting next to each one of them and telling them stories about reindeers and elves.

He sat back and took in the whole scene. Every part of

his body ached, knowing he was losing his child again. He would have to tell his family about his decision to let Winter stay with Nora, but not today. He wanted them to enjoy the next week. Then he would have to break their hearts too.

"How about if I make some lunch?" his dad said. "Winter, do you want to help Grandpa?"

Winter grabbed the cooking apron Brooklyn had bought her along with some plastic red kitchen utensils and skipped into the kitchen. The doorbell rang again.

"I wasn't expecting anyone else." He wasn't seeing his cousins today, and Raf had promised to stay away since he was having his brothers over. Raf wanted to spare him time with Tino after the other night.

"I'll get it." Brooklyn jumped up before he could.

"Is Cordy coming back early?" Caleb inspected the scarf Brooklyn had knitted by sticking his fingers through the big holes that weren't supposed to be there. Even he could see that.

"Not today. And she wouldn't ring the bell. She'd just walk right in, shouting hello to everyone." At least Cordy would be back in time to meet Winter before she returned to Vermont.

"Brad, someone is here to see you." Brooklyn's face had drained of color. Definitely not good.

He stood, ready for trouble. If Lyra had shown up, he'd walk her back. She had been irresponsible. He couldn't trust her. But it wasn't Lyra. Nora came around the corner with her luggage in her hands. Anger twisted her face into an ugly snarl. Her dark eyes were flat and cold—empty even.

"I've come for my niece. I'm taking her home today."

Brad led Nora onto the front porch, closing the door behind him. "You're back early." Fire burned in his veins. She could have given him these last days. It wasn't a lot to ask.

"Do you seriously think I would leave Winter in your care for even one more minute? You let her get hurt and not just a bump on her head this time. Something terrible could have happened."

"But it didn't. You have no right to be here, trying to ruin our Christmas."

"I don't see how it matters that she only got a little hurt. I also don't see how taking her a few days early matters either. She was never going to stay with you. I would never allow that to happen. She belongs with me."

"Why is that exactly?" He wanted to hear why she thought she was the perfect choice even if she was a better choice than he was. He wasn't ready to admit that to her yet.

"For one, I've been around her entire life. I know her. She knows me. For another, she's my sister's daughter. I've already lost Maggie. I can't lose Winter too."

"So, it's about you."

"No, it's about Winter and who she's safer with. She isn't safe with you. How will you keep her safe on that orchard of yours? And if you're willing to go running to help a drunk friend when you have a child to worry about, what other foolish things will you do?"

He had no argument. He went running when he should have stayed put. He didn't know how to put his needs second. "You're right. I don't know what I'm doing here.

I've been flying by the seat of my pants. Winter is better off without me."

A gasp came from behind him. He spun on his heel. Winter's red face screwed up with disbelief. "You lied. You said we'd be together." She bolted into the trees—again.

He ran after her, but she was small and could duck around the brush and branches better than he could. His shirt stuck on a twig, yanking him back. He tripped over a fallen limb and fell to the side, landing on his hands. The pain shot up his arm and vibrated in his jaw. He probably just refractured his wrist.

"Where did she go?" Nora skid to a stop beside him.

He climbed to his feet. His hand pulsed. "She ran next door. It's where she goes when she's mad at me."

"How often does she get mad at you?"

"Only one other time." He rubbed his wrist through the brace. "Give me a minute. I'll go next door and get her." He went into the house, leaving Nora on the lawn.

"Dad, I need your help. Winter overheard me say something I shouldn't have. Will you come next door with me to get her? She'll come back with you." Because she must hate him. He was going to have to send his little girl away with anger in her heart. He rubbed the pain in the center of his chest.

"What's going on?" Silas grabbed his coat.

"I'm sending her back with Nora."

"You can't do that," Brooklyn said.

"I can. It's what's best for her."

"You're wrong," Dad said. "But let's go get her from Lyra first, then we'll all sit down and talk about this."

They walked over to Lyra's and knocked. He held his breath until she answered.

"Oh, Brad, Silas. Merry Christmas. What can I do for you?" She looked beautiful in a red sweater and dark jeans. Her face was wiped clean of makeup and her hair fell around her face.

He wanted to grab her and pull her into his arms and tell her about what he was thinking. He wanted her to tell him he was doing the right thing for Winter and that the pain would go away. But he shoved his good hand into his pocket instead.

"I came to get Winter."

Her eyes narrowed. "Winter isn't here."

CHAPTER TWENTY-NINE

"Let me call the police," Lyra said.

"We will if we need to." Brad fought the urge to pound his fists into something, anything. Winter was missing, and the day was growing dark. But his family was around him. Brooklyn, Caleb, Dad, and Raf. He had called Raf asking for help, and Raf had come. That was what family did. And even though he shouldn't have left Winter with Lyra, he would always be there for Raf. Raf was his brother.

"Nora, you stay at the house in case Winter comes back," he said. The snow was coming down and sticking. An inch or more was on the ground, and Winter didn't have a coat.

"I'll take Main Street and the town area," Raf said.

"Caleb and I will go over to the orchard near the store and the apple trees," Brooklyn said.

"I'll drive around," Dad said. "She couldn't have gone far."

"I'm going to drive around too. If we don't find her in

the next hour, we call the police." He'd comb through the tree-lined streets in case she was hiding somewhere.

Lyra gripped his arm. "Can I come with you?"

"Don't you think you should stay with your children?" He wanted to get out of there and start looking and not explain why he didn't need her help.

"My parents are on their way. I asked them to come so I could help with the search. Please, Brad. I feel like I'm responsible for this."

"Fine. Two pairs of eyes are better than one." He hurried to his truck and jumped in. She could keep up or not. Now was about Winter.

He drove up and down the streets of Candlewood Falls, desperately searching for a glimpse of pink. "I can't remember if she even had on shoes," he said. Winter would be freezing by now. She might try to find a hole to get warm in. They would never find her if she did that.

"We're going to find her." Lyra squeezed his leg, reading his mind.

Her touch was comforting, but he couldn't think about his feelings for her. His feelings didn't matter. Only finding Winter mattered.

"I hope it's soon." He took a right turn. The streets were quiet as dusk settled in and stripped the color from the day.

"Does she have a favorite place?"

"Besides my dad's house?" Winter actually liked the little cabin even though she didn't like the bathroom situation. She always went before she left the house, and then she would ask him to stop at Brooklyn's afterward if she had to go again.

He slammed on the brakes. Lyra shot forward in her seat.

"Do you see her?" Lyra screeched.

"I know where she is." He pointed the truck in the direction of the alpaca farm.

Lyra shivered inside her coat. Anger, fear, and stubbornness rolled off Brad in waves. The tension in the truck could snap it in half. She kept her hands in her lap, even though she wanted to touch him, to bring him some comfort.

If Winter wasn't at the alpaca farm, where would they look next? It was almost dark. The truck shook and jostled as he navigated the gravel driveway. The farmhouse came into view first with its white clapboards and wide porch. She had never been to the alpaca farm before. She wished it had been under better circumstances.

He parked by the barn. "Stay here."

It wasn't a request. She owed him her cooperation. After what had happened under her watch, it was the least she could give him. "Of course."

He pushed out of the truck and walked around the front. Even in this crisis, he stole her breath with his size and strength. He was the strongest man she knew, and the kindest. That heart that he wrapped up in armor to protect, had to be crumbling like old stone about now. And he would never let anyone know how he was dying inside.

She needed air. Even though she had promised to stay, she opened the door. The snowflakes brushed against her heated cheeks. She would give him three minutes. If he didn't return, then she would go to him whether he liked it or not. They would need to call the police.

CHAPTER THIRTY

B rad held his breath as the frozen ground crunched under his boots. If Winter wasn't in the barn with the alpacas, he was out of ideas. And would be out of his mind.

Lucy started screeching from the female's side of the barn. She was the farm's danger warner. "Lucy, girl, it's just me." He thought by now that alpaca would know his smell, but she was a worry wart. All that noise had Ethel running in circles.

He flipped the light switch on the wall. A burst of white light spread over the inside of the barn. After the fire a few months ago, Brooklyn and Caleb rebuilt the barn and added a few extra touches that it didn't have before.

Chewpaca, the black alpaca, came up to him. "Hey, boy. Is she here?"

Alistair poked his head out around the bales of hay. They made eye contact. Alistair ducked back behind the hay. He'd start there.

He hurried through the barn. His fast movements made the alpacas scurry. He came around the bales of hay and stopped short. A gasp of air left his lungs. Tears filled his eyes. He swatted them away.

Winter was propped against the corner with Alpacino sitting on the ground next to her. She had one arm wrapped around his neck while she cried. Alpacino hummed. Brad swore that damn alpaca looked at him with a smug smile that said it took you long enough.

"Hey, kiddo." He dropped onto the ground beside her, wanting to pull her to him, but she turned away. "You had us all pretty scared there. You shouldn't run away like that." His voice shook with relief to see she was unharmed.

She kept her back to him.

"Are you cold?" He shrugged out of his jacket and wrapped it around her shoulders. She didn't say anything, but she buried herself inside the down parka. At least she had shoes on.

"Winter, why did you run away?" He tapped her on the shoulder.

"Go away."

He had no idea how to make this right. This was just another example of why he was a lousy father. "Alpacino, man, how do I fix this? You got any advice for me? You're the smart one in the group."

Alpacino continued to hum. Alistair had come over and dropped his rake. "Thanks, Alistair, but a rake won't solve the problem this time."

Winter looked over her shoulder. "They can't talk."

"They can't? Are you sure? Alpacino's making a lot of noise now." He leaned back against the wall and stretched out his legs.

"Aunt Brooklyn said they hum when they're happy. That's not like words." She wiped at her pink cheeks.

"I guess not. He must be happy then that you're here. How did you know how to find the farm by yourself?"

She rolled her eyes at him, but she turned so her back was against the wall too. She stretched out her legs beside his and pulled the coat closer. "Grandpa told me how to find my way. He gave all the marks on the road."

He shook his head. Of course his dad did. "He told you to look for the red house and the sign on the telephone pole, right?"

"Yup. He told me street signs were for suckers."

"You ran away because you heard what I said, right?" He might as well cut to the chase. The barn was cold, and he needed to tell everyone to stop looking, but he wanted to talk to her first.

"You told Aunt Nora I was better with her. You promised we'd stay together. Are you mad because I hurt my hand?"

"Heck, no. I'm not mad at you. I'm mad at myself. I let you get hurt."

"You didn't do anything. I saw something pink, and I tried to grab it even though Lyra told me not to. I lost my balance and fell. I should have stayed in the car like Lyra said."

"She wanted you to stay in the car?" And she had told Winter not to reach inside the dumpster. He had believed the worst. He owed Lyra an apology.

"She took me for a ride because I wanted to stay up and wait for you."

"Why did you want to wait for me?"

"Because I was afraid you wouldn't come back. Like my mom." She peeked up at him through her lashes.

He really was a screwup. "I'm sorry, kiddo. I completely

messed that whole thing up. I'm not a very good dad. I think it takes a lot of practice, like when I played football. I practiced a lot to get good at it."

She jumped into his lap, knocking the wind out of him, the coat forgotten. "I think you're a nice dad. My friend Rachel, the one that likes Luke, her dad isn't nice at all. He yells and hits her. She told me. He doesn't make her laugh. And you're funny. Dads should be funny."

He choked out a laugh. "If you say so." He needed more than a few laughs if he was going to keep her safe, but the compliment warmed his insides.

She brushed his hair away from his shoulders. "Why can't I live with you?"

"Is that what you really want?" Because he did. Did he ever. But if he wasn't the right thing for her, then he would have to give her up. Winter's needs were more important than his ever could be.

She nodded, but kept her gaze averted. Her bottom lip trembled.

"Aunt Nora doesn't like that idea."

"I know I'm supposed to listen to adults because they know best, but you're an adult. If you say I can live with you, she has to listen."

"It isn't that simple."

"Please. I'll be good."

He cupped her head. "Hey, you're the best. I'm the luckiest dad in the world. I just want to do the right thing for you. And I don't know if I'm it. Your mom didn't think I was so good."

She threw herself into his arms, gripping his neck. "My mom said we were better off without you. She told me I wouldn't like you. She said you were mean. But she was wrong. You're a great dad. And I love Grandpa and Aunt Brooklyn and Uncle Caleb. And all the alpacas. Please don't make me go. Please, Daddy. I love you."

Tears wet his shirt. When she took her small hand and wiped at his cheek, he realized those tears were his. "I love you too." He gripped her tight and soaked in her strawberry smell.

She eased back. "Can we be a family with Lyra?"

Oh, boy, she was killing him here. He didn't know how to juggle all these emotions in one night. "I don't think so. I said some not nice things to her. She's pretty mad at me."

"You should say you're sorry. That makes it better." She hopped off his lap and gripped Alpacino in a big hug. "Alpacino says so too." She giggled. Alpacino hummed and gave him another smug smile.

"Um…is everything okay in here?" Lyra stood a few feet away with tears in her eyes too.

"How much did you hear?" He pushed off the ground to stand before her.

"Enough."

"Winter, call Grandpa and tell him to call off the search." He handed Winter his phone. "Stay with the alpacas a minute. Lyra and I need to talk, okay?"

"Okay, Daddy." She took the phone, then turned to Lyra and puffed up her chest. "I'm staying with my dad."

His chest followed suit. He would keep his daughter. He'd figure out the legal issues later. Nora could fight him all she wanted. He would never back down. He wouldn't lose. He never did.

"I'm glad. You two belong together." Lyra's watery smile didn't reach her sad eyes.

"Can I talk to you out there a minute?" He pointed toward the barn opening.

"Sure."

He gave another glance at Winter as she put the phone to her ear. "Hi, Grandpa…"

CHAPTER THIRTY-ONE

Lyra followed Brad back out into the night air. The snow covered her coat. The gray clouds didn't offer any light, but the light from the barn and the porch lights cast enough glow that she could see his face.

His eyes were hooded, and he had a crease between his brows. She wanted to wipe away the hurt and the fatigue. He had been through enough thanks to her.

"I'm sorry." She needed to try and explain. "I shouldn't have taken her to the dumpster. I'll never forgive myself for that. It's just…" She stumbled over the right words. "I lost the group of women I counseled. One of the women made it look like I wasn't licensed. I thought the dumpster diving would make me feel better. I was wrong." She had been so wrong. What would have made her feel better would have been to tell Brad about her bad day.

"I'm sorry too. I shouldn't have said those things to you. I was mad. Scared actually. I don't know what I would have done if something had happened to her." He glanced toward the barn.

"It's every parent's nightmare. You have nothing to be sorry about."

"I still shouldn't have thrown you out of my house or insulted you by trying to give you money. I was a jerk."

"I've been the jerk. Can you forgive me?" Even if they couldn't be together, she could live with knowing she had his forgiveness.

"I do."

"Thanks. I'll wait in the truck." She turned, but he grabbed her arm.

"I want to be with you. All of you. Even the bad stuff. But you have to let me in to see it. Would you do that for me?"

"I'm tired of pretending I'm something special. I realized the other day when those women believed I had lied to them, that people can believe whatever truth they want about me. It's exhausting to please everyone else. I know who I am. And I'm a big, fat mess at the moment. But if you want me like that, then Brad Wilde, I would be the happiest woman in Candlewood Falls."

He stepped closer and put his hands on her face. His warm touch pushed the cold away inside her. "Babe, there isn't anything I don't like about you. You're everything I've ever wanted in a woman. You accept me exactly as I am. You don't judge me or expect me to be someone I'm not. You showed me how to be a dad when I had no idea what I was doing. Well, I still don't, but I'm a little better now."

He made her heart full. "You're a fantastic father. I promise you."

"I love you, Lyra. And if you'll let me, I want to tell you every day. I want to show our kids what love looks like. And

I want to sneak off whenever we can so I can get you naked and underneath me."

Her knees wobbled at the idea of stripping him free of his clothes, even out in the snow. "Do you think your dad would watch Winter for a few hours?"

He growled and possessed her mouth with his. The kiss burned her from the inside out.

"Yuck. You two are gross." Winter interrupted them, breaking them apart. She put the phone back to her ear. "Grandpa, can you come pick me up? Daddy and Lyra are kissing again."

"Looks like we have a few hours to ourselves." She stood on her toes and placed a sweet kiss on his wet lips.

"I'm going to owe my dad a better Christmas gift."

"I love you, Brad Wilde."

He kissed her again and wrapped her in his strong arms. The very place she was meant to be.

READY FOR ANOTHER TRIP TO CANDLEWOOD FALLS?

If you would like to find out who the guy is checking out Lacey Wilde at the Victorian House Christmas Tour, be sure to read Wilde Christmas by K.M. Fawcett

And if you want to learn what secrets were uncovered by the town's new doctor Trey and the sassy Riesling River, pick up a copy of The Buried Secret by USA Today best selling author, Jen Talty

When it's too late to fix the past, only forgiveness can rebuild the future.
Defining Chances by Stacey Wilk

Thank you for visiting Candlewood Falls!

Be sure to leave a review to help readers like you find and enjoy our small town.

Join our exciting community of authors and readers at the Candlewood Falls Facebook Readers Group for cover reveals, sneak peaks, deleted scenes, and excerpts from upcoming releases. Plus games and fun!

ENJOY MORE CANDLEWOOD FALLS FUN!

Join our exciting community of authors and readers at the Candlewood Falls Facebook Readers Group for cover reveals, sneak peaks, deleted scenes, and excerpts from upcoming releases. Plus games and fun!

ACKNOWLEDGMENTS

My team is a small one, but we're mighty. I would like to thank my two partners on this small town crossover series— K.M. Fawcett and Jen Talty. Without you, who would I spend countless hours with talking about Candlewood Falls as if it's a real place? Wait...it's not????

I also need to thank Robin Rottner for all her input and feedback. I hope the day never dawns that you tire of my prose.

And always to my copyeditor, Kimberly Dawn, because I will never learn where a comma belongs. As long as I have her, I won't. *Kidding.*

Most importantly, I have to thank you, my readers. I am humbled each and every time you choose my books. Thank you for sharing your free time with me. I hope I have given you a chance to escape real life and find a little romance along the way.

ABOUT THE AUTHOR

From an early age, Stacey Wilk told tales as a way to escape. At six she wrote short stories in composition notebooks, at twelve she wrote a novel on a typewriter, in high school biology she wrote rock star romances in her binder instead of paying attention.

But it wasn't until many years later, inspired by her children and a looming birthday, that she finally took her storytelling seriously. And published her first novel in 2013. Since then, she's gone on to publish nineteen more so women everywhere could fall in love and find an escape of their own.

She isn't done telling stories. Not by a long shot. If you want to read her best selling, emotional, and honest books about family, romance, and second chances, visit her at www. staceywilk.com

Made in the USA
Columbia, SC
29 April 2022

59494725R00176